DATE DUE			
HIGHSMITH #45114			

THIS PLACE HOLDS NO FEAR

by

MONIKA HELD

translated by

ANNE POSTEN

Originally published with the title *Der Schrecken Verliert Sich Vor Ort* by
Eichborn – A Division of Bastei Luebbe Publishing Group
Copyright © 2013 by Bastei Lübbe AG

First published in Great Britain in 2015 by
HAUS PUBLISHING LTD
70 Cadogan Place, London SW1X 9AH
www.hauspublishing.com

English translation copyright © Anne Posten, 2015

ISBN: 978-1-908323-90-3
eISBN: 978-1-908323-91-0

Typeset in Garamond by MacGuru Ltd
info@macguru.org.uk

Printed and bound in Spain by Liberdúplex

The translation of this work was supported by a grant from the Goethe
Institut, which is funded by the German Ministry of Foreign Affairs.

The house stood at the end of the street, its garden turning into woods without a fence. They couldn't make up their minds, as if their fate hung in the balance. On their first visit the sun was shining and Heiner said: The living room is friendly. Lena liked the plum trees in the garden and imagined herself making jam. The realtor gave them the house key. Take your time, she said, see if you suit each other. How can you tell whether a house suits two people or two people suit a house? They didn't know. They walked around, approached the house from every side. It's bored, Lena said, it's been alone too long. Heiner asked the house about their future. What awaits us here – disaster or happiness? The house didn't answer. If they painted the window frames white it would look friendlier. On their second visit the sky was grey and Heiner thought six rooms would be too many for two people, but Lena had a plan for every room: Living room, study, and laundry room on the ground floor, a bedroom and two guest rooms on the second floor.

Heiner inspected the neighborhood. There were no shops, no pubs, no news-stands – only new houses, hard to tell apart. Even the gardens were almost identical: a lawn with a rhododendron bush or a lawn with French broom. Fine. He walked up and down the streets. Dirty little shoes outside the doors, yards with swing sets. There was a playground with a slide and a sandbox full of children. A girl with blonde braids whizzed past the houses on rollerblades, while her mother called to her from the kitchen window: Jenny, watch out! The sight of the nimble child brought back a name that made Heiner feel sick: Kaija. These children would grow up, and when their parents were old, they would still be younger than he was today. He would sleep poorly in a neighborhood filled with people his own age. The neighborhood is fine, he said, but shouldn't a new house be like love at first sight? They returned the key and looked at houses in other new neighborhoods. A month later, when the house was still on the market, they paid it a third visit. It was early evening, the day muggy and oppressive – weather that would make any house look dreary. They sat on the porch swing that had been left out on the patio. Lena put a thermos and two coffee cups on the table; they waited without knowing what for. Patches of fog settled on the pine branches and floated down to the forest floor. The birds were silent, as if the fog rested heavily on their beaks. Lena put her arm around Heiner. What do you think? she asked. Will your soul be at home here?

It smells nice, he said, that's a good sign.

It smelled like Lena's hair when it had first fallen over his brow, blanketing his closed eyes, tickling his nose – long ago when he didn't know whether the hair of the woman bending over him was blonde, brown, or black. It lay on his face, warm and smelling of mushrooms.

They rocked on the porch swing, uncertain whether they suited the house or it them. Six rooms are too many, Heiner said, and this place is so lonely. He poured himself more coffee. There are only young couples and children in the neighborhood. More cats than dogs. They watched the silent trails of fog. The silence is nice, Heiner said. He had barely spoken when Lena grabbed his hand: Listen. A crackling sound came from the woods, as if someone were creeping over rotten branches through the undergrowth, approaching the patio. Then a stag with huge antlers stepped out of the trees.

It can't be, whispered Heiner, it's impossible. Tell me this isn't true.

The animal looked at them calmly and without fear – perhaps it didn't notice the two motionless people. It lowered its head and slowly turned around. The stag was sunk up to its belly in fog and seemed to float back into the woods on a white cloud. They heard the crackling of branches under its hooves.

Lena stood up. She packed up the thermos and led Heiner away from the patio. His hands were ice-cold and he was trembling. It's a sign, he said. Fate can't speak more clearly than that. I see, she said, you hear fate – and what does it say?

Buy it, Heiner said. And when we live here, if it comes back, I'll tell you about the most terrifying night of my life.

They kept the key and bought the house. They painted the window frames white.

The porch swing became Heiner's summer sofa. He'd often sit there long after midnight, listening to the muffled thud of pine-cones falling to the ground, feeling more certain every day that he would be happy here for a good while to come. Impatiently he waited for the stag to return.

His winter sofa, in the living room, had two bare patches: one from sitting, and the other near the right armrest, where his head lay when he got tired during the day and even Lena's coffee didn't help.

The cuckoo clock hung over the sofa: a twelve-inch-tall, wal-nut-brown little house framed by five hand-carved leaves, with a pointed roof and faint writing under the face, which read "Made in Germany." When the cuckoo called four times it was time for coffee and cake; when it called eight times it was time for the evening news. The cuckoo clock was the ugliest thing in the room, in the house, probably in the whole neighborhood. Every hour the little door sprang open and a pale, shabby bird made of light wood shot out, shrilly calling out the hour. Day and night, around the clock, 156 sharp cries. All that was left of the painted beak that opened when it cuckooed was a red dot that looked like a speck of jam. The left eye was paler than the right, making the bird seem to squint. Heiner loved the ugly clock. It had once hung in his parents' sitting room. It had cuckooed when Heiner was born, and it had cuckooed when the Germans invaded. Eight cries were the last thing Heiner had heard as the police handcuffed him and hauled him away. His mother had stayed behind in the kitchen so that Heiner's last image of her would not be her tear-streaked face.

Martha, his girlfriend, had gripped the doorframe and whis-pered "Rotfront." And because a whisper was too quiet for what they were doing to him and for all that they were going to do, at the cuckoo's last cry he had turned. Louder, darling, say it louder. Before he stepped into the street, he heard her despairing cry from the stairwell: "Rotfront!"

Come back soon, his mother had said – but when is soon? Is four hours soon, or three days? If he had known the future, a month would have been soon, or even a year. But when Heiner was taken for interrogation, he hadn't been thinking about a long separation. He'd thought he was going to die.

After the war, when he picked up the keys from the caretaker and stepped into his parents' apartment, he was prepared for anything except for the orderliness that greeted him. In his room the bed was made. The pillows and bedspread were as smooth as if they'd been recently ironed. How often he had dreamed of this red-and-white-checked linen! An old volume of Seneca lay on the nightstand. A bookmark was stuck between pages 260 and 261. The chapter was titled "Man is Man's Wolf," and it was only thirty lines long. He had underlined the most important ones: *Even the storm, before it gathers, gives warning; houses crack before they crash; and smoke is the forerunner of fire. But damage from man is instantaneous, and the nearer it comes the more carefully it is concealed. You are wrong to trust the countenances of those you meet. They have the aspect of men, but the souls of brutes...*

He snapped the book shut. The sentences were of no use to him anymore.

Heiner's childhood in Vienna had been quiet. Few cars were on the streets – it was mostly horse-drawn carriages. In his district there was a fountain where horses were serviced by a man they called the waterer, just as cars would later be serviced at a gas station. In winter he sledded down the steep streets. In school he sat on brown wooden benches with forty other boys, their backs as straight as if they had swallowed sticks. Hands were supposed to remain on the table, never under it, so nearly every good school-boy kept his ten little fingers scrubbed clean – but not Heiner. He smeared dirt under his pointer finger and let the teacher slap him with a ruler. He showed his father the welts, and the teacher never hit him again, no matter how black his nails were.

The picture that had so revolted Heiner as a child still hung in the kitchen. In it a dead pheasant with glazed eyes lay on a bed of carrots, celery, and leeks. Its claws were spread, and a slug crept from its open beak. Heiner could no longer understand his child-hood fear. The picture was an idyll. Pure peace.

There was still a jar of Nivea on the rim of the bathtub. His mother's toothbrushes still stood in a green ceramic mug. His grandmother had once brushed her long hair in front of the mirror over the sink. She would bend over and brush her hair a hundred strokes from back to front. Then she'd straighten up and throw her head back, brushing the hair off her forehead and down her back with another hundred strokes. No more and no less. Why do you do that, grandma? So my hair stays shiny and doesn't turn grey. Look, child: No grey hairs. Can I help brush, grandma? Yes, she said, but careful, child, don't pull your grand-ma's hair out, she still needs it. Sometimes in the evenings Heiner was allowed to brush her hair, so he learned to count to a hundred before he even started school. When he gripped the brush right near the bristles, her hair would glide through his fingers. It felt like silk. Sometimes sparks flew from her hair. When that hap-pened his grandmother would say that a storm was in the air. She was an old lady who wore long black dresses, so long they dragged on the floor. She had fought on the barricades for women's suf-frage. When it was finally granted on November 12, 1918, Heiner's grandmother declared November 12 her birthday. Because of the barricade incident and her long hair, the family called her "wild Hilde."

Heiner went into the living room. The white lace tablecloth used for family celebrations lay on the table. The silver salt shaker that was never cleared away stood on top. Salt on the table brought good luck. His father sat at the head of the table with grandmother across from him and mother to his right; next to her sat Greta, who was so young she still needed help with her food. Heiner sat to his father's left, beside his sister Alma. For a moment he saw them all there, the whole family. They didn't pray. They joined hands and his grandmother said: Even in our greatest need, let us have salt and bread.

Carefully, as if it were a relic, Heiner took the silver salt shaker in his hand. It was tarnished; he shined it on his jacket. Nine tiny clogged holes. The salt shaker exuded quiet, as if it had been holding its breath for years. Heiner licked the top – Even in our greatest need, let us have salt and bread. The meal began after his father bade them "Guten Appetit." Heiner had only ever seen his father in a suit. A civil servant in "Red Vienna," he had returned from the war a radical Social Democrat. Dinner was not always followed by dessert, but there was always a little lecture from his father on politics. His grandmother would nod in agreement while his mother let it wash over her; the girls were bored, but Heiner was rapt. It was only outside the Rosseck home that Vienna was a quiet place. By age five Heiner knew that there had been a great war, and that Austria had been left without a kaiser. He was six when his father brought him to the Social Democratic Youth Organization. By then he already knew that Vienna belonged to the "Reds," and all the rest of Austria to the "Blacks." Heiner was listening to the hooves of the horses, the rumbling of carts, the screeching of children, all the sounds of the cozy

Viennese world outside, when one day his father did not pick up his silverware and begin the meal as usual. Instead he stared at his bare plate and finally broke the silence by saying: The Justizpalast is burning. Heiner was seven and would have let any soup in the world get cold if his father would just explain why the Justizpalast was burning, who had set it on fire, and whether this was a good thing. And for whom it was good – the Reds or the Blacks.

Heiner sat in the chair he had used as a child. He heard his father's voice: curt, lecturing like his schoolteacher. In Schattendorf, a town in Burgenland, two people had been shot in a clash between the right-leaning "Frontkämpfer," who were loyal to the Kaiser, and the left-leaning Social Democrats. A man and a child. Yesterday, on July 14, 1927 – remember that date, child – the killers were acquitted by the grand jury. People were so outraged by the "Schattendorf Verdict" that they took to the streets. Crowds marched on the courthouse and broke through the barriers, pushing closer and closer; stones flew, glass broke. Brave men stormed the building, destroying the furniture with hatchets and setting fire to everything that would burn. The fire devoured the roof and smoke rose to the clouds. The people can stand up for themselves – never forget that, child. Let's go, begged Heiner, let's go look! It's no place for children, his father said. He left the apartment after lunch; later at dinner he summarized the events of the day. The police had opened fire on the crowd. Eighty-nine people were dead and thousands wounded. Watch out, child, the Right is gaining power. He picked up his silverware. The murderers are free, he said softly. These are radical times. Take my word for it – this is the first step towards civil war. Let us enjoy this food. To Heiner, his father seemed like a prophet.

When he was eleven Heiner joined the Red Falcons, where he was introduced to Marx and to Martha. She was a slim girl with thick braids, the first in the group to ask his name. Other boys daydreamed about heroes from adventure stories, like Hadschi Halef Omar Ben Hadschi Abul Abbas Ibn Hadschi Dawuhd al Gossarah, but Heinerle, as Martha called him, dreamed of the dictatorship of the proletariat and fell in love with the slim girl who shared his dream. Like Heiner's grandma, she was ready to take to the barricades in the name of justice.

When he was thirteen, Heiner's father died. A year later the civil war began. Heiner and Martha handed out pamphlets. There were only two sides: Right or Left. Left stood for justice, Right for exploitation. They knew where they belonged. The Right wanted to do away with everything the Reds had done for the poor in Vienna. Affordable apartments, rent control, luxury taxes on people who had servants and housemaids, riding horses and private cars. Many districts in Vienna were no longer cozy. The high and mighty battled in parliament while the common folk brawled in the streets. Heiner got into fights with other children in defense of his mother, when, as his father's second wife, she was denied her husband's pension. Stubbornly she begged for a reprieve, for an orphan's pension for her children, and began cleaning rich peoples' apartments ten hours a day. Now Heiner sat at the head of the dinner table and played at being head of the household. He gave political lectures, quoted Marx, and said "Rotfront" before starting to eat. When he called his mother a "dishrag of the bourgeoisie" she threw her empty purse on his plate. Buy some bread and meat, she said, and then come back. Furious, he ran through the city, rang Martha's doorbell, and found out that her mother also cleaned houses. He grew quiet. Without their mothers' hard work, they would both have starved. Cleaning for class enemies – they swore this humiliation wouldn't go unpunished.

In the mornings he left the house without coffee, without even a bite of bread. He saw swirls of red and black, and would hole up in doorways to wait for the dizziness to pass. His view of the street sharpened. He saw people in rags. Old coats, pants, and jackets weren't thrown away anymore, they were patched. He looked down at people's feet and saw their shoes falling apart. Beggars now stood in the alleys where his father had once marched resolutely to work. He wasn't the only boy who sat in doorways fighting red and black whorls of hunger. He realized that Marx alone could not alleviate poverty – more was needed. Stalin became his god, revolution his dream. He couldn't imagine anything better than writing pamphlets with Martha and distributing them during the night. Love and danger – it was intoxicating. After the revolution, they planned to take their exams and go to university – in Vienna and Moscow. In the meantime, Heiner tried to find an apprenticeship as a draftsman, and when none was to be had, his mother apprenticed him to a bookbinder. A bookbinder! It was slave labor. At the crack of dawn he was harnessed to a wagon full of books. He hadn't known that mere paper could be heavy, but he quickly found out. It took him four hours to pull the cart from the fifth district to the seventeenth. He unloaded the books, loaded the cart up with fresh paper, and travelled back from the seventeenth district to the fifth. He collapsed in the street like a malnourished nag. People stopped and stared: look – the poor boy! They helped him up and pushed him onward as if he were a stubborn mule. Once a woman gave him a bit of sausage.

Heiner encountered new words in this changing world. Suddenly every family he knew had a night lodger – these were men who had work, but not enough money for a room, so they rented beds for just a few hours. Martha's family had one too, and one day Heiner's grandmother brought a stranger home. According to the rules, he could only arrive after nine in the evening and had to leave the house at seven in the morning. These men had no family, and on Sundays they slept on park benches. In comrade Paul's house Heiner noticed chalk marks on the floor. There was a line in front of the sitting room, one in front of the room where Paul slept with his son, and one in front of the kitchen. What game are you playing? he asked his friend. It was no game. Paul had marked off areas where the night lodger wasn't allowed. Heiner never met the man who stayed in his own home. Once Alma saw him in the hallway at night. He's a dwarf, she said. He's punier than Greta, two of them can fit in one bed.

How long ago that was. Another lifetime. Heiner stood up. He pushed his chair under the table. His whole family was scattered, yet he could feel their presence in this room. He put the salt shaker back on the table, right in the middle, over the hole in the lace tablecloth.

A thick layer of dust covered the chairs and the floor. Cobwebs hung from the ceiling with motionless spiders, either sleeping or dead. Should he rescue the apartment from this dusty stillness, or leave it to the spiders? Should his new life begin in a new apartment? The carpet was full of holes. While he'd been gone the moths had had more to eat than he.

As he was about to leave the apartment he noticed tracks in the dust, the imprints of shoes larger than his own. Whoever made them had just walked through the hallway into the living room, over to the sofa above which the cuckoo clock hung, and back to the door. There was just this one path. The steps were longer than his. They hadn't gone into the nursery, the bathroom, or the kitchen. On his way out Heiner heard a muffled knocking. He went back to the living room and saw that the door of the cuckoo clock had gotten stuck. When he opened it, the little bird shot out and belted its familiar "cuckoo."

A hundred thousand bombs were dropped on Vienna, forty thousand apartments destroyed, half the world shattered, millions of people killed – and in the middle of the inferno some crazy person must have come and wound the cuckoo clock every eight days. And on returning home, he, a survivor of the madness, had freed this wooden cuckoo from imprisonment. Heiner stood looking at the clock and laughed his strange laugh. It sounded like an asthma attack.

Softly, so as not to wake Heiner, Lena closes the door behind her, pushes the motor scooter out of the garage, and drives three miles down ruler-straight streets to the town. She wouldn't have wanted the house by the woods if this little town hadn't been close by. Her eyes crave more colors than the dark brown of the tree trunks, the velvet-brown of squirrels and the green of pine needles, and her ears need more sounds than just screeching birds and cracking twigs. She needs the voices of the merchants at the Saturday market, the sounds of traffic, the feeling of being part of things. She'd liked this place from the very beginning. The tall half-timbered houses along the square were five hundred years old, red and white, with shiny slate roofs. Pigeons bathed in the sandstone fountain and in the summer tourists sat on its edge.

It's just after eight when Lena gets to the bakery and picks up her standard order of "two poppyseed and two caraway for Rosseck." Then she drives to the news-stand, takes a copy of the local paper from the stack and adds a *Vienna Courier* for Heiner. She sits down to read in the dusty old Café Plüsch on the square and drinks two strong black coffees. The travel section is her favorite. Lena dreams of the South Pacific. Four weeks of sitting under palms and swimming with colorful fish, burying her hands in hot sand – but marrying a man like Heiner meant either giving up the South Pacific or traveling alone. One time, right after the wedding, she'd succeeded in carrying him off to the Adriatic. They had stayed in a little hotel by the sea. The water was as blue as the sky, and they could see the ocean floor from the window of their hotel. Heiner stayed in the room while Lena swam and lay in the sun. He wasn't bored. He read and slept and made notes for an essay on life as a survivor. He enjoyed making love to Lena. She smelled like the sea and tasted like sand – he never wanted to let her go. If that meant traveling to a Croatian island called Dogi Otok, then so be it. Heiner didn't find beautiful places relaxing, Lena learned after that vacation. Beauty dazzled and tormented him and made the images he carried inside even gloomier. And besides, he had his own sand to stick his fingers into every now and then. He kept it at home in a mustard jar on the sideboard, three steps from the sofa.

How is your husband? drawls the waiter at Café Plüsch. He asks every morning between Lena's first and second coffee and Lena always says: My husband is well, thank you, even when he isn't. At nine she drives back home. On Wednesdays and Fridays it's not until ten, because on those days the pastor's wife practices the organ. There is a ritual connected with this organ-playing, though no one knows just how it began. The pastor's wife enters the church and closes the heavy door. As soon as she hits the first note, someone opens the door again so that the music can flow out over the square. Twice a week Lena watches, fascinated by the way just fifteen minutes of Bach or Bruckner are enough to loosen the grip of routine. A woman pauses in her shopping and sits down on the church steps. The baker opens the bakery window, the bookseller stands outside her shop and Lena puts down her newspaper. The butcher says there's a difference between slaughtering a lamb on a Monday and slaughtering it on a Friday. When it's accompanied by organ music, he says, even butchering becomes holy.

When Heiner and Lena moved into the house by the woods in the fall of 1966, they counted as an old couple amid all the young families. He was in his mid-forties, she was ten years younger. Fifteen years later, only newcomers to the neighborhood wonder what they're doing together. She's a jolly woman who loves to laugh and laugh loudly, who makes the best plum jam in the neighborhood, speaks Polish and French, and wears crazy hats and dangerously high heels when she drives the old Daimler into the city. A sign hangs on their front door: Lena Rosseck, Certified Translator. She lets her long hair fly free in the wind when she drives the scooter and could almost be the daughter of the old man with the deeply wrinkled face. The way he says "Servus" in greeting is quite charming, but then his smile fades a bit more quickly than other people's. That's the interesting thing about them: They seem like an unremarkable couple, but one can spend a long time talking about them. The Rossecks often keep the living room light on all night, and a thin yellow strip spills through the curtains and onto the street. People say the man didn't work, even when he was younger. He reads at night – maybe he's a scholar. Now and then the Rossecks have house guests who stay for a long time, sometimes as much as two weeks. People from Poland who roll their "r's" strongly, and there are often cars with Austrian plates parked in front of the house. You can talk to the Poles – they speak good German. No one knows why such a lively woman would love such an odd man. Still, she must have her reasons. Perhaps he's rich and she has a lover in the city. The Rossecks are the only people in the neighborhood who never put up a Christmas tree. They celebrate the holidays with guests from Poland and Vienna – you can tell from the license plates. Everyone knows that Lena has a friend in town – Gesa, the woman who owns the cinema. When no one wants to see the movies that Gesa has ordered, the two women sit alone in the theatre, watching the movie and drinking wine. Besides Gesa, the doctor, and the postman, no one has ever seen the inside of the Rossecks' house. Their patio is visible from the woods, and everyone knows you can set your watch by "the Viennese," as they call him. It's three o'clock when he ends his afternoon nap on the porch swing. Then he goes for a brisk walk in the woods for an hour, as if there's no other way he can wake up. It's four when "the Viennese" drinks his coffee on the patio. The news is over when he takes his evening walk through the neighborhood as if performing an inspection, always with a glowing cigarette in his left hand. The man isn't unpleasant, just somewhat peculiar. He gets a lot of mail and puts thick envelopes in the mailbox several times a week.

Lena rolls the scooter back into the garage, sets the breakfast table, makes coffee, and quietly opens the bedroom door.

Are you awake?

If he doesn't answer, she lets him sleep. If he moves his head slightly he's awake, but not yet ready for the day. Then Lena goes into the study, starts working on a translation and listens carefully to the sounds from the bedroom. When she hears the shower she makes scrambled eggs and bacon for Heiner and two soft-boiled eggs for herself. His hair is damp. He smells of lavender. He wears the velvet bathrobe that she gave him for his birthday. Two poppy-seed rolls for Lena and two with caraway for Heiner. Sometimes he says: Even in our greatest need, let us have salt and bread.

We're having a guest on Sunday, Lena says.

Who?

A colleague. She's new to the area. She's nice – I like her.

Good, says Heiner, then I like her too. What's her name?

Ninja. Don't scare her off with your sand. Or do. See how you feel.

His eyes were closed when Lena's hair fell on his face. He couldn't see what the woman bending over him looked like, but he liked how she smelled.

Nor would Lena forget her first sight of Heiner. A tall, gaunt man leaning against a wall in the hallway of the courthouse, slowly slumping, sinking down inch by inch. She had spent the last few hours sitting in her office translating the testimony of a Polish witness who had refused to come to Germany. Her windowless office was stuffy, but her feeling of suffocation had more to do with the text. She put the transcript in a binder to send to the judge's office. It was a Friday, June 5, 1964, a warm summer day; Lena had planned nice things to get the witness's testimony out of her head. She'd go swimming, doze by the pool, then go to the movies with Tom and drink some wine with him somewhere in the warm summer night.

The face of the sinking man was very pale. Lena ran to him and held his shoulders until he was safely squatting. Watch this binder, she said, and ran into the cafeteria. She found a chair, bought water and a chocolate bar with nuts and got a pillow for his head. His brown curls were stuck behind his ears, and his forehead was sweaty. She knew who he was. He was the witness from Vienna, summoned for 8:30 am on June 5, 1964, the 52nd day of hearings. She wiped his brow dry with her handkerchief and he opened his eyes. They were blue and very bright, the color she had painted the sky with watercolors when she was in school.

You okay? she asked.

He drank a sip of water, took a bite of chocolate, and let Lena help him onto the chair. Later he confessed that he'd been less concerned with his weakness than with Lena's strong hands and the smell of her hair. Lena's first thought was: What a gentle face. The first word he whispered was a greeting: "Servus." On this day of all days the last thing he wanted to do was answer more questions, but Lena asked more than the judge and wanted to know everything all at once. Are you alone here in Frankfurt? Are you staying with someone? How long have you been here? How long are you staying? Are you staying at a hotel? What do you do at night?

The man, who was slowly regaining his color, said faintly:

I'm trying to walk around the city.

Why "trying"?

Because it's not working. Whenever I leave the hotel I'm back in ten minutes.

Why?

He smiled. There are too many Germans in this city.

Hmmm, Lena said, too many Germans. That can't be helped – they live here.

Young people aren't the problem, he said. I just can't handle the ones who are my age or older. I stare at them until they stop and ask if we know each other. Then I say: Good God, no – that would be terrible! and I turn around.

Hmmm, Lena said. It could have meant anything. I understand, or: this man is nuts.

She laid her hand on his shoulder and considered. Swimming. Movies. Tom. Wine in the warm summer night. It was a nice plan – but could she leave this poor man all alone in Germany, struggling to take just a few steps? Why didn't he let someone sponsor him here in Frankfurt? Usually all witnesses were taken care of. Should she take him with her, include him in her plans? Not a good idea. Ten minutes ago the man had had tears in his eyes. She looked at him. He looked good. He smiled and let her help him without being ashamed of his weakness. The longer her hand lay on his shoulder, the more curious she became. She didn't know anyone like him. Once he went back to Vienna, she'd miss the chance of getting to know him. May I…Lena said, and at the same time Heiner said Shall we…and then their sentences overlapped: "Buy you a beer this evening?"…" Eat some cream-cake?"

He'd first come to Frankfurt a year ago. At the time his feet had been leaden, and the road to the detention center where prisoners were kept during investigation had felt like a second deportation. The judge who escorted him had been kind, but no matter what friendly terms were used for what awaited him – a lineup, a meeting – it didn't make the trip any easier. He was to identify two men who could have killed him whenever they felt like it back then: Josef Klehr and Oswald Kaduk. He was supposed to say what he had seen to their very faces. Kaduk had spent the last five years in prison awaiting trial after a former prisoner had recognized and denounced him. As if nothing had happened, Kaduk had been working as a nurse, just as he had before the war. The patients called him "Papa Kaduk," because he was so friendly. He was a powerful man who still terrified Heiner. What if he suddenly lashed out? Would the judge be able to protect him? His fear of Klehr was more diffuse. The man no longer held a lethal syringe, but the cold fear that had overcome Heiner when the Oberscharführer inspected him still lay in his bones.

The judge reassured him: It will be fine, Herr Rosseck. Don't worry. When they entered the small interrogation room, the two men were already there, and Heiner saw them for the first time without uniforms, without weapons, away from the surroundings that had given them their power. He exchanged a quick look with Klehr, whom he'd seen every day in the camp. Why the charade? Klehr said coolly. I've never seen that man before in my life.

Heiner believed him – how could Klehr recognize him? He was no longer a striped skeleton. He had let his hair grow and wore a suit, a white shirt and a tie: he was a gentleman. Of course Klehr didn't know who he was. Klehr stuck out his hand and Heiner took it, although he had planned not to shake hands with any of the men – it was just a reflex. You shake the hand that's held out to you. Klehr was not angry, but exasperated by the accusations: Yes, yes, I gave injections, he said. How many times do you want to hear it?…I kept records…everything is in those diaries… yes, 12 400…it was a mercy for those people, why won't anyone believe me?…in the gas chamber they would have had to suffer for more than eight minutes…but inject them, right in the heart, and they fall over, dead…And this man here – he looked at Heiner again – I've never seen him in my life. Heiner could hardly recognize Klehr, either. He looked like anybody now, though at the time Heiner would have been able to pick him out of a crowd of hundreds, from any distance.

Kaduk didn't stand up. He threw his head back and looked at Heiner as if to say: What do you want, you little shit? Please, Herr Rosseck, said the judge, describe your first encounter with Kaduk.

Now he was allowed to speak, and he said what he had planned to say. Everyone there had a specialty, Your Honor, but it's something you have to see to believe. I remember this so clearly because it was my first day of work, and I had arrived just the day before. Kaduk killed with a club.

The detainee jumped up, fists clenched. Heiner recoiled as Kaduk screamed: Just put it all on me, ha! And suddenly it was him again, the old Kaduk. The bellowing and the "ha" at the beginning or end of a sentence. Ha, they pin everything on the little guys, and nothing happens to the higher-ups. They run free and we get life. He stared at the judge. Do you want to know how it was? The judge nodded – that's why we're here. It was how it was, Kaduk screamed. The great commanders have no right to deny it now. The transports rolled into the camps like rolls hot from the oven – everyone did shifts on the ramp, and of course children went to the gas chambers first, that's logical, and then the mothers who were clinging to the children. But I didn't send anyone, not me – I just watched like a hawk to make sure that none of the condemned snuck off. Yes, sure, I was an attack dog. Working at the camp took a toll on my nerves, believe me, it was hard work. But I wasn't the kind to fall apart – it's only here in the cell that I had a breakdown – and do you know why? Because I'm being tried in a court of double standards.

Heiner pressed himself against the wall. Kaduk was a tough customer. Heiner couldn't let Kaduk see him trembling, no matter what. The judge tried to calm the accused: Sit down, please, Herr Kaduk, just sit down. When Kaduk finally sank back into the chair, Heiner took a deep breath as he tried to wrangle the whirl of images in his head into the sentences upon which everything depended. His voice was soft and firm. *Kaduk did it with a club,* he said, *and Klehr with a needle.*

As the two men who had often come so dangerously close to Heiner in the camp were led out of the interrogation room, the judge pushed Josef Klehr's chair over for Heiner to sit in. Please, Heiner said, let's leave. I can't sit in that chair.

That had happened a year ago, and now he was to stand in court and repeat what he'd seen. As precisely as possible. When, where, how. The transcript would later state that the questioning of the Viennese witness Heiner Rosseck on the 52nd day of hearings had to be interrupted because the witness broke down in tears and was unable speak. But it wasn't the memories that overpowered him. He could talk about what he had experienced

– that was why he had come to Germany. What did him in on that morning was the search for truth in terms of the penal code. He knew that a trial dealt with facts and data, not with feelings, but he had overestimated himself. The judge's tone was reproving, as if he were questioning some inept witness of a traffic accident. An entire world would have fit between the images Heiner carried inside him and the facts the judge wanted to hear. His skin wasn't thick enough for such a performance. The murderers sat behind him. He didn't need to turn around to know that they were sneering and taunting him. Klehr smirked. Kaduk threw his head back insolently. Their lawyers' questions were sharp or smug: And where is this supposed to have happened? On which day, in which month, at noon or at night? How far away were you when you saw this? Ten yards, twenty yards? You were able to recognize a face from fifty yards away? And the weather? Was there snow? Rain? Was it foggy that day? The door through which you say you saw Herr Klehr giving injections, was it on the right or the left, at the back or the front of the barracks? Was there even a door, or just a curtain? Was it brown or blue? It was easy to fluster him. The defense attorneys were like the dogs in the camp. Lurking, vicious, ready to attack.

He felt dizzy, and began to stutter. He broke down in tears and asked for a break.

On the evening of the 52nd day of hearings Heiner and Lena were the only customers in Café Stern. The café was in the Gallus area of town, close to the court. Lena drank wine and Heiner smoked two cigarettes with every coffee. They found the right tone quickly – earnest, cheerful, and already rather familiar, after their meeting in the hallway. Heiner let Lena describe the way he had slowly sunk down the wall, and she wanted to know what he had first noticed about her. Your hair on my face, he said. It was like a cool silk cloth. And your scent. Have you ever picked cèpes on a sunny day in September? That's how your hair smells. Your hands seemed bigger and stronger than they do now, lying on the table like that. A surgeon's hands. Are you a doctor? He felt good. He hadn't felt as light as he felt on this evening, with this woman, in a long time. He wanted to please her, to entertain her, he wanted to make her laugh. He liked her laugh – it was easygoing and loud. For Lena he turned his crying fit in court into comedy. He spoke with a Viennese accent. Heiner gestured to the man eating bratwurst next to them. Imagine this: After twenty years this man is summoned and interrogated. Heiner sat up straight and played the defense attorney: How long was the bratwurst that you ate – 3 inches, 5 inches, 10 inches? Was the skin notched or smooth? Was it brown or pale, crispy or limp? Hot or cold, or perhaps just lukewarm? Herr Witness, what color was the mustard? Was it light yellow, golden, orange, or brown? Mild, spicy, or medium-spicy? Whole-grain or smooth? Or did you eat the sausage without mustard? Was there ketchup or mayonnaise involved? White or dark bread? Was your waiter German or foreign? Heiner was a good actor. He waited for Lena to laugh, but she didn't laugh. She looked at him as if he'd told a terribly sad story, and he liked that even better. He felt her looking at him, registering that his nose looked like he'd lost quite a few boxing matches, and that his chin was a little crooked. He felt like falling in love, but it would have been a miracle if that were to happen in a place where he already had to struggle with so many feelings. Falling in love – what chaos that would bring. It was something to fear more than to celebrate. And if she didn't return his feelings and was just sitting with him out of pity – here, in this city? It would do him in. Better not to see her again. Tender feelings are like young plants. You can just pull them out before they take root.

They sat in Café Stern on the evenings of the 53rd, 54th, and 55th days of the hearings. He told Lena, as if it hardly mattered, that he had been divorced for five years, and that he had a daughter in Vienna – Kaija. He had lost contact with her. So he wasn't completely free, but he wasn't really attached, either. And you? Lena answered tersely: I live in an apartment alone. I don't have children. I have an attachment named Tom. On the 56th day of hearings Heiner walked through the city for a whole hour, led by Lena's hand, and he still wasn't sure whether the hand was only meant to protect him or whether her heart was pounding like his. He gained confidence, ventured a few shy glances at people and stopped thinking that he had seen every face before. When he appeared in court for the second time, Lena sat in the gallery, listened to the judge's questions, and heard Heiner's clear voice responding. Just knowing she was there gave him strength, but he still felt as if he were walking on a wire over a deep canyon. He couldn't allow himself to fall, not again. He had to simply remember, without seeing any of the images that went along with his memories. Evidence in the eyes of the law: that was all that mattered. Murder, even the murder of thousands, had to have a place, a time, and a date. Where had he seen Klehr? In Block 20? Why there? He worked in Block 21. How did he get from Block 21 to Block 20? Which door had he used? The one on the long side or the one on the short side? Or on the gable side? In what room did Klehr kill people? Was it to the right of the hallway or to the left? Was Klehr alone or were there prisoners in the room? Did Klehr wear an apron during the killings, or a lab coat? Was it purple, red, white, or yellow? Did he have a needle in his hand when the witness saw him? Was it in his right hand or his left?

Did the witness see the people who were killed? How many were there? Was it closer to twenty or to a hundred? And where were the bodies taken afterwards? Was there a door between the hall and the room, or just a hanging blanket? How often did killings take place there? Once a week, or every day?

He wanted to be a reliable witness – that was why he had stayed alive. He couldn't let them confuse him. He couldn't think about the men who sat behind him, haunting his every word. He couldn't imagine their eyes, their smiling faces. The effort was inhuman. Kaduk put on a show: he paraded into the courtroom with his hands stiff at his sides and his head thrown back proudly. He ridiculed the court, the witnesses, and even the men next to him in the dock who couldn't remember anything. Klehr laughed and spoke just as he had back then. Selection was called "making the rounds," and killing with the disinfectant Phenol was called "inoculation." He said what he thought: the method was cost-effective, odorless, easy to use, and completely dependable. He found the judges obtuse. Why fuss? A quick death is humane! The syringe was hardly empty before the man was dead, he explained. Murder? Your Honor, sick ain't the word for those people. In plain German: They weren't ill, they were half dead.

Heiner made it through his second testimony, barely stuttered, and did not let them confuse him. He did not break down. He was proud of himself, but only made peace with his performance later, after he had written down what he actually wanted to say. Whenever he was asked, even years later, he could recite the text like a ballad.

Your Honor!

I worked as a typist in Block 21, the prisoner's infirmary. That's where I learned to use a typewriter, practically overnight, otherwise I wouldn't be standing here.

The typing room is on the ground floor of Block 21, just on the left as you come in. Sixteen men type constantly, day and night. We have quotas. We type death records. The first shift runs from six in the morning until six at night and the second begins at six at night and ends at six in the morning. Death records, you have to understand, are written only for people who have numbers – those are the ones actually admitted to the camps – most people on each transport don't even make it that far. No records have to be written for people who are to be killed immediately. Several times a day an SS man brings us a list with names and numbers of the dead. We don't know how these people died. We can choose from thirty different illnesses. According to my typewriter people die of heart failure, phlegmons, pneumonia, spotted fever and typhus, embolisms, influenza, circulatory collapse, stroke, cirrhosis of the liver, scarlet fever, diphtheria, whooping cough, and kidney failure. Under no circumstances is anyone tortured, beaten to death, or shot at Auschwitz. No one starves, dies of thirst; no one is hanged, no one gassed. We write death notices twenty-four hours a day – eight hundred to a thousand every shift – and we write doctor's reports for the relatives, but it's all an empty clattering of keys.

Here Heiner paced his speech as if chanting a hasty Our Father. You could see him typing: Prisoner 128 439, Otto Schnur, born 24.9.1905, previously residing in Hannover, admitted to Auschwitz Concentration Camp on 19.10.1942. Period. On 28.11.1942 Prisoner 128 439, Otto Schnur, was admitted to the camp infirmary. Period. A clinical and radiological examination found typhus, which resulted in cardiac failure, and he collapsed and died on 2.12.1942 at 19:35. Period. If the deceased was a citizen of the German Reich, a copy of the report was sent to the relatives. I don't know what Prisoner Otto Schnur actually died of.

Your Honor!

Do you know what phlegmons are? Phlegmons are inflammations of cellular tissue, primarily in the legs, as a result of hunger and filth. The legs swell – they get thick like Doric columns and the feet start to look like cannonballs. The skin cracks and pus is secreted through the cavities. And – here he holds his nose – it smells rotten and sweet…you can't imagine the stink! Sometimes I smell it in my dreams, and I get sick and have to vomit. Otherwise, I must say, the work was perfectly pleasant. Except that sometimes it broke your heart. You come across the number of someone you saw in the morning and now it's afternoon and he's dead. What happened to him? Was he shot? Did he get his head bashed in? When it's for someone you know, when you have to invent a cause of death for a friend – that's a terrible thing.

Your Honor!

The death-ledgers from the infirmary in the main camp survived; 130 000 numbers from the summer of '42 to the summer of '44. It's hard to fathom what human beings can get used to. We ate our bread next to half-decayed people. We chatted. Sometimes we made jokes and laughed.

Now, for Klehr. It's as if I saw him every day. When Klehr made his selection, the prisoners had to leave the infirmary naked and stand in the corridor, each holding his medical card. The cards were laid on the table before Klehr. He smoked a pipe and singled out sick prisoners with its stem: Step forward! You and you and you and you. Klehr picks up the first card. He has time. He looks at the card. The entries reveal how long the person who stands naked before him has been in the infirmary. He puffs on the pipe. Fourteen days! He puts the card aside, picks up the next one, shakes his head. Just two days in the infirmary and already a Muselman! He sets the card aside. No one has ever survived more than fourteen days in the infirmary. During every selection one of us typists sat out in the corridor. Klehr announced the numbers and we wrote them down. These were the numbers of people he had chosen to die. The people were still alive while we were pecking out their death records. Dead of heart attack, dead of phlegmons, pneumonia, kidney failure, spotted fever, typhus, embolism, influenza, circulatory collapse…Everyone whose cards we had sorted out was picked up and brought to Klehr in Block 20.

Your Honor, in Block 20, Klehr injected Phenol into the hearts of the people he'd selected. He killed them in the "dressing room" – the room behind the curtain. There was a small table with the needle and the Phenol. Next to it was a chair where the victim was forced to sit. Most of them were so weak and their minds so worn down that they just let themselves be killed. But one time I was there when a man cried out and begged for his life and tried to protect his heart with both hands. Klehr ordered his assistants, who were prisoners too, to twist his arms so that the right arm lay against his back and the left could be pressed to his mouth. Then it was quiet. The area around his heart was free.

Once I had to deliver a message to Block 20. The curtain to the "dressing room" wasn't closed. I saw Klehr with the needle in his hand. He looked into my eyes, annoyed, as if I had interrupted his breakfast. He lifted the needle and snarled at me. Beat it – or do you want a shot too?

We had this crazy fear of Klehr because he had no anger towards us. He killed with a light touch, without hatred.

Your Honor!

The perpetrators of these crimes weren't sick in the head – they weren't any crazier than you or me. If this playground of murder in Poland, if I may call it that, hadn't existed, Klehr would have stayed a carpenter and Kaduk a nurse. Or a firefighter. Dirlewanger would have remained a lawyer, fat Jupp a dumb gangster, and Palitzsch, if he hadn't died in the war, would have been Chief of Police or Secretary of State, and Boger would have been manager of the local insurance company. Or a teacher with a secret lust for punishing children. He wouldn't have built the Boger swing. The perpetrators, Your Honor, were young and ambitious. They wanted to succeed at what they did. What it was didn't matter. They acted like employees, hungry for praise and advancement. The sadists aren't the most dangerous. The most dangerous are the normal people.

Your Honor, if you and I were to meet again in such a place, I would stand among the prisoners. You don't know where you'd stand, I'm one step ahead of you there.

At this point Heiner paused to free himself from the sentences that could have driven him mad. End of the ballad.

Your Honor. You hear our stories. You record them. They touch your mind. They touch your intelligence. Perhaps even your imagination. But you're not one inch closer to us than you were before the trial. Nothing in the world can bridge the gap between your imagination and our experiences.

At six in the morning on Monday, June 15, 1964, Heiner and Lena stood at the main Frankfurt train station. Every day, five trains traveled to Vienna and from Vienna back to Frankfurt – a journey of ten hours each way. Seven more minutes, Heiner said, and for the first time he took Lena in his arms and she kissed him – not like someone in need of her protection, not like a person she was teaching to walk through a German city. When they heard the loudspeaker say that the train would be twenty minutes late, they simply remained there, clasped together as if stuck with glue. And when they heard that on that day the train would be leaving from Track 12 instead of Track 9, they didn't budge. Please stand clear, doors closing, the voice from the loudspeaker said. They left Heiner's suitcase in a locker and took a taxi to Lena's apartment. Heiner said: Every man knows that he is born to die, yet we all forget, and squander our time on earth. Death is my shadow, it accompanies me like a mild headache. It's there to say: Do not forget that each moment is precious. With this in mind, Heiner made love to Lena until the night train left. My treasure, he wrote from Vienna, I don't know if there can be a future for us. The truth is, I'm a wreck. I've survived spotted fever, typhus, and tuberculosis. I suffer from acute exhaustion and chronic bronchitis. I have a circulatory disorder. I'm forty-five years old and I've already had a heart attack. At forty, when I was manager of a print shop in Vienna, I was sick more often than the workers. Once my sickness outlasted my vacation days, and I hadn't gotten any better, I was dismissed. I trained to teach at a vocational school and taught printing, and after three double periods I felt worn to the bone.

Do you know what a wreck is? Lena wrote. A wreck is a "drifting object" that has become unusable due to decay or damage. Decay certainly doesn't apply to you.

Treasure of my heart, Heiner wrote, there are days when I wouldn't want to be friends with myself. The camp has infected every part of my body, and as far as I know, scientists have not been looking for a cure. There are nights when I can't sleep and nights when I cry out. There was already one woman for whom it was all too much, and a child who no longer asks about me. They sent me away. I barely survived that – I don't have the strength to go through it a second time.

The cure has already been discovered, Lena wrote. It has four letters. You've experienced it and it did you good.

Before we make any plans, he wrote, I have to show you something that belongs to me as much as my head and my heart. You may well find that you don't want to face sharing an apartment with me and it.

His letters were tender and shy. He tried to warn her off. He was desperate for happiness yet terrified of happiness.

Lena packed a bag and traveled to Vienna unannounced. She had a taxi take her to the twentieth district – the envelopes said 37 Rauscherstraße. At three o'clock in the afternoon she stood before a decaying Jugendstil building, her heart pounding. She found his initials, HR, next to a brass doorbell. On the train she'd neither read nor slept. What did he want to show her? What was as important as his heart and his head? What kind of possession could be so earth-shattering that it required a warning? She put her finger on the doorbell. What might she not want to face living with? A sick mother? Did he have cats, dogs, birds, poisonous snakes? Lena pulled back her finger. She looked up at the façade – he lived on the third floor and must have a nice view of the Augarten. She heard his voice in her head. *Treasure of my heart...*

Treasure was a word she knew. She knew it was not a word that was bestowed lightly. Her father had called her mother treasure because she was the most precious thing in his life. The bible says: For where your treasure is, there will your heart be also. For Lena, "treasure" was a key. In Danzig it had unlocked her father's study, where there was a family treasure that Lena would later inherit. In Zurich, the key unlocked the drawer of her father's desk. Lena's treasure was the diary of Franziska, her great-great-grandmother's grandmother, who had been born in the free city of Danzig, which at that time was part of the Kingdom of Prussia. In 1813, when Franziska was eleven, Danzig was attacked by French-Polish troops and lay under siege for eleven months. In her diary, the young girl described the panic when forty thousand French soldiers invaded the city. They looted shops, burned down buildings, ravaged churches. The streets were filled with garbage and excrement. "We are all under house arrest," the girl wrote. "Theyre is bread and horrible preserved fish. I hidd my dolls in the shoeclosset. Mama's jewelry is in the honey jar. Papa says we will put the cowardly Frenchmen to flight. We are afrayd."

When the French were forced to yield to an army of Russians and Prussians, Franziska wrote: "Papa says: Hurrah, we are Prussians again!"

Eighteen years later, when she was twenty-nine, she wrote to her husband, who was stationed in Vienna: "They took a census. Seventy-six percent of the people in Danzig speak German, and only twenty-four speak Polish. Danzig is a German city. Now it's official."

Nearly a hundred years later, ninety-five percent of the citizens of Danzig claimed German as their mother tongue, and Lena's father threw an orgy for his friends, which was still stuff of legend when Lena graduated in Zurich. Lena found her family's history interesting and unusual. Born in Danzig, with Poles as neighbors and friends, but no Polish relatives. When Hitler invaded Poland, Lena's parents moved to Switzerland. We're Prussians, her father said, we're not Nazis. Lena was six at the time, and her heartache over the move turned into a malady her father called "Nasty-itis." She hit anyone who attempted to touch her. She spat food in her parents' faces or at the wall. She'd lost her friends, two grandpas and two grandmas, uncles, aunts, nieces, and nephews – the whole beautiful city had been taken from her. The sea and the harbor. Lena screamed the name of her nanny for hours on end: OlgaOlgaOlga, as if her heart were breaking. Olga had sung Polish songs with her and had read her Eichendorff's

Danzig poem so often that both knew it by heart: *Dark gables, high windows, towers gazing through the mist. Statues looming pale as ghosts, standing silent at the doors.* Lena loved the poem because the image of towers gazing through mist was uncanny, and it was creepy to imagine pale statues standing silent at the doors, though she didn't even really know what a statue was. Olga knew whether statues were good or bad and what it meant for them to stand pale and silent at the doors. Are they sick or dead? Neither, Olga said, they're just old. Olga started university a year before, and to Lena she was the cleverest, most beautiful playmate one could wish for. She had black eyes and she was soft and round like Lena's teddy bear. Swiss nannies didn't last a week with Lena. She bit their hands like a mad dog.

She learned Schwyzerdütsch and French, and as a reward, her father allowed her some Polish time – lessons on Sunday from eleven to one – which cured the "Nasty-itis" and brought back Lena's sweet temperament. Her father's wise choice determined her path in life. Without Polish, there would have been no trips to Poland. Without Polish, no degree in translation. Without the degree, no job at the court in Frankfurt. Without the job, no walk down a hallway in the Gallus quarter, where on June 5, 1964, on the 52nd day of hearings, the witness from Vienna was leaning against the wall, his eyes closed and face white as chalk.

Lena took her finger from the doorbell. She decided to sit on a bench in the Augarten and consider whether it was a good idea to ambush a person without warning. Heiner's face – what would it look like if she suddenly appeared at his door? Would he wear the exhausted expression she knew from the courthouse hallway, or the laughing, mischievous one with which he parodied his questioning when they were together in the café? She knew his face when he made love to her and his lonely face behind the train window when they parted. Did he get angry when someone disturbed his schedule? He wouldn't have a chance to cover up his reaction if she surprised him like that, no way to even feign politeness if he wasn't pleased. He would show her the only face available to him in those few seconds of recognition. That face might show joy, or fear. If it was an angry face, it would be over between them.

She sat on a bench in the Augarten for an hour, on the big avenue. Most people were in a hurry. A hurdy-gurdy man with a black top hat stopped and played for her because she clapped after every song – a quarter of an hour, just for her. Waltzes – the most cheerful kind of music. She gave him five Marks – he accepted any currency. When he moved on, she decided to let chance decide. If in the next half hour more women passed by her than men, she would ring the bell at 37 Rauscherstraße. She looked at the clock – it was half past three. No one came for a long time, and then, as if chance were teasing her, two couples. Then came a girl walking a dog and a mother pushing a stroller, but she couldn't tell whether the child inside it was male or female. Lena looked at the clock. Ten more minutes and there was no one on the avenue. In the final minutes, two old men turned onto the avenue from a smaller path and a boy ran after a girl with a dog. The time was up. Lena stood. She caught a taxi in Wallensteinstraße and said: To the train station, please. The next morning she sent a postcard to Vienna: Tell me what it is that belongs to you that I won't be able to bear.

Treasure of my heart, Heiner wrote. Come to Vienna. I'm plagued by hallucinations. Two days ago my heart stopped because through my window I saw a woman who looked just like you. A crazy hat, your quick steps. She came out of the park and walked toward Wallensteinstraße. I almost ran after her.

Look around, Heiner said, I'll make some whipped cream.

His kitchen was narrow, clean, and tidy. A still life hung over a small breakfast table. A dead pheasant with glazed eyes lay on a bed of carrots, celery, and leeks. Its claws were spread, and a slug crept from its open beak. Was this the "something" from which he could not part?

Who cleans the house? Lena asked.

I do.

The bathroom was painted green. Lena felt like she was in an aquarium. Two hairbrushes stood in a stoneware jar. Why two? He used lavender soap; she sniffed his aftershave. Sandalwood. His face and neck smelled of it. Four toothbrushes stood in a glass. Why four? The furniture didn't look like what a forty-five-year-old man might choose – it looked more like he had inherited it. There was a heavy sofa in the living room, Biedermeier style, freshly covered in dark green velvet. A baby blue wool blanket hung over the back, neatly folded. Books were stacked on bookshelves or piled on the ground; they lay open on the windowsill, chairs, and table. On the sideboard she found a crumpled picture in a silver frame: a girl with blond braids and braces, smiling shyly. A game of Halma was set up on the coffee table, seemingly abandoned mid-play. Black and red marbles were clumped in the middle of the board – it wasn't clear who was going to win. A cuckoo clock hung on the wall.

Are you playing with a child?

I'm playing with myself, Heiner said. Or against myself. It depends on who wins.

Lena walked into the dining room. Heiner had set the table with an old coffee set: white porcelain with narrow gold rims.

He'd whipped cream and set two thermoses of coffee on the table, as well as a tray of plum cake. There was no ailing mother, no cat, no snake.

Did you see the bedroom? Heiner asked. If not, go and look. Was the secret object from which he did not wish to part in there? Cautiously, she opened the door.

The room was bathed in warm light, as if an evening sun were just setting. Heiner had arranged five small lamps on the floor: one stood at the foot of the bed, another behind the armchair, two on the wardrobe and one on the windowsill. In the middle of the room was a single bed strewn with fresh rose petals.

Welcome to heaven, Lena said.

Heiner took her in his arms: That's how our life should be.

So. An obliquely lit life.

What she was looking for wasn't here, either.

What is it that belongs to you like your head and your heart that I won't be able to bear?

Later, Heiner said. Let's have some coffee.

I'm not touching that coffee until I know what's in store for me.

Look, Lena, Heiner said, and for the first time she heard the two words that were to accompany her everywhere, like a melody composed for her alone. Look, Lena. At that moment, she had no idea in how many different ways he would use those words. Depending on his tone, they could be soft – Look, Lena, I'm telling a story – or commanding: Look, Lena! They could sound arrogant, encouraging, cautioning, impatient – Look, Lena. How could you possibly not know? On that afternoon in Vienna, as Heiner took a round mustard jar filled with light-colored sand off the bookshelf, the words sounded gentle, almost seductive. Look, Lena. Look what I have here. He set the jar down next to the plum cake. What might this be?

It's definitely not an egg-timer.

Guess. Hold it.

A souvenir from a nice vacation. The South Pacific?

Stick your finger in it. It's rough, right? Guess again.

Broken shells? Gravel?

Casually, as if discussing the weather, he said: In Birkenau, when you walk from the women's camp to Crematorium II, you see a small path – nothing special. People don't notice, he said, when it crunches under their feet. Little stones, they think – gravel, sand. But what's really crunching underfoot are the remains of people who've been burned. Tenderly, he took the jar out of her hand. Do you understand? The rough pieces are tiny bits of bone. Each from a different person. The paths there are covered with the bits of bone that trickled off the truck. In Birkenau pools and tarns are filled with this stuff. The lane that leads into the camp is white. You walk on the dead and don't even notice.

He cut slices of plum cake and poured coffee.

I could have turned into one of those tiny bones.

He laid a slice of cake on her plate. Dig in.

Lena pushed the plate towards the middle of the table. Plum cake, whipped cream, and bits of bone. You're really quite a host.

It's not the cake's fault if the ground in Birkenau is white.

That jar is going to accompany us everywhere?

I'll be buried with it.

It's going to live with us?

I have to have it near me.

I don't know if I can live with a mustard jar in which the dead are still so alive, Lena said.

Since Lena hadn't touched her cake, Heiner too ate nothing. They sat across from each other in silence.

Say something, Lena.

What a lovely coffee hour this has been.

He stood up and carried the plates with the cake into the kitchen. He cleared away the cups and saucers, the bowl with the cream, and the forks. He bustled back and forth between the kitchen and dining room as if he wished he could keep cleaning up forever. He washed the dishes, dried them, and put everything back in the cupboard, plate by plate, cup by cup. Lena watched.

The jar, she said. You need it as much as your head and your heart?

He nodded.

When there was nothing left to do in the kitchen, Heiner set a bottle of champagne and two glasses on the table. He wanted to toast to Vienna, to her visit to his apartment. He opened the bottle and poured two glasses. Lena stared at her glass as if trying to count the bubbles. A mustard jar full of sand stood between them.

Once a large family had sat around this table – everyone he loved. Father and mother, his sisters Greta and Alma, the grandmother with the beautiful hair whom they called wild Hilde. *Even in our greatest need, let us have salt and bread.* Everything important was discussed around this table. The Schattendorf Verdict. The burning of the Justizpalast. And then, one by one, they'd left the table. First his father, then him, his grandmother, his mother, his sisters. Heiner stood up and walked around the table, straightening the chairs. What could he do to convince Lena that living with a jar filled with bones was no worse than living with photos of relatives who were no longer alive? He could say: Look, Lena. What's the difference between a yellowed photograph of your dead grandmother and the bones in this jar? Both are mementos of people that don't exist anymore. The bones are clean, they don't smell bad, and they have one great advantage: they don't have faces. They're reminders of the way the people lost their lives, I admit that. But don't photos do the same thing? If you had an uncle who was stabbed to death, and you looked at a photo of him when he was young and full of life, wouldn't you think about the horrible way he died? So the sand is the same – no more than a memento. We can call the jar South Pacific, if you like. He left the table and stood by the window.

Down below, children used to whistle when they wanted him to come out and play. The waterer watered the horses. These were the streets his father took when he walked to work – Heiner could still see his straight back, his energetic gait, and his face when he came home and waved up at Heiner. When the wave seemed tired, Heiner knew his father had had a hard day. *The Justizpalast is burning. These are radical times.* On the day before the invasion, Vienna felt like a bubbling cauldron, and Heiner was right in the thick of it, with Martha at his side. They would have given their lives to defeat the Nazis. Carl Zuckmayer had described March 11, 1938 in his memoirs, and when Heiner discovered the text, he copied it down word for word into his notebook. That's how it was, exactly like that. *That night hell broke loose. The underworld opened its gates and vomited forth the lowest, filthiest, most horrible demons it contained. The city was transformed into a nightmare painting by Hieronymous Bosch; phantoms and devils seemed to have crawled out of sewers and swamps. The air was filled with an incessant screeching, horrible, piercing, hysterical cries from the throats of men and women who continued screaming day and night. People's faces vanished, were replaced by contorted masks: some of fear, some of cunning, some of wild, hate-filled triumph. I saw the early period of Nazi rule in Berlin. But none of this was comparable to those days in Vienna... What was unleashed upon Vienna was a torrent of envy, jealousy, bitterness, blind, malignant craving for revenge.*

All better instincts were silenced. Here only the torpid masses had been unchained. Their blind destructiveness and hatred were directed against everything that nature or intelligence had refined. It was a witches' Sabbath of the mob. All that makes for human dignity was buried. From this window he'd seen a fire burning in the city on November 9, 1938, and had rounded up his friends: Comrades, the temple on Hubergasse is burning! He saw how the fire brigade protected apartment buildings and let the synagogue turn into ashes. He watched two Nazis no older than himself force an old man to scrub the sidewalk with a toothbrush. They spat and screamed at the man: Keep scrubbing, you dirty Jew! You've contaminated a German sidewalk with your stinking, sweaty Jew feet. Heiner stood with a group of people who were staring in silence and he yelled: You pigs! You're not men, you're pigs! They jumped on him. For the first time, Heiner was beaten by Nazis, who only let up when his friends threw themselves over him to protect him from their blows.

The city was unrecognizable – even his own street was transformed. Flags with swastikas hung from the windows, and neighbors raised their arms: Heil Hitler! Servus, Heiner replied. The Nazis had taken over Austria eight months ago. The country had greeted the annexation with excitement. The Führer gave speeches on Heroes' Square and Heiner's countrymen rejoiced. He couldn't walk through the city without seeing Adolf Hitler's face. It was plastered on every wall, in every street, on every column where advertisements were posted, in every tram. Thousands were imprisoned: Jews, Social Democrats, artists, Communists. Lists were made and the first transports left for Dachau. Only a few of Heiner's comrades remained. The Nazis broke down their doors before they could flee. And the few who managed to escape the first wave of imprisonments printed and distributed pamphlets:

Fight the fascists! Get the Nazis out of Austria! Soon there were only three of them: Heiner, Martha, and Paul, who was like an older brother to him. He was from Hungary, and had a son named Laszlo, whom he called Lassi. Paul Szende rented films in the 1st district. When Heiner and Martha looked after Lassi in the evenings, Paul would cook them sausage soup or give them money. There were no more chalk marks in Paul's apartment – the night lodger had moved out once the Nazis came. The night Paul found out that his shop had burned down, he packed two big suitcases and drove with Heiner and Martha to the train station early the next morning. Lassi was wild with excitement. He didn't understand that their adventure was actually an escape. He waved out the train window with both hands, as if he were going on a two-week vacation. As the train pulled out of the station, Paul raised a fist. Rotfront. I'll see you back in Vienna someday. When he waved his fist it looked like he had lost his fingers. Now it was only the two of them. Martha and Heiner, fanatical and brave. Stalin was their god: his gulags were full of class enemies – that was only right. The world was that simple.

A year later, the German Reich sent him to do Arbeitsdienst in a barren, isolated area. Donauwörth, it was called. No trees, no bushes, no mountains, just brown fields. In Donauwörth Heiner learned to march in lock-step, and to position the tips of his boots during muster so that they formed a line with the hundreds of other boots standing next to him. In Donauwörth he learned that his country no longer existed.

Where are you from?

Vienna, Austria.

He received a kick in the stomach.

Austria? No such thing. Where are you from?

Austria. Vienna.

They stuffed mud in his mouth.

There is no Austria. Where are you from?

They didn't wait for his answer. They took his spitting and choking for what they wanted to hear: Vienna. Germany.

The war against France began on May 12. Heiner was twenty when he boarded a truck with fifty other young men, which was later unloaded in the place where their war was supposed to begin – an empty landscape between Belgium and France. He received a uniform, a helmet, a knapsack, and a gun filled with cartridges. With the gear he was seventy pounds heavier, and he marched thirty miles every day. They were the reinforcements, accompanying horse-drawn carts laden with food and munitions to the front. Where exactly that was, they didn't know. Heiner was the only Austrian, but he was by no means the youngest soldier. Hermann, who marched next to him, was seventeen, and Meinhard, his neighbor to the left, was nineteen. Hans, who marched in front of him, was excited for battle, until he saw his first corpse. It was a farmer in rubber boots, who lay headless in his field. Hans retched and cried out in the night "Mama, I want to go home." Meinhard said that the Frenchman deserved it – it was revenge for Versailles – and Heiner prayed: Dear God, if you exist, teach me French. All I know is Résistance. While they marched, he practiced two simple sentences with Hans: My name is Heiner. Je m'appelle Einér. Je suis Communiste. I'm a Communist. Résistance. Heiner. Communist. Would it be enough? Hans, how do you say "I want to fight the Germans with you"? Too complicated. He learned "I hate the Germans." Je hais les Boches. But where were the people he could say this sentence to? In Paris, Marseille, Bordeaux, Lyon – not in the abandoned farmhouses they were marching past. He'd never felt as lonely as he felt in a marching column.

On May 21, 1940, they entered the town of Abbeville on

the Somme. It was a Tuesday. It was Hans's birthday – he was eighteen. Abbeville had been bombed by the Germans the night before. Heiner and Hans stalked through the ruins and wondered that there were somehow objects that had remained unharmed in the face of total devastation. A rocking horse. A section of wall with a cross hanging on it. A kitchen table with four bowls of soup, now covered in a thick layer of plaster dust. Every step they took in Abbeville felt obscene. Their boots made too much noise, they had no respect for the dead. No one knew what the city had been bombed with. Hans guessed phosphorous. The people were shriveled into little black parcels, yet Heiner could still discern facial features – sharp lines that looked chiseled by a sculptor. He saw children lying on the street with their mothers as if welded together. When you touched the dead with your foot they crumbled to dust. Meinhard liked kicking the little black Frenchmen. Heiner watched a face – a face in which he could still see wrinkles fall apart after a kick from Meinhard. He vomited. He had witnessed a second murder.

A week later he was shot during an ambush. The bullet stuck in his shoulder. Perhaps he'd been targeted by the very soldier to whom he'd so wanted to say Je suis Einér. Je suis Communiste. Je hais les boches. He was given emergency care and sent home. To Vienna, in Germany.

After the war, he came back to visit Abbeville. He was hoping to replace his bad memories with beautiful new ones. Like an artist painting over a canvas when displeased with his work. He walked through the town. He memorized the most beautiful places, photographed them with his eyes. He sat in a café and looked at the people. He said to himself: There are people living here. There are children playing. There are old people who must have managed to flee. He walked along the bank of the Somme – it flowed fast and clear. When Heiner closed his eyes, he saw the little black parcels. His head couldn't accept the new images.

Je suis Einér. Je suis Communiste. Je hais les boches. While in France he'd forgotten that they were looking for him in Vienna: the Gestapo had set aside the order for his arrest, but not forgotten it. He was on their list: RPR. Resumption of Proceedings upon Return. He lay in a hospital on the Chiemsee, writing pamphlets against the Nazis and their accursed war, with no inkling that gendarmes were on their way to arrest him for continued illegal activities.

Yes, the head doctor said, Herr Rosseck is my patient. Please, sit down. He let them take Heiner away – immediately, and with no warning. Heiner had no chance. It was the day before his twenty-second birthday. Two plump gendarmes escorted him to his room and asked politely for permission to sit on his bed while they let him pack his suitcase. Out of the corner of his eye he saw them pocketing the sugar cubes that lay on his night-stand. He offered them chocolate cookies, which interested them more than what he was doing. He tore up his notes for the next series of pamphlets and destroyed addresses and telephone numbers: the next patient was to have a "clean" room. Then they goose-stepped through Prien with bayonets fixed, Heiner between them. They did not handcuff him. He could have run – his wardens certainly weren't the brightest: they asked directions to the train station three times, even though they'd arrived there less than two hours before. He followed them to the train. Trying to escape in a city he didn't know was risky – in which corners could he hide, from which corners would he be shot at? They sat in a reserved third-class compartment and chatted about the bad times they lived in, the war, and how everything would be better one day, just as sunshine follows rain and everything comes to an end. At some point the guards' eyes closed. The train was going too fast for him to jump off. In Salzburg the gendarmes allowed him to call Martha. He had time only for a quick message: Darling: arriving in Vienna at midnight. Be there. And there she stood, at the train station. With silver tongues, they convinced the gendarmes not to deliver him to the Gestapo – not right away, not in the middle of the night. Look, Heiner said. What are the Gestapo going to do with me at midnight? Maybe no one will be there. Then what? And if someone is there, Martha said, they'll be really, really mad at you for waking them up.

Later, Heiner acted out the story like a skit.

But miss, the gendarmes whined, we're supposed to guard this guy! An order's an order.

Sure you have to guard me, Heiner said. But you can do that just as easily at my house. The two amiable gendarmes looked at each other.

At your house?

Sure, Martha said, his mother will cook a nice meal, and in the morning you can deliver him to the Nazis. They linked arms with Heiner's guards, knowing they'd won. They took the last tram to Rauscherstraße. Heiner's mother covered slices of bread with sausage spread and watered down the already thin vegetable soup. The gendarmes gobbled it all up greedily, as if they hadn't eaten in weeks. Then the four of them went to sleep in his parents' bed: two fat policemen with bayonets, with the prisoner and his fiancé between them.

That night they clung to each other as if they could melt into one, as if in Martha's arms Heiner could become invisible. The next morning Martha whispered: Heinerle, my Heinerle, happy birthday. He remembered an old children's song, and sang it softly in her ear: Marthale, you have to buy me something nice. And she sang: Heinerle, Heinerle, I've got no money/Marthale, I want to go to see Kasperle. She rocked him like a child: Heinerle, Heinerle, I've got no money. Martha, I wanna lick a lollipop/Heinerle, Heinerle, I've got no money. But when I do have lots of money, Heiner will get everything that he wants. Lollipops, Kasperle, carousels, there's nothing in the world I won't give him then. For my sweet little Heinerle – you, your Martha will do everything, you.

Heinerle, she sang, I'll wait for you, and Heiner sang: Marthale, I love you. Darling, he sobbed, my dearest darling…

At six they got up and had breakfast with his mother in the kitchen. Bread with no butter, red rose hip jam, and coffee. The still life on the wall no longer disgusted him – it frightened him. The dead pheasant with glazed eyes. The stiff, spread claws. The slug. Death and decay, and he had just turned twenty-two. The gendarmes bowed to his mother. Thank you, madam. They marched Heiner between them. In the stairwell he heard the cuckoo clock. Seven times it sounded, and between the cuckoos came Martha's cry: Rotfront!

He thought of trying to escape, but was trapped. They would have taken Martha. If he and Martha had fled, they would have taken his mother or his sisters. Or his grandmother. The other reason he didn't resist when they led him away was because the gendarmes were so dumb and so decent. He reassured himself: It won't be so bad – a few slaps in the face wouldn't kill him. He didn't believe his own words.

The Viennese gendarmes delivered him into police custody. They shook his hand as they departed – after a night sleeping in the same bed, they were practically friends. Servus, they said, God bless you. A German policeman locked Heiner in a solitary cell with no light and no bed. He was given a cup of soup at midday and in the evening two slices of bread with rancid sausage. He didn't sleep. He sat on the stone bench and tried to prepare himself for the day to come. They were going to interrogate him. They would ask for names and codenames. His comrades had been imprisoned – if any of them had talked, things wouldn't go well for him. He'd been the leader of a group, responsible for agitation and propaganda. He swore by his love for Martha: I will betray no one.

They let him wait. They let his fear grow. Soup at midday, bread in the evening, no light, no bed. No one spoke to him. After four days, two Gestapo officers came for him – two men whose voices were far too gentle. A little walk, Herr Rosseck. Are you hungry? Are you thirsty? Do you want to smoke? They took him to a cozy pub. He ate as much as he could, smoked their cigarettes, drank beer. They paid the bill. We just want to chat, they said. All it takes is a little honesty and tomorrow you're a free man. He talked much and said nothing. They brought him back to the jail and came for him again the next morning. Heiner ate dumplings with bacon, ordered two servings of red cabbage, drank, smoked, and ignored all their questions about names and addresses. On the third day, they led him past the pub to the luxurious hotel Metropol on Morzinplatz, where the Gestapo had made their headquarters since March 12, 1938. Everyone in Vienna knew that the basement vault had been turned into Austria's most notorious torture chamber. The Nazis were meticulous bookkeepers: twenty thousand interrogations between March and December.

They entered the hotel through the back door. They led him to a small office. Sit down, Herr Rosseck, said the man behind the desk in his far too gentle voice. Just tell us what you know, and you'll be free. He placed his right hand on a thick file. You won't be betraying anyone, we already know all your contacts, my boy. When the man who just yesterday had paid for his food and beer began using the informal you with him, he knew this "you" was a matter of life and death. The man who had been leaning impassively on the door swung his fist at Heiner's face.

They beat him for twelve days. They took him out in the mornings, and when he lost consciousness, they threw him back in the cell; they took him out, beat him up again, and Heiner remained silent. They broke his nose and kicked in his jaw. They knocked out his teeth. He lost all sense of time. He was nothing but a bundle of blood. With every blackout his hatred grew. He would have let them beat him to death before he gave them any names. They asked about all his comrades, but they did not know about Martha: Dear God, let it remain so. Martha was the most important contact between all the groups in Vienna.

Heiner survived the torture, somehow. He emptied his head and engraved two commands inside: Hold on. Hold your tongue. He took a comrade's advice: When you're tortured, imagine you're outside. Leave your body. Fly to heaven and tell the most beautiful angel the most beautiful story of your life.

In August 1942, Heiner Rosseck was sentenced by the seventh senate of the Viennese Volksgerichtshof to one and a half years in prison for inciting treason. When the judge asked: Is there anything you wish to say, Herr Rosseck? he nodded. Even if you hang me, he cried, your power will not last forever! They locked him in the dark cell and he began to dream over his bread and water. He dreamt of Martha, he dreamt of home, he dreamt of the fight against the Nazis and their defeat in every country, he dreamt of peace. He wanted to get a diploma and go to university. Politics and History. Je suis Heiner. He wanted to learn French. Marry. Have children. He imagined Martha's face on the wall of his cell and heard her voice: Hold on, Heinerle. Rotfront! I swear it, darling, I swear three holy oaths on our love, I will hold on – but he had little strength left. The night he found out that the Gestapo wanted to see him again, he looked around his cell. It was no use. There was nothing: no bars over the window, no doorknob. Only smooth walls and a bucket for urine and feces.

The Gestapo, he learned the next morning, had no interest in interrogating him further. They came to give him a short message: You're being taken into protective custody – you'll wait for the

Schutzhaftbefehl and then off you go, my boy! That's when he knew. No freedom, no Martha, no more political work. Protective custody. Custody to protect the German people. A camp, he thought. But where? Dachau, probably. And for how long? Six months? A year? On the evening of September 9, 1942, a Thursday, he was sent away on the "transport." It was a long train with many cars, carrying 1 860 people.

On September 11, they were herded through the gates. Men in black uniforms barked orders and hit the new arrivals with clubs. He quickly realized that screaming and beatings were tactics they used to instill confusion. He said to himself: Keep your eyes open, learn the structure. People stood on the camp road in striped pajamas, at attention like soldiers at muster. Hands pressed to their sides, eyes glazed. Blind. There must have been thousands of them. Fog crept over the camp, it was drizzling, he couldn't make much out – but he did see a bizarre mountain of limbs piled next to each row of people – yet he couldn't believe what he saw. Naked people with their mouths open, eyes open, heads smashed. Large numbers written on their chests in indelible ink. Three rows of electric barbed wire between the camp and the world from which he'd come. What kind of a place is this, he thought, where the dead lay piled in the street like garbage? Your treasure is being sent to one of the good camps, they'd told Martha, he'll have it easy. Of the 1 860 people on his transport, four survived.

The first night they stood naked in the rain for four hours. It was cold, the rain was icy. The man next to Heiner was called Simon. A Jew from Vienna, a lawyer – Heiner knew him. A strong man. After two hours, he fell down dead. Heart attack – the nicest possible way to die in the camp. They were disinfected with stinking petroleum, shorn like sheep, dressed in prisoner's clothes, and photographed – three shots, like passport photos. Profile: Sullen, lop-sided chin thrust stubbornly forward, head shaved, and at the bottom left-hand corner, his new name – 63 387. Three-quarter view with prisoner's cap: crooked nose, lips pressed together, high forehead. In the middle photo, a young man's haggard face stares at the camera, eyes wide. Later, when he was no longer a prisoner, he got the photos from the camp archives. Whenever he was asked for his ID, he presented these photos as well. He kept the protective custody mandate with its stamped "R.U." in his wallet. Who but Heiner could go for a stroll with his own death sentence? R.U. Return Unwanted. At that time he had no idea what the letters stood for.

His first block was number nine. It was next to Block 10, then came Block 11. It was a deadly neighborhood, but he wasn't aware of that at the time. They were forced up to the second floor. Two thousand people crammed into two floors. The Kapo assigned the new arrivals to wooden bunk beds. One, two, three, four – this bed, he screamed. One, two, three, four – that bed. Two and a half feet for four men, how could that work? The Kapo raised his club. You and you and you and you. Two with their heads this way – he pointed to the foot of the bed – and two with their heads this way – he pointed to the head. Head, feet, head, feet. They stared at each other, but when the Kapo began to beat them they leapt into the beds. They lay on stinking, sagging, piss-soaked straw mattresses with no straw. It was nearly four in the morning and nothing mattered anymore. He had no thoughts, no dreams – he slept like a dead man. But clubs are magic wands – they can wake the dead. Up, up, up, dalli, dalli! The Kapo screamed at five. The new arrivals stood by their beds and scratched themselves like monkeys. He looked at his skin. His arms, legs, chest, belly – all were bright red. What a welcome. Ten thousand flea bites in an hour.

Keep your eyes open, learn the structure.

As if the route were a one-way street, it was always Lena who traveled to Vienna, never Heiner to Frankfurt. My treasure, he wrote, going to your country and walking down the street is like entering a haunted house. I never know when a ghost or devil might jump out at me.

Dearest treasure, Lena replied, we bought two tickets to this haunted house – don't forget that.

My treasure, Heiner wrote, it's a stupid question, but I'm asking it anyway: How can you love someone like me?

Lena was more scrupulous with language than Heiner. I don't love someone like you, I love you.

She put down her pen. Lena knew exactly why she'd fallen in love with the man who had collapsed before her very eyes. It wasn't his weakness that attracted her; it was the defiance and pride in his pale face and the tone of his "Servus" when he opened his eyes. He had needed her help, but he hadn't surrendered himself to her. His "Servus" was a combination of thanks and scorn. He let her help him, and watched her as she did so. He didn't attempt to hide his curiosity about the woman who found him a chair and fed him chocolate. She loved him, she just didn't know whether she would be able to tolerate a man who lived with a mustard jar that he wanted to be buried with. He would set it next to other peoples' plates and with a hint of typical Viennese mockery in his voice, he'd ask: *Look, what might this be?* The same guessing game every time. South Pacific? Broken shells? Gravel? A short pause, a little smile, his gentle voice. *They're tiny bits of bone...* How many times could one bear that?

He didn't like to cook, but it didn't bother her, since he set the table with such ceremony each time – as if the smallest snack was cause for celebration. He washed dishes as if it were a special treat, his cool hands warming in the hot water – but the way he ate! Meat, bread, eggs, vegetables – he chewed everything he put in his mouth into a mushy paste. He analyzed every fiber, tasted, wrung out, sucked the taste from every morsel until the paste in his mouth had become a dry ball that he divided into portions with his tongue before swallowing them. He ate to quiet the huge old hunger that could never be satisfied. She didn't know if she could ever get used to such desperate exploitation of food.

In Vienna Lena learned to play Halma, a board game from his childhood collection. The rules were simple. Each player got fifteen little men, which he could place in one of six triangular areas. The goal was to reach the opposite triangle by shrewd jumps over your own and your opponent's men. He called the triangles blocks and the men comrades. He always chose red men – his chevron in the camp had been red – and Lena could choose between black or green, since he'd gotten rid of the yellow ones. Choose! Black or green?

Black chevrons were for the Asocials, the Asos, though no one knew exactly what the Nazi definition of Aso was. A homeless person, a person without a job, a thief, a beggar, a loafer, a prostitute – anything was possible. Green was for Berufsverbrecher – "professional criminals." The Bv's did the Nazis' dirty work. Lena liked green better than black, but under these circumstances she chose the black comrades. Heiner had learned to play Halma from Kostek, a typist in the prisoners' infirmary. Kostek had drawn a six-pointed star on a stolen scrap of paper. For playing pieces they used little stones they found on the camp road – light ones and dark ones. Two work groups, called Arbeitskommandos, were trying to cross the camp road and each used the other as a springboard. Heiner had a good eye for clever jumps. He liked the game because the opponent wasn't eliminated, just outsmarted. He was dead serious about the game. Often the red comrades jumped far outside the boundaries of the game.

When his typing shift was over, he crept up to the attic. He knew how dangerous it was; one could be killed for "attic peeping." From a tiny window he looked over into the yard of Block 11, which was called the "Death Block." You couldn't see the yard from street level – it was sealed off by a gate. Inside the yard was the "Black Wall" – the wall of death. For two years, whenever he could get away, Heiner stood at the window in the attic. That was his mission – to be a witness, so that one day he would be able to stand before a judge and say: I saw it with my own eyes. Sometimes he stood there frozen, paralyzed by what he saw. Watching a murder was more horrific than being murdered. He stood behind the glass and cried and counted: One afternoon, in retaliation for a partisan attack in Warsaw, 278 people were dragged to the wall and shot in the head. 278. And Bunker-Jakob, his poor comrade, had to bring them to the wall, one after another. 278 naked men and women. Some raged, some screamed and cried, but most of them went to the wall quietly, knowing that chance and luck were of no use to them anymore. Bunker-Jakob was big, and strong as a bear. He held their arms tight until they fell, even those who tried to struggle. A sweet guy. A prisoner, just like those he marched to the wall. He didn't choose the job.

That afternoon, Heiner was standing once again at the little attic window. Be a witness. Count. Each shot was like a shot in his own head. Don't forget. 278 in one afternoon. Say the number out loud, then you'll remember it better. After it was done, they brought wooden wagons with slanted sides and a tow bar, like the kind farmers use in the fields. So he wouldn't forget, he said: *Then they brought wooden wagons with slanted sides, like the kind farmers use in the fields.* The dead were loaded on and pulled to the crematorium by other prisoners while blood flowed through the boards onto the camp road. His eyes didn't want to stay open – keeping them wide was hard work.

Once, standing in the attic as usual, he watched Rapportführer Gerhard Palitzsch, scourge of the camp. A plague. A woman walked in front of him with a baby in her arms. Next to her was a man holding two children by the hand: a girl and a boy, maybe four and seven years old. The girl had long braids, the boy a black newsboy cap. *The girl had long braids, the boy a black newsboy cap.* They were walking to Block 11. He heard a sound behind him, a door creaking, and he spun around. If he were found here, the path to the Black Wall would be short, only a few steps – one more death wouldn't matter. It's me, Kostek whispered. Heiner moved over, and then there were two faces watching from the window. He's bringing a family – it's going to be bad. Palitzsch opened the gate. The woman and the man did not resist as they were brought to the wall. The yard was quiet. Palitzsch raised his gun. Heiner heard his heart pounding, knowing what was going to happen. Kostek bit his knuckle. The family held hands. Palitzsch knew what he wanted to do, and only an order from a superior could have stopped him. He shot the infant in the head and it flopped like fish in its mother's arms, not yet dead. Then Palitzsch shot the little girl. The parents stood as if made of ice. Suddenly the boy with the newsboy cap tore away from his father and zigzagged across the yard in the crazy hope of saving himself. Palitzsch watched him, let him run back and forth. He had time – he knew there was no escape. When the boy realized there was nowhere in the yard for him to hide, he fell to his knees and raised his folded hands. They saw his lips moving, begging for his life. Later, whenever Heiner saw a newsboy cap, he saw that child's pleading face under it. Palitzsch calmly circled the begging boy, kicked him down, then stood on his back and shot him in the back of the head. Then he shot the woman, who was still holding her baby, and then the husband. Heiner was wracked with tears. Kostek held his hand over Heiner's mouth. They stared into the yard. Palitzsch took the small-bore rifle from his shoulder, his work done. He walked toward the Rapportführer's office – he was a young man, not yet thirty, a Hauptsturmführer in the SS. He wiped his left hand on his pants. As long as he lived, Heiner could never forget the gesture. As if he were wiping dirt off his fingers, and the dirt was not his deed, but the people. Before Palitzsch disappeared into the barracks, he looked briefly up at them. Smooth forehead, narrow mouth. They threw themselves to the floor. They'd seen his face. He looked satisfied, as if he'd just eaten a nice meal. Heiner and Kostek clung together until they stopped shaking.

They watched Boger, too. Friedrich Wilhelm Boger, a commercial clerk who in the camp had mutated into a specialist in shooting people in the head and in taking interrogation to the next level. He was the inventor of the "Boger Swing," a horizontal bar over which a shackled body would hang, every naked inch exposed to his lust for torture. He called his invention "my little conversation device." Heiner had seen people before an interrogation by Boger, and after. If they survived the torture, they had to be carried out. They no longer looked like people. He'd heard their screams. Heiner coughed up green phlegm. There was no name for this sickness. It was the vomit of despair. The vomit of panic. The vomit of pain, of sympathy. The vomit of rage. He held his hands over his ears. The screams of the victims were high and sharp, they pierced his head. If there was a God in heaven, he must have heard those screams.

They watched Ernst Krankemann, called Jupp, who'd been a crook in his civilian life in Cologne, and was one of the cruelest

Kapos in the camp. No one had ordered him to force priests and Jews to pull the heavy road roller like work horses. Kapo Jupp was a colossus, a "mountain of flesh." He, the "fat pig," had a favorite game. He stood atop the roller as if it were a Roman chariot and hit the prisoners with a long stick: Onward, you vermin, dalli, dalli! He didn't stop the roller if one of the harnessed prisoners collapsed.

They often saw Unterscharführer Bruno Schlage crossing the yard. Block 11 was his workplace – he was the supervisor in the Detention Block. He unlocked the cells of the inmates who had been sentenced to death; he was older than the other Nazis, nearly forty. He moved less briskly, he crossed the yard in an easy way, as if taking stock of his vegetable garden. When the weather was nice he'd sit on the steps in the Death Block and sun himself as if on vacation. Twenty thousand people were shot at the Black Wall; blood soaked the earth thirteen feet deep.

Heiner and Kostek risked their lives. They had no watches and no calendar, no paper and no pen. They couldn't write down the month, day, or time of what they saw, and so from a legal perspective they were bad witnesses.

But Heiner was unbeatable at Halma.

I don't love someone like you, Lena wrote, I love you. She'd quickly banished any vague doubts. But she didn't know how long her love for the part of this man that had stayed in the camp could last.

On a warm summer evening, Heiner stepped off the train in Frankfurt. It was August 5, 1965. He was wearing a linen suit and a beige hat. He'd had his hair trimmed a bit. You're the best looking man on the train from Vienna, Lena told him.

This trip hadn't been particularly difficult for him, as it was part of his mission. He'd come to Germany to hear the closing

statements of the defendants. He didn't expect remorse, he didn't
expect any of them to break down on the stand, but maybe, just
maybe one of the defendants would say: Yes, I am guilty. I did
what I am charged with. I don't understand why I did it – I must
have been a different person. It was in this absurdly slight hope
that Heiner had come. If it happened, Heiner's world would look
just a little less bleak.

A year had passed since Lena found Heiner unconscious in the
hallway. The trial was coming to an end. Three hundred and fifty
witnesses had come to the stand, the record stood at eight thousand pages, and the committee of judges, prosecutors, defense
lawyers, and joint plaintiffs had taken several trips to Poland to do
research with a ruler. They had paced out distances and recorded
them. How many feet along the camp road from Block 21 to the
Black Wall? Could one recognize Palitzsch's face from the attic
window in Block 21, or Boger's? Was it possible to tell the faces
apart? The committee was meticulous – they were not there to
judge morals, only provable acts. What if Boger claimed he had
been on vacation during the time Heiner said he'd seen him? If
Bruno Schlage swore he'd heard and seen nothing in Block 11?
And so they measured out what they'd heard from the witnesses in
the courtroom, inch for inch. They played perpetrator and victim.
Who could have seen whom from where? Who couldn't possibly
have seen whom from where? Could a person be recognized from
three hundred feet away? Can you tell who a person is if you only
see him from behind? Because you know the build, the way he
moves, because for you it means danger? How many feet between
the attic window of Block 21 and the Black Wall? The court pho-
tographer took five thousand pictures from the scene of the crime.
No prisoner would ever have been able to write captions for the
pictures, he would have choked on the words: "It was determined

on site that three railroad tracks are present and that, looking in the direction of the crematorium, from left to right one can see the following facilities: a) a paved road, 18 feet wide, b) a ditch, 23 feet wide as measured from the top, c) the first track, at a distance of 17.7 feet from the right edge of the ditch, d) the second track, at a distance of 11.5 feet from the first, e) a graveled loading ramp with a paved edge, 34.4 feet wide, f) the third track, 3.9 feet from the right-hand edge of the ramp, g) an irregularly shaped ditch, 12.5 feet wide, 5.9 feet to the right of the third track."

This was the ramp.

Language, too, was measured. The following sentence was supposed to be taken into the record: *Thereupon the commission betook itself to the grave where the corpses were burned.* The defense lawyer was concerned that it ought rather say: *where the corpses may have been burned.* The concern was registered and the sentence was formulated in the conditional: *where the corpses may have been burned.*

The committee inspected Block 20, where Klehr had killed with Phenol, or rather, where he *might have killed.* There was no longer anything to be seen. The walls had been torn out – there were no rooms as there had been then. Dust and debris had turned everything gray. No one could imagine a man with a needle here, no one could imagine Heiner fearing for his life.

Among the most perfidious instances of torture were the four "standing cells" in the cellar of Block 11. They were barely three square feet. Four prisoners at a time had to crawl in like dogs through an opening at the bottom of the wall, which was barred behind them. Inside the cell it was blacker than the darkest night – no light even came through the two-by-two-inch air hole. They couldn't stand, couldn't squat, they couldn't lie down; they were just squeezed together, unable to move. They screamed, moaned, cried – prisoners lost their minds in the standing cells. Could anyone hear them? Were they being listened to? Could a person be a supervisor here and not have known of the cells? For such a question, no ruler could help the committee. Since there were no longer people screaming in the cellar, they had to produce the sounds themselves, to find out what was heard back then if someone screamed – or *what could have been heard if someone would have screamed* – and whether Unterscharführer Bruno Schlage was telling the truth when he claimed never to have heard anything.

Indeed, since no member of the committee was keen to imitate the prisoners' screams of fear and death, Sergeant Lanz was asked to sing *Once a boy a Rosebud spied* in one of the cells, the song the prisoners sang when marching back to the camps, broken-down from hard labor, carrying their dead comrades on their shoulders. The sergeant belted at the top of his voice, he was easy to understand. This was the volume at which the prisoners had screamed or *might have screamed*.

Heiner laughed at the inquiries of the committee into the "Audibility Quotient" of the cellar of Block 11 until the end of his days, with his Heiner-laugh, which sounded like an asthma attack.

He went to bed early and clung to Lena, but even in her warmth he could only sleep for a few minutes before he'd awake with a start, frightened by his own moans, which were uncannier than any scream. Lena had bought little lamps that gave off a weak light, like the ones he had in his apartment in Vienna. She didn't want him to have to stare into darkness when he woke up during the night at her house. It was the night before the day when the accused were to make their closing statements.

Let them speak, Lena said. Then they'll be sentenced and locked away – what are you afraid of? Not the verdict, Heiner said, it's their voices that terrify me. Lena got up around four and made pitch-black coffee, which she poured into two thermoses. Heiner sat in bed and gulped down the hot coffee. No sugar, no milk, but with a cigarette to accompany each cup. Lena called Heiner's first meal of the day a hooker's breakfast. On August 6, 1965, he prepared himself as for an exam. He dressed nicely – black suit, white shirt – stood for a long time in front of the mirror shaving carefully, and brushed his brown hair. On that day he looked every inch a gentleman, sweet-smelling and elegant. He wanted the distance between him and the accused to be greater than that between the earth and the moon. After twenty months, the trial was coming to an end, and none of the perpetrators was going to recognize prisoner number 63 387.

With hands intertwined, Heiner and Lena crossed the big bridge and passed the train station to enter the Gallus quarter. The courtroom was full, yet it was quieter than it had been on the other days. The audience whispered as if they were in the theatre and the curtain was rising. The blue curtains were drawn and it was hot in the room; the faces looked pale under the neon light.

The accused entered the courtroom in the same order as they had on all the days, weeks, and months before. Detention Cell Supervisor Bruno Schlage was at the head of the line. Heiner looked at the clock. At eight twenty-eight, the judges and jurors entered, and the accused rose and greeted them, each in his own fashion. Boger smiled. Kaduk stood stiffly with his hands at his sides and his chin up – a defiant attempt to mock the trial – and Klehr grinned. That was too much. Heiner turned away as if pulled by an unseen hand. He wanted to see the perpetrators, he wanted to hear what they had to say, but his eyes and ears wouldn't obey him; they wanted to flee. He squeezed his eyes shut, breathed deep into his belly and tried again. Slowly, he turned his head back. He didn't want to forget the faces, in any case. Learn the system – what was happening here belonged to those days. Of the twenty men accused, he knew five. All of them had killed. Of the millions of dead they'd left in their wake, 17 670 could be proven, and none of the men looked like they'd slept poorly in the last twenty years. Heiner saw nondescript faces. On the defendants' bench sat conventionally attired men, bald or with white hair. Sedate husbands, fathers, grandfathers. Only Boger had retained the harsh face he'd used to instill panic wherever he went. Boger, the devil of the camp. Heiner compared the faces of the defendants with those of the witnesses. Even if no one else would have been able to tell the faces of the perpetrators from those of the victims, he could see the difference. It was in the eyes. Even when they laughed, the eyes of his comrades had the deep sadness of eyes that have seen more than they can comprehend. And behind that, like a kind of badge, was a deathly terror that had nothing to do with the normal fear of death.

The perpetrators wouldn't recognize him – they wouldn't have recognized a single one of their former prisoners. To the Nazis, they'd all looked the same back then – just umpteen thousand stinking shapes. Their clubs hit shaved heads in striped rags. Now these beings were wearing suits, they had brown, blonde, or white hair, which was long or short, straight or curly, they had distinctive faces and individual names. They were people. Heiner looked up. The judges were arranging their files, cleaning their glasses; the prosecutor tore up a note that a court attendant had brought him. August 6, 1965, the 180th day of hearings, was a major event for everyone present.

For a while Heiner had been feeling that one of the men who sat among the accused was looking at him. Heiner tried to ignore him – under no circumstances did he want to be recognized or greeted. Lena nudged him. Heiner, she whispered, someone is looking for you. He turned his head and the man looked him right in the eye – a grandfather, almost bald. The black pupils – piercing and huge – they hadn't been three feet from him back then. It was him. Rottenführer Emil Hantl, the fish-face, who was accused of being involved in selections and of killing people with a syringe full of Phenol. Did Hantl recognize him? Was his slight nod a greeting? Did he remember their nights in Block 21?

Prisoners' infirmary, night shift, sixteen typists at work, keys clattering. Dead of phlegmons, pneumonia, typhus, spotted fever. The door opens and Rottenführer Hantl enters the typing room. He's not a big man, five-six perhaps, stocky, heavyset. His mouth is always slightly open, as if his bottom lip had gotten stretched out. Heiner, who's the shift supervisor tonight, leaps to his feet, stands at attention, and yells: Prisoner 63 387 working with fifteen men.

Continue!

Yes sir, Herr Rottenführer!

He was linked to Hantl, if such a thing could even be said, by a brief proximity, an episode, a few minutes, when Hantl had asked why he was in the camp, and Heiner had told him of Vienna, of the war, and of the little town of Abbeville on the Somme, and Hantl had told of his father, who'd been sent to the eastern front. It was a little exchange – almost a chat. Hantl had trained to be a baker but couldn't find work after his apprenticeship, so he'd become an errand boy at the textile factory in his town, where he discovered his love of sewing. He took home fabric remnants and started to make clothes at night. First he sewed simple undergarments, later he managed vests and shirts. He'd loved to do gymnastics in his free time, but after the annexation of the "Sudetengau," his whole gymnastics club had been swallowed up by the SS, after which he was sent to one place after another, here, then there, like a package no one wanted, until one day he landed at Auschwitz and became supervisor of the prisoners' infirmary.

That night as he opens the door and walks into the typing room with his half-open mouth, he looks to Heiner like a man deranged.

What's happened, Herr Rottenführer, sir? Has your father been killed?

Let us sit in my office!

It's an order. Heiner feels queasy – sitting in an SS man's office wasn't something to be done lightly, it could cost you your life. Hantl reaches into his coat pocket and tosses a pack of cigarettes on the table.

Wanna cigarette?

I'd love one, Herr Rottenführer, sir.

They smoke in silence. Heiner sits on the edge of his seat, ready to jump up at any moment. The world is upside-down, this isn't the way things are supposed to go here. He has to type death notices, he's the shift supervisor. This cigarette could cost him his life. He makes another feeble attempt.

Herr Rottenführer, sir, I can see from your face that something's happened.

Leave me alone, have another.

Yes sir, Herr Rottenführer.

If it strikes his fancy, Hantl can shoot him, simply because his mood has changed between the first cigarette and the second.

What's your name? Hantl asks.

Heiner jumps to his feet: 63 387.

Say your first name!

Heiner, Herr Rottenführer, sir. My name is Heiner.

Have another one, Heiner.

Heiner takes out two cigarettes – one for himself and one for Kostek. He calculates. Ten minutes per cigarette, and he's on his third, so they've been sitting across from each other for thirty minutes, and Hantl has only stared at the table in silence. Heiner feels like he's in the electric chair, waiting for the deadly shock. Suddenly Hantl lifts his head.

How long have I known you?

Heiner jumps up and tears the cap from his head. One year, Herr Rottenführer.

Sit down.

Yes sir, Herr Rottenführer.

You're a decent guy, you won't betray me – right?

Heiner jumps up. One stands at attention when addressed by an SS man.

But Herr Rottenführer, sir, what would I betray?

Sit down, have another.

Yes sir, Herr Rottenführer.

Hantl's pupils are huge. The man is mad, Heiner thinks. What should I do? If I don't meet his eyes he'll shoot me. If I look away, he might shoot me anyway. Heiner speaks softly, as to a child.

Honestly, Herr Rottenführer, I can be silent as the grave.

And then Hantl speaks. Quietly, haltingly, at first, then faster and louder until finally he screams: One hundred and forty-seven trains! Four hundred and thirty-eight thousand Hungarian Jews! And I, Hantl, assigned to the ramp! Three hundred and sixty thousand led to the gas chambers immediately, and – you must believe me – I can't do my duty! I can't do it!

Heiner looks around in terror. Thank God there's no one around. He doesn't care that Hantl's risking his neck, he's afraid for his own life. Sitting at a table with an SS man, holding a ciga-rette – it's worse than being caught stealing.

Because, you see, there aren't enough crematoriums to burn the mountains of corpses, Hantl screamed, and to keep the corpses from rotting and stinking, graves are being dug: Three hundred feet wide and a hundred and fifty feet long. Dump the corpses in, dump on some petroleum, and light it up. Funeral pyres are burning in Birkenau – you can't even imagine – gigantic funeral pyres!

What he'd most like to do is clamp Hantl's mouth shut. He has to go to work – he's the shift supervisor tonight, he mustn't sit here any longer. He tries to get up so slowly that Hantl won't notice.

Sit, have another.

Yes sir, Herr Rottenführer.

Do you know about the children?

No, Herr Rottenführer, sir, which children?

A command from high-up: send the children to the funeral pyres – the gas chambers are full. I've seen it: they grab them by the arms and legs and then – living children! Into the fire! Infants! They fly into the fire like butterflies, their arms wide.

Hantl reaches for Heiner's hands. He whispers. The same

sentence, over and over: I can't do this job, I can't do this job, I want to go to the front, do you understand? I can't do this job. Why are you staring at me like that, are you going to give me away?

No, Herr Rottenführer, sir. Word of honor!

Hantl stands up and reaches under his coat with the dull movements of a sleepwalker, to where he keeps his pistol.

That's it, Heiner thinks, my life for this Nazi's confession. He's not afraid, he feels cold and calm. He'd long ago prepared himself for the moment of his death. He never imagined a slow death – he pictured his death as quick, surprising, and without any chance of escape. That was the first lesson that he'd learned: You can die. For looking too curious, too horrified, too bold, too submissive or not submissive enough. For walking. Too fast, too slow, too casually. You can die for saying your number wrong. Too softly, too loudly, too hesitantly, too slowly or too fast. You can be killed for not knowing the words to a song. If a person wants to kill, any reason will do. Bed not made properly. Shirt not tucked in correctly, or tucked in correctly, but looking wrong. Taking one's hat off too slowly or too fast when saluting. No reason was also a reason, as was boredom, but above all, sitting at a table and smoking with an SS man and telling him your name was Heiner was a reason. If Hantl has good aim, it will be over soon – he is prepared for this moment. He doesn't want to take anything with him but the memory of Martha. He doesn't care what happens after death. He's already in hell, and he doesn't believe in heaven. It's comforting to imagine that Martha's face will accompany him. He'd read an essay that said death consisted of memories, of a thought, and the more he thought about that, the more he liked it. He wants his memory to be of a face – he needs nothing else, just that face. But in the second in which Hantl reaches behind him,

Heiner sees more images than could possibly fit in a second. They whirl pell-mell, as if a storm had torn them out of a photo album. Father, mother, grandmother, his sisters with red ribbons in their hair, trips to the mountains, picnicking on a woolen blanket. He doesn't want to take these images, he has to find Martha's face, but it doesn't seem to be in here. Where should he look? That last night, in bed with the gendarmes. There it is. And as he fills his entire mind with the face he fell in love with as a child in the Red Falcons, small and fresh as a boy's, he closes his eyes. Death is memory. *Marthale, you have to buy me something nice, Heinerle, Heinerle, I've got no money. But when I do have lots of money, lollipops, Kasperle, carousels, there's nothing in the world I won't give him then. For my sweet little Heinerle you, your Martha will do everything, you.*

Heiner sits on the edge of his chair, hands clutching the seat, eyes squeezed shut. He hears the harsh tapping of keys. His comrades type out their quotas: pneumonia, phlegmons, heart attack, spotted fever, typhus. His heart pounds. He breathes. He's freezing. He opens his eyes. He's alive. Hantl continues his movement from the moment when Heiner began to look for Martha's face. Hantl takes the pistol from its holster and releases the safety.

Herr Rottenführer, sir, I give you my word of honor, I won't say a thing.

Hantl sets the pistol on the table.

Shoot me, Heiner.

It was quiet in the courtroom. How long had he been looking at Hantl? How long had Hantl been looking at him? Were they both thinking of that same night twenty years ago? They took their eyes off each other and looked to the front of the room. The president of the senate told them that closing statements were an opportunity, not an obligation, and that each defendant should consider for himself whether he might want to break his silence at the last possible moment. What they were looking for that morning in the courtroom was atonement, not revenge.

Lena laid her hand on Heiner's, which was ice cold. The twenty defendants were being charged with 17 670 provable murders. The perpetrators' closing statements whizzed past Heiner like a multi-voiced choir singing the song of innocence, interrupted now and then by solo voices. Mr President, Your Honor! Gallows? We saw gallows, but not prisoners being hanged. Whole transports forced to the gas chambers? There were rumors, but we saw nothing. Our memories are not so good. We don't know anything about starving prisoners. We didn't notice the many dead people. Boger, solo: *Your Honor, at this moment let us remember all the prisoners, irrespective of race or religion, who perished in the concentration camps. But let us also remember all the SS men who had to serve at Auschwitz.* Choir: Mr President, Your Honor. Beaten to death with bull whips? We know nothing about bull whips. We overheard some things about gassing, people said all kinds of things in the camps. Mass executions at the Black Wall? Funeral pyres in Birkenau? Rumors! Mr President, Your Honor. We did what we had to do. We didn't hurt anyone. We're not guilty, but we have the deepest sympathy for the unlucky victims. Klehr, solo: *I was a small cog in the wheel, not master of life and death. I simply carried out the commands of the doctors, and with the greatest reluctance.* Mr President, Your Honor. We didn't mistreat, beat, or drown anyone. We're the victims – we did what had to be done. We were soldiers under orders. Hantl, solo: *I acted purely according to reason, without regard to race. No one died at my hand.* Mr President, Your Honor. We say what those before us said. Those who were human before the war remained so.

For two days the accused said what they had to say. Mr President, Your Honor, ladies and gentlemen. We are innocent before God and man.

The air was warm on that Friday afternoon of August 6, 1965, and it already felt like the weekend. The river glittered in the sun like a sparkler. On any other day Heiner would have taken Lena out for ice cream, or for a boat ride on the Main, and he would have said that Frankfurt was a city full of cheerful people. But it was that day. People laughed. What was there to laugh about that day? In the evening, the sun drenched the city in warm orange light, as if mocking the cold light of the courtroom. The river flowed indifferently by, and the birds mimicked the courtroom's choir of innocence.

Heiner and Lena followed the river east to a fence, behind which lay the industrial zone. They walked back westward the way they'd come until their path was blocked by a construction site. They walked without speaking, arm in arm, leaning on each other. Back and forth, always the same path. When their feet began to hurt, they sat on a bench and watched the ships beat slowly against the current or glide quickly as the current pushed them downstream. Colorful containers were sent from east to west and from west to east – and on that day, this too seemed pointless to them. I'm still in the courtroom, Lena said. It's holding me tight, it's chasing me, it won't let me go. It's like I'm locked in there and can't get out.

For Lena it was new to be tormented by a place she'd already left. For Heiner such attacks were part of everyday life. They caught him on the street, at the movies, while talking with friends – everywhere, and for no reason at all. Last time it had been on a beautiful afternoon at a café in Vienna. He was sitting alone at a table, smoking, waiting for the chocolate cake he'd ordered. A couple sat at the neighboring table eating schnitzel, which had been pounded so thin and wide that they hung over the edge of the plate. She spread ketchup on hers while he used mayonnaise. They ate with pleasure. It was a Saturday. The radio was playing hits from the sixties, and the waiter pranced over with his chocolate cake, singing cheerfully along: *Blame it on the bossa nova, what could I do? Blame it on the bossa nova, believe me, do!* Suddenly the sickly fog of the past clouded over the good mood in the café. The eating couple disappeared along with the plates, the schnitzel, and the prancing waiter, and suddenly he was freezing. He was sitting in the typing room typing his quota with two fingers: dead of spotted fever, heart attack, typhus, phlegmons, tuberculosis. He felt his comrades next to him, felt the old fear, and he knew he had to withstand this attack, and that it would pass. The worst part wasn't the images that tore him away from reality; it was the loneliness – the immeasurable distance between himself and other people. He didn't hold the couple's enjoyment of their schnitzel against them, nor the waiter's love of the bossa nova. Tears came to his eyes because he found it so monstrous that they knew nothing of his world. Because they could eat, dance, and live without knowing about a single image from his past. He was an alien.

Late in the evening, in the Sachsenhausen entertainment district, once they had somewhat recovered, they wondered who was crazier – the people out having fun, or themselves, carrying the weight of the day inside them. *Innocent before God and man.* They went to an Indian restaurant where they were the only customers. The Indian waiters floated silently from the kitchen to their table and back again. They brought coffee for Heiner and cold, sweet plum schnapps for Lena.

What do you think, Lena asked, do they really believe they're innocent?

I don't care.

The waiter brought Lena chicken curry and Heiner duck with pineapple.

Talk to me, Lena said.

She ordered a second plum schnapps. You know what bothers me? Heiner shook his head.

Boger, Lena said. I'm trying to imagine what happened before the trial. When the war ended, Boger was thirty-nine, and suddenly instead of Oberscharführer, he's a Swabian clerk again, a reliable employee for the next thirteen years. A hard-working man. Settled. He doesn't flee – he has no reason to hide out overseas, he doesn't have a guilty conscience. Auschwitz has nothing to do with his daily life. He has two sons from his first marriage and three daughters from his second – he loves his children and they love him. He plays Pachisi and Halma with them. On Sundays they go for picnics in the Swabian Alps. He's content with his life, he sleeps well, his wife has never heard him scream in the night. It's March 1, 1958, and he has no clue that a former prisoner knows where he lives and has denounced him. Right?

Heiner looked up impatiently from his food. What are you getting at?

Bear with me. I'm trying to understand something. One day two police detectives knock on Frau Boger's door and ask for her husband. She's alarmed, and asks whether something's happened. The policemen reassure her. Everything's fine, Frau Boger.

It wasn't like that, Heiner said. Don't make it sound so idyllic. After Boger was denounced, nothing happened for months. No Swabian prosecutor took up the inquiry, no one took the denunciation seriously – Boger was a model citizen. That's how it was. Things only got rolling when my comrade Langbein from the International Auschwitz Committee produced eleven witnesses against Boger. No one knocked on Frau Boger's door; her husband was arrested at work eight months after having been denounced.

That's not the point, Lena said. You won't let me finish.

What's the point, then?

I want to understand the wife. At some point she finds out what her husband is accused of. And then? Does she ask him about it? Can you imagine the scene? What does he say?

What should he say? That the accusations are nonsense! That no one died by his hand. Weren't you listening this morning? Or do you think he'd say: Darling, all I did there was invent a little conversation device that no one could resist.

That's the point, Lena said. Does Frau Boger want to know where "there" was, and what happened "there"? And if she doesn't hear it from him, does she try to figure it out by herself? There are reports, witnesses, the bill of indictment…

Heiner threw down his fork. He laughed angrily. Research? he asked. You think she wanted to know? Talked to those who survived? That's how you imagine it? Maybe the lady buys a first class ticket to Vienna, rings the doorbell of witness Heiner Rosseck and chirps: Good morning, Herr Rosseck, my name is Boger – I'd like to talk to you about my husband.

Would you have let her in? Would you have told her what you've seen?

Lena, he said sharply. It didn't happen! None of the perpetrators' relatives ever stood on anyone's doorstep trying to find out the truth. I don't know of any wife who divorced her husband for what he did. They didn't turn away in disgust. They let their husbands continue to touch them, they slept beside them and made babies with them.

Because they believed them?

Lena! His voice was shrill. These women were Nazis, just like their husbands! Himmler's words touched their souls – their husbands were doing a hard job, they were the real victims, you heard what they said. The men endured the mountains of corpses and returned from the war covered in glory.

His face was white, his eyes full of hatred. It would have been better to change the subject or remain silent – but whom else could she have asked the question that she was turning over and over in her mind?

And when the children find out what their fathers…

The German Woman! Heiner screamed. This is exactly how I imagined her! His hands shook. Sympathy for the wives of murderers! Tears for their brood! Do you know why I can't live in Germany? Your ability to empathize with the monsters in the camp will do me in!

He pushed his plate aside, as if disgusted by the remainder of the duck and sauce. The waiters looked on in horror. Lena stood up. She said quietly: You will never speak to me that way again, you understand?

He paid the bill and they went back to Lena's apartment, a wide gap between them. He didn't undress. He spent the night on the sofa. His face was frozen; she felt sorry for him. She sat next to him and tried to free him from the prison he'd locked them both in. The victim and the German woman. She made coffee and warmed his hands. Heiner remained silent. Silently they drove to the train station the next morning, silently he boarded the train to Vienna. She saw his face behind the window. He was looking at her. The voice from the loudspeaker informed them that they were waiting for passengers from another train that was seven minutes behind schedule. That was too long for her to bear looking in his eyes, when she didn't know if it would be for the last time. She wrote six letters on the window: Get off. She put her hand to his face through the glass. He leaned his head against it. When the train left, Lena's hands and Heiner's forehead were both cold.

Before even unpacking his suitcase, he sat down at his desk. Lena, he wrote, I have to say it again: I can't live in Germany. Our conversation will repeat itself with anyone who finds out about my past. You don't want to know what I've seen, you want to understand the perpetrators and find out if perhaps you too could have become a monster. You look for the causes of evil and discover dysfunctional parents, children drilled into submission. Your reckoning tallies – evil comes from evil – and you're comforted. And good? Are you sure that good can't emerge from the abyss too? Come to Vienna!

How is Vienna different from Frankfurt? Lena wrote. Are there no Nazis there? Wasn't your country ecstatic when Adolf brought you into the Reich? In your city I can't do the work that I love. And besides, we're too old to blame each other for the countries we were born into. This is about you and me, not "you all" and "your country."

She accepted a translation job, threw jeans and pullovers into a suitcase, and went to see Olga, her former nanny. She posted the letter to Heiner from the train station before getting on the train to Danzig. His letters received no answer, his calls rang in an empty apartment. After defending his touchiness in his first and second letters, in the third letter, he wrote: Treasure of my heart, let's see if we can make it work with "you" and "me." I love you.

He didn't go to Frankfurt for the announcement of the verdict, because Lena was not there to protect him. He read the verdict in the newspaper. A life sentence for Oberscharführer Boger, who was proven to have personally committed one hundred and fourteen murders, and to have been accessory to the joint murder of a thousand – by participating in selections on the ramp at Birkenau.

Six years for the supervisor of the detention block, Unterscharführer Bruno Schlage, for at least eighty cases of joint murder. Life for Unterscharführer Oswald Kaduk for personally committing ten murders and jointly committing at least a thousand. Life for SS Oberscharführer Josef Klehr. The man with the syringe of Phenol was accused of at least four hundred and seventy-five cases of murder and was, according to the punctilious language, joint accessory to joint murder in at least six cases; in two cases committed against at least seven hundred and fifty people, in the third case against at least two hundred and eighty, in the fourth case at least seven hundred, in the fifth case at least two hundred, and in the sixth case at least fifty. Klehr did not accept the verdict.

Heiner got a pen and paper and listed the numbers – 475+750+280+700+200+50 – and added them. 2 455. He saw the man, he saw the room with the table and chair, he saw the people on the chair accepting the needle as if it brought release. He felt himself getting sick. What had this trial done to him? He was adding up the dead as he'd add figures in an arithmetic lesson. He brewed black coffee, sat down by the open window, and kept reading. Rottenführer Emil Hantl was proven to be accessory to murder in two hundred and ten cases. *Shoot me, Heiner*. His three-year sentence was waived on account of the time he'd already been detained during the investigations. *Smoke with me*. Emil Hantl left the courtroom a free man. Most of the defendants were disenfranchised – for three years, in Hantl's case. Heiner read the remarks of Laternser, the celebrated defense lawyer, aloud slowly in order to understand their full import. The murderers hadn't carried out selection, they'd tried to hinder it. Hitler had ordered the murder of ALL Jews, and those who choose people for work – thus not sending all straight to the gas chambers – were actually decreasing the number of victims. Heiner read the passage until he understood that the argument wasn't as outrageous as it initially seemed. The murderers as saviors. They believed their own logic. Heiner closed the door behind him and walked to the Augarten.

He'd wanted to survive the camp in order to be a witness. He'd survived – but what was the point? The perpetrators were convicted and would serve their sentences without remorse, without understanding, without any shock over what they'd done. He took long strides through the park. If the world grew radical again, would the little boys on scooters be tomorrow's Kaduks and Klehrs? He couldn't think coherently. What was going on with Lena? She didn't answer his letters, she didn't pick up the phone. He called her early in the morning and late at night. To keep from going crazy in his apartment, he walked in the park. After a week he knew every path, every bench, every tree. He knew the rabbits that played in the fields by moonlight, he knew the kids on scooters, the dachshunds and pugs on their leashes, the stray cats. He knew the Augarten in sun and rain, hail and wind. After two weeks he'd become part of it. He was greeted, expected. He was the man with the long stride, hat, and cigarette, the man with the long hair who always said hello, but seemed so absorbed in thought that no one tried to start a conversation. He moved his lips as if talking to an invisible person. Only once did he take a different route. He walked through the section of town where he'd lived for a few years with Martha and his daughter. He tried to imagine her. Kaija. The girl with the blond braids was twenty now – a young woman who wouldn't recognize him if she saw him on the street. They would pass each other like strangers. He found the house and their names on the doorbell: Martha and Kaija Rosseck. They'd kept the name. That was nice, but also sad, because there was nothing else left of him. Cautiously he touched the bell, but when he heard steps inside, he pulled his hand away and never returned to the neighborhood. He felt safer in the Augarten. He'd played there as a child; there comrades had mingled with the strolling people and secretly exchanged information. The Augarten was where he'd stuck his first love letter to Martha in the hood of her anorak and waited a week until he found her answer in his coat pocket: Heinerle, I love you too. This is for always, he thought then, and later, every letter he wrote and received in the camp was a promise: This is for always. He wrote tiny letters in pencil on the grey camp paper. Six by eight inches, fourteen lines; writing more than twenty-eight lines was not allowed. Every letter had to contain the line: *I am healthy and doing well.* The letters were censored and the slightest hints about daily life were blacked out. He wrote: My dearest darling, here the winter is white, just as it is where you are. It is very cold. If I were home, we could go skiing. I celebrated my birthday with a few comrades. They stole a potato for me. *I am healthy and doing well.* I love you. This is for always. Martha answered: Heinerle, sweetheart, I moved to Bad Aussee. I have a new job. I guide hikers through the mountains that are now part of Germany. I know interesting trails. The men and women who entrust themselves to me are tough. I love you. This is forever. He understood the message. Martha had joined the partisans and was hiding those who were in danger from the Nazis in remote huts. On July 4, 1943, he wrote: My dearest, best darling, I'm happy to hear of your progress in your new profession. I have always been proud of you, and of course I am especially so now. There's nothing new here. The summer is long. There are no birds in Auschwitz. *I am healthy and doing well.* I love you. This is for always. A thousand kisses, Schutzhäftling Heiner Rosseck, Auschwitz Concentration Camp, Block 21, Prisoner Number 63 387.

She could see that he wasn't well. His handwriting was as shaky as an old man's. Martha too kept the truth to herself. She didn't tell him that she'd fled Vienna after the third visit from the Gestapo. On the first visit the man had come in and asked her for names and addresses, the second time he'd punched her in the face and ravaged the apartment, and the third time he'd put a gun to her head and told her his patience had limits and that when he came again she'd have to come with him. My dearest, beloved darling, Heiner wrote during his third year at Auschwitz, I've met a lot of people, and many interesting characters, but very few who compare with you. We will be the happiest human beings whom the sun shines upon during the day and the moon watches over at night. We will fill every minute with happiness. I love you. This is for always. *I am healthy and doing well.*

He never lied – healthy was relative. He wasn't lying on a bug-riddled mattress with half-rotted legs. He'd survived typhus and tuberculosis, he typed death notices twelve hours a day, he didn't break down, he met his quotas. He only collapsed when his body realized that the war and the struggle was over, as if it wanted to drag him down to his long-overdue death. No doctor had a name for what happened to Heiner. He swam in a sea of stinging sweat and acrid feces and tears that burned as if pepper was pouring from his eyes. He was hot as an oven and cold as ice. He had the disease he hadn't allowed himself to have for all those years – he had Auschwitz. Martha didn't dare to leave the apartment. She didn't sleep, and together with Heiner's mother she held a death vigil over a living person. Neither believed that the stinking creature he now was could ever become a person again. After twenty-one days, he emerged from a hurricane of voices that he didn't understand and a sea of colors he'd never seen before. R.U. He had been where he was supposed to go long ago. Afterwards he knew that the beyond was not comprised of memories, but of a colorful confusion.

His daughter was born on Christmas day, 1946. They named her Kaija – life. Our Christ Child, Martha said. Our little partisan, Heiner said, with whom we'll build a new world. He was the first man at the hospital who had ever wanted to watch the labor, but then he couldn't bear it and ran away.

Martha's cries during labor were cries of death, and her blood was the blood of his murdered comrades. The child came, and he searched inside himself for some feeling, but found none. He wanted to love it, and he tried – he kissed the baby's tiny fingers. They were soft and tender, but a stolen potato for his birthday in Auschwitz had meant more to him. Maybe you've lost your feelings, Martha said – but that wasn't true. He had feelings. His heart overflowed when comrades from the camp happened to be traveling through Austria. Then nothing in the world could stop him from seeing them. If Martha had chained him to the table, he would have run through the streets of Vienna dragging it along. He was overpowered by emotion when mail came from Poland. He would sit weeping over those letters, but he didn't hear his daughter speak her first words.

In Auschwitz he had never cried out in his sleep, but in Vienna, Martha had to free her screaming husband from the camp every night. In his dreams he smelled the smoke from the chimneys – he jumped out of bed and held his nose. He gasped in fear. The old Heiner, who had wanted to drive the fascists out of Vienna, was a sweet man – charming, witty, and intelligent, a pig-headed radical, but the new Heiner was a stranger to her. After five years, Martha's patience ran out. Your bed is in Vienna, God damn it, not in Block 21! I can't stand living with a man who screams his prisoner number in the middle of the night: 63 387.

They had no friends. No one wanted to hear his stories, and he couldn't stop telling them. They didn't believe him, but the fact was that he'd long before stopped even telling the whole story. You're exaggerating, they said. That can't be true, you made it up. His mother tapped her forehead: You're not quite right up there. The war was over and everyone just wanted to laugh again. The only visitors who would come gladly, and then wouldn't go to bed before dawn, were people like Heiner. Gruesome memories lurking behind marked faces. He could laugh with his comrades, but as soon as they left he'd go back to screaming in his sleep. Martha threatened to divorce him if he didn't make some effort to free himself from the nightmares. She gave him three years. Heiner went from one therapist to the next, but he quit every treatment after a few weeks. How could he talk to people who didn't believe him? They gave him pills to take at night, and he'd take a double dose. There was no medication that could prevent his dreams.

He tolerated Viktor Frankl's couch the longest. Frankl was Viennese. Like Heiner. He'd been a prisoner at Auschwitz. Like Heiner. He'd lost his wife, his mother, and his brother. Frankl was a socialist. If Frankl couldn't help him, no one could. Heiner could look into Frankl's face and talk to him, and when Frankl sat behind him, he felt warmth and solidarity. Heiner cried on the couch, he blamed and cursed himself because he knew that the dead were better people than he, since they hadn't survived at the cost of others. On Frankl's couch he could talk about his revenge fantasies – but what good did that do? After a hundred hours he had not one nightmare fewer. He embraced his friend and never returned. Martha filed for divorce; it broke Heiner's heart, but there was nothing he could do. He was a burden – he left without protest. He embraced his daughter. Goodbye, my beautiful child. He would have liked to cry, but he had no tears for this farewell. The child looked at him as if she knew that her silent father wasn't just going on a trip. She tucked a photograph in his jacket pocket. He shook Martha's hand. Darling, what can I do? His walk down the stairs felt like an endless descent. When he reached the bottom, he listened in the stairwell. He heard Martha shut the door.

Many years later he realized that he'd developed his very own method of therapy on Frankl's couch: Friendship with Auschwitz. He adopted the past, made it his twin brother who followed him down the street, accompanied him to the grocery store, sat next to him on the terrace and followed him in dreams through the night. Faithful unto death. Anyone who wanted to be Heiner's friend got his twin brother too. Heiner-therapy meant: remembering. Telling stories, shaping and reformulating them until they were perfect, like an Arabian storyteller. It was too late for Martha and Kaija.

Two loves were too much for one man to lose. Before Heiner gave up his apartment, he called Frankl. He was in luck, without even knowing it. Frankl was a guest professor at Cambridge, but he was in Vienna for two weeks. Help me, comrade, Heiner said, I'm guilty.

Olga pours flour into a bowl, forms a well in the middle with her fist, crumbles in yeast, and fills the well with lukewarm milk. Lenchen, she says, butter the baking sheet for me. When Lena comes to Gdańsk, they always have pierogi the first evening: filled with chopped egg, onion, ground meat, and fresh herbs. Even if it's two or three years between visits, there are always pierogi, and Olga is always Olga – calm and round. Whether she's showing visitors around her amber museum, giving a lecture, or kneading dough, haste and anxiety never dare to enter her presence. That must be what happens when one spends one's time with spiders and insects, bugs, woodlice, and beetles who were trapped millions of years ago in sticky resin and now sleep their eternal sleep in translucent graves, Lena thinks.

Tell me about him, Lenchen, Olga says, chopping onions and herbs into fine pieces.

If he had a beard, he'd fit right in at the Last Supper. He has brown curls like St Philip, and bright blue eyes. I never tire of looking at him and touching him.

Olga dusts the table with flour.

Sounds good.

Olga cuts the lump of dough in two pieces and rolls them out. She scores the dough into twenty-two squares with a sharp knife. She's made pierogi so many times she doesn't have to think about what she's doing. The squares come out the size they're supposed to be: five inches by five inches. Olga brushes the edges with egg yolk. Go on, she says. What's the catch? Does he stutter? Does he have a limp? Is he a hundred?

Forty-five, and not in good health.

What's the catch?

He was at Auschwitz.

So?

I don't know quite how to explain it, Lena says. It's a feeling I don't have words for.

Try, Lenchen, Olga says, as if she's still Lena's nanny. She dusts her hands with flour, puts a little pile of meat in the center of each square, and folds it in two, creating twenty-two filled triangles. She presses the edges together and places them on the buttered sheet. I'll get some wine from the cellar, Olga says. Brush the tops with egg yolk and pierce them with the fork. And when I'm back, tell me what you don't know how to explain.

Lena sets the table the way Olga likes it – with a white table-cloth and the china that her mother hid in the cellar during the war. Two point four billion cubic feet of rubble was removed from the bombed-out city, but in the cellar of the small building in the old city where Olga's family lived, twelve plates, wrapped securely in old felt, survived without the slightest crack. When everything is bombed, Olga once said, but twelve gold-rimmed plates can survive the war in the basement of an old house, it has to be a sign. Of what? Lena had asked, and Olga replied: Of a happy life. Nowadays she could afford an expensive place in a restored building near the harbor – but there no stone had remained unharmed during the war, which was not a sign that one should expect a happy life there. Olga lives in the old city in the building her parents had lived in.

Lena puts the baking sheet in the oven, and as Olga sets glasses on the table, she says, I can't put this love into words – let me try to paint you a picture. Imagine you've just bought a new radio with lots of stations and programs.

Olga uncorks the wine.

Are you listening?

Olga pours wine in the glasses. Go on, Lenchen!

You turn on this nice new radio and find a station, and you like what you hear. You try another station and realize it's playing the same thing. You search and search and are amazed to find that all the stations are playing the same program.

One good program is better than ten boring ones.

Imagine you love Verdi – do you want to hear Verdi every day?

Olga clinks her glass against Lena's – na zdrowie, Lenchen. Verdi composed over thirty operas.

And if I know all of them, I'll sing along – and then?

Olga shakes her head. Lenchen, she says sternly, there are newspapers and television shows. You can read books, watch films, talk to people – you translate articles and novels, you don't have to listen to the radio all the time!

The man I'm talking about is named Heiner, not Verdi. He consists of one leitmotif with endless variations. This is what I mean: He sees a brick chimney and says: Look, Lena, Birkenau. He sees thin, white smoke coming out and says: They're not very busy today, otherwise the smoke would be thick and black. Do you have any idea how often the ramp comes up in our everyday life? The post office has a ramp, there's a ramp at the train station, every warehouse has a ramp but for Heiner there's only one ramp. I buy myself a nice new coat and what does he say? Look, Lena. The brand name is *Selection*. Everything has a false bottom, and memories lurk around every corner.

And afterwards can you talk to him about filled dumplings?

No problem. Until we run into another ominous word.

That's good, Olga says, taking the baking sheet with steaming pierogi from the oven.

Oh Olga, can't you see what I mean?

Na zdrowie, Lenchen. Tomorrow we'll visit Uncle Amszel, then we can talk a bit more.

After breakfast Olga fills a thermos with hot soup and puts bread and butter, a jar of honey, a pot of tea, sausages, and a big piece of cheese in a dinner pail. When they get down to the street, Olga turns back and fetches a bottle of vodka to bring along as well. For inner warmth, she says, he's always cold, even in the summer.

Olga had inherited Uncle Amszel like a piece of furniture no one wanted. Strictly speaking, Olga had inherited not just a man, but also an apartment no one cared about in a building that belonged to no one. It stands in an area of the old city that hadn't been rebuilt, and it's bordered by similarly dilapidated buildings. The building they stop at has four stories and a crooked chimney; tiles are missing from the roof. The windows are too dirty to see through.

Olga points to a window on the third floor. Lena can see that a circle has been rubbed clean to make a kind of peep-hole. Olga waves, even though she can't tell whether there's a face behind the glass or not.

How long have you known him? Lena asks.

Three years.

How did you find him?

Because I heard a noise in the night that didn't belong. I was on the way home from a girlfriend's birthday party. It must have been almost two, and I felt like going for a walk. I love this ram-shackle part of town, you know. It reminds me of the old days – I used to play here as a child. I must have been hearing the music for a little while, but at some point I really noticed it and stopped – although music isn't quite the right word. Someone was picking out notes on a piano. Sometimes a very shrill note, sometimes a deep one, sometimes the same note played quickly over and over. It would stop and there would be silence, and then it would start over again. It was like a summons. As if someone was sending out notes and waiting for an answer.

Lena looks around. Where were you standing?

Here, Olga says, right where you're standing now. It was a clear night.

Weren't you scared?

Olga laughs. Me?

She'd survived the Nazis, the bombing of Danzig, the Russians, the Communists – she'd used up her supply of fear.

The tones were coming out of this building here, and when I found the source, I thought I saw a candle flickering on the third floor. I walked up to the door and found four names listed on the doorbell – faded, mildewed, but still legible:

Szymerman S.

Szymerman P.

Szymerman A.

Szymerman M.

You went into this ruin?

Why not? Murderers don't play piano at night.

Olga had climbed the creaking stairs. She couldn't find the light switch in the stairwell, or maybe there wasn't one. She'd clung to the rickety railing. The doors on the first and second floors were nailed shut with wooden slats. She listened. The sound had stopped. Hello, she called, Is anyone there? It was silent for a while, then she heard steps, then more silence. Tentatively, the third-floor door opened, just a crack. By the light of a candle she saw a man's round head. A kippah covered his baldness, and when he saw her he cried: It's you, child, you've found me! Where are the other children? I've been calling you every night.

He was…?

Crazy? Call it what you will, that's the way I inherited him.

From whom?

From the war. He was the only one of the Szymermans to come back. The other apartments remained empty.

And what happened that night?

Nothing. He told me his name – Amszel – we drank some vodka, I promised to come back, and then I walked home.

And then?

I realized someone must be bringing him food, or else he'd have starved. But when this person noticed that there was someone else coming to see him, namely me, he stopped coming. I was his replacement. I don't know anything else – we never met. I've been cooking for Uncle Amszel ever since, and I make sure the place is clean. I won out against the authorities who wanted to have him put away. I had the piano tuned. Olga laughs – the notes he calls the children with at night actually sound good now.

She opens the door to the stairwell and calls up: It's me, Uncle Amszel – Olga. She climbs the stairs to the third floor, seemingly unafraid of rotten steps, knocks on the door, and calls again: It's us, Uncle Amszel, the children. They don't hear proper steps approaching the door from inside, more a quiet shuffling of felt slippers, a rattling of keys, and then the door opens slowly to reveal a bowed old man, who raises his head with great effort. He reaches out both hands. He beams at them: Come to me, my dear children.

At the threshold Lena hesitates. Linens spill from the cupboard, and everywhere – on the table, the chairs, the floor, the bed, the stove – are piles of yellowed newspapers and a plethora of half-made shoes. Heels of every height, soles, legs of boots with no feet, scraps of brown leather. He was a cobbler, Olga says, this apartment was his workshop.

Olga makes room on the table for a plate and a glass.

He looks at Olga and points to Lena: Has the child seen my scars? Shall I show her? He begins to unbutton his cardigan.

No, Uncle Amszel, Olga says quickly, not today. Lena knows all about scars.

They stay with him until he's finished his soup. They drink vodka with him. Olga looks to see if the pantry is stocked, and Uncle Amszel brings Lena the leg of a boot made of soft leather.

Touch it, isn't it nice?

Very nice.

Take it, my child. I knew that you'd come needing shoes.

Olga packs up the dinner pail. She embraces the old man. I'll be back in two days, Uncle Amszel.

Be well, dear child, he says, and take care of my little friend. He takes Lena's hands and kisses them both.

He hid children, Olga says when they get down to the court-yard. They were discovered. He survived the ghetto by making shoes. What are you bawling about?

Lena strokes the leather. Why did you bring me here?

I was thinking of Verdi, and how it's harder with the living than with the dead.

Oh, Olga.

No one Lena knows sees herself so much as part of the history of the earth as Olga does. Her path as a scientist began with an amber necklace her grandmother gave her for her first Holy Communion – that was what incited her passion. Olga learned from her grandmother that the stone warms the skin, wards off demons, chases away witches and trolls, and that millions of years ago there must have been a damaged tree that healed its wound with resin. The liquid bandage had dripped onto the trunk and gently covered the woodlice, spiders, and beetles that lived at the foot of the tree – as it had the winged ant that now lay in Olga's amber necklace, as in a translucent coffin. When light strikes that part of the necklace, the stone flashes red like the Baltic at sunset. That was how Olga had come to learn the meaning of awe early in life. A being from the beginning of the world lay between her collarbones, and she was carrying it into the future. Olga needed no religion to feel she had a place in the universe. When she touched the stones, she understood where in creation she belonged. And then, on the day of her first Holy Communion, she learned a word that captivated her and determined her path in life: death assemblage. Lice and leaves, worms and feathers, pine needles and spider legs could form a community in death, without any effort on their part. It was the loss of Olga and her amber necklace that had made Lena scream and bite after leaving Danzig, until she could learn Olga's language and become her friend.

As on every visit, Olga shows her friend her new discoveries. Each piece of amber is unique. They can be white like milk, yellow like acacia honey, red like blood, or blackish-brown like the earth of a tilled field. Whenever Lena watches Olga submerging herself in a long-ago era she herself can't even image, she understands her friend's tranquility a little better – though not her ability to handle pain. In the past few years, three men had left Olga, and the last one, whom Olga had said she'd loved like no one else, had lied and betrayed her. Olga spoke of it without tears, without anger. A shrug and four words: What's done is done.

On the last evening Lena says: You use your amber coffins like a drug.

And?

You don't take your troubles seriously, Lena says. Your lover lies to you and you smother your grief with the whole weight of the earth's history.

That's the way it is, Olga says, unmoved. What's a man

compared to a bark beetle immortalized by a drop of resin fifty million years ago?

I know, Lena says. It's easier with the dead than with the living.

When they say goodbye a week later, Olga lays an amber necklace around her friend's neck. Yellow, like acacia honey, with inclusions, as trapped animals and plants were called in Olga's terminology – delicate threads of leaf called "star hairs" in common parlance and "Trichome" by Olga.

Which part of me can help? asked Viktor Frankl. Do you need the doctor, the comrade, or the psychiatrist?

I need all of you, Heiner said, but I'm not going to lie on your couch. Words can be suffocating.

We can do it whichever way you like, Frankl said.

What I'd like most is to run away.

Run towards your memories, then.

Three weeks after the end of the Auschwitz trial, Viktor Frankl convinced his comrade to return to his couch on therapeutic grounds. At Heiner's desperate request that he not sit behind him, since those who stood, sat, or walked behind him posed a threat, Frankl pushed his armchair next to the couch, so that Heiner could see his face.

Unburden your heart, I'm here.

It was quiet in the apartment. Somewhere a clock ticked. Heiner heard his friend breathing, and closed his eyes. He quickly reached his destination – it wasn't far. It must have been the winter of '43, it had been snowing for hours, and he was glad that he'd kept his job in the typing room. It was cold and damp, but no one froze to death there. On the day that was to haunt him forever, he had been sorting the record cards of prisoners who had been admitted to the infirmary from the sub-camp Monowitz, the coal mine. He stumbled upon a familiar name. Czende. Paul, Prisoner number 123 145. Could it be his friend who'd rented films in Vienna, whom he and Martha had brought to the train to Budapest? He saw Lassi, Paul's son, waving cheerfully, as if he were going on vacation. Heiner looked carefully at the card. The year of birth was correct; the previous residence was Vienna, Zieglergasse, in the 7th district. He saw the chalk line on the floor of the apartment where he and Martha had looked after Lassi.

Shaken, Heiner ran through the halls of the infirmary. How could he find Paul, when eight hundred men lay in each hall, and none of them looked anything like their former selves? They were skeletons, bare-shaven, disfigured, feverish faces, so similar they could have been twins. Heiner hoped he would be able to sense when he was close to Paul. Nonetheless, he cried out: Paul, it's me, Heiner – Heiner from Vienna. He bent over every man that reminded him even vaguely of his friend, a big man with bushy eyebrows. Paul, he shouted, it's me, Heiner from Vienna. He was about to give up the search when he came upon a man with white eyebrows.

Paul?

Slowly, the man turned to face him.

Paul, is that you? It's me, Heiner, from Vienna.

Paul Czende had phlegmons on his legs, which was bad, but his frostbitten hands were the real catastrophe. His fingers were black, with no flesh, no nails. Just stay here, he said, as if his friend could possibly have moved. I'll get the prisoner's doctor, he's a friend, a great guy, Dr Steinberg, a Jew from Paris – he'll save you. He begged the doctor: Help him, Doctor! He's a friend, a comrade – a Jew from Budapest.

The results of the examination came as a shock. Third degree frostbite was incurable. Both hands would have to be amputated. A man without hands here, the doctor said, you know what that means. Everyone knew. Help him anyway, Heiner said.

Dr Steinberg amputated Paul's hands, and during the next selections, Heiner let Paul's card disappear, so no one could see how long Paul had been at the infirmary. When Klehr came to inspect the halls, Heiner hid his friend among the dead. He traded his bread for cigarettes and the cigarettes for medicine. How long are you going to keep this up? his comrades from the Resistance asked. This business with Paul can't go on. The medicine, the extra food…you're giving your bread away, we're risking our lives for a man who can't work here, and if he can't work – you know what that means.

Heiner leapt from the couch and stared at Frankl. Do you know what they said? The effort was too great – we could save two or three other lives instead. Heiner, they said, Paul can't be helped. He's closer to death than to life. No hands in Auschwitz, frozen feet – which Arbeitskommando should we put him in? There isn't one. Yes, I said, that's true, but he's my friend. They said in this place that was too little, everyone has friends here, but we can only save those who are important for the Resistance, and then they said: Enough talking, we'll take a vote. Except for me, everyone was in favor of letting Paul go. I hoped for a miracle. They forbade me to hide him amid the corpses, and so at the next selection, it was Paul's turn. Heiner stared at Frankl as if behind his eyes he could see the place where, the next morning, the truck came to pick up the men whom Klehr hadn't been able to kill with his needle on the previous day, because there were simply too many.

Frankl brought Heiner a glass of water and sat him back down on the couch. Go on, my friend.

If only that were where the story ended, Heiner said. But Paul's son, little Lassi, was also in the camp, and though visits to the infirmary were forbidden, I'd brought him to see his father a few times. He knew where to find him.

I'm listening, comrade.

The sky was blue, a shameless blue, and the prettiest snowflakes I've ever seen were falling on the roofs, the camp road, covering the roller, covering everything. Anywhere but here one would have said: A fairy-tale kind of day – but here every snowflake in this lovely scene was a mockery, because here, under this sky, twenty naked men were being loaded from a ramp onto a truck. Everything happened very quietly and peacefully, as if in eerie agreement. The Kapos didn't need to yell – the men knew all was lost, they didn't try to defend themselves.

Heiner straightened. He felt ill, as if he were about to vomit. He screamed as he should have screamed then – but back then he'd been mute. He reached for Frankl's hand.

What happened next could only have been the work of the devil: Suddenly, as if he'd fallen from the sky with the snowflakes, there stood Lassi, that gaunt child, who should have been at work outside the camp. He saw his father and screamed: Father, father, they're taking you to the gas chamber, take me with you.

Heiner wept. Take your time, my friend, Frankl said.

You're the only person I can tell, Heiner said, only you can understand what lives inside me. The truck drove off, and the boy ran after it and grabbed the tailgate, and before the Kapo could hit the boy's hand with a club, one of the naked men pried the boy's fingers away, forcefully and tenderly. Lassi fell into the snow.

"Father" no longer existed for Heiner. Whenever he heard the word, all he could hear was the boy's cries: "Father, father, take me with you."

Frankl, he said softly, what kind of man am I? Sacrificing one life to save another – what a rotten moral.

They were silent together – they were in the camp, both of them. That time was ruled by other laws, Frankl said, we didn't make them. We made choices, it's true. But half-dead men can't take part in the Resistance – that's also true. It wasn't a matter of love and friendship, it was a matter of life and death.

Frankl gave his weeping friend a sedative. He covered him with a blanket. You'll sleep for a while, he said, and then you'll feel better.

I should have fought for Paul, Heiner said. I am guilty.

The circumstances made us guilty, they implicated us.

Before Heiner fell asleep on Frankl's couch, he said: Does someone like me deserve love?

Any man who has no wife lives without joy, without blessing, and without goodness.

When he awoke, he wasn't sure whether Frankl had really said those words from the Talmud, or whether they belonged to his dream of a life with Lena.

Heiner sent only the bare necessities from Vienna to Germany. Two thousand books, fifty filing folders, ten photo albums, the sofa, the cuckoo clock, and a new wool blanket, baby blue like the one in Vienna. Why always this blue, Lena asked, do you owe the color something? Can one owe something to a color? He hadn't thought about it, he'd simply replaced the blanket with a new one in the same color when the old one grew threadbare – another color wouldn't have comforted him when he got cold, and he was often cold, even in the summer. It was forty below when word spread among the comrades: Blue blankets have come from Holland – as if they'd traveled under their own power.

Heiner turned the living room on the ground floor into a hermit's cave. He hung curtains over the wide window and heavy drapes over the first curtains. When the cuckoo chirped eight times, it was time in Heiner's cave for the television news and dinner. Lena decorated the rest of the house. She arranged bright furniture in front of the white walls, and got a stove with six gas burners, because Heiner's vision of happiness included being able to entertain guests with a lavish feast at any moment. The kitchen cupboards reached the ceiling, and pans of all sizes hung on the walls. Lena was the cook, and Heiner cleaned, set the table as if every meal was the last celebration of his life, and made sure the cupboards were always well stocked. He bought groceries as if famine was a daily threat.

Rituals that gave him a sense of security were a big part of their life. In the evening he said: Be with me through the night. Lena had never slept with a man who held her as if afraid she might be stolen from him. They used only one side of the double bed. As in Vienna and in Lena's old apartment, they slept in gentle yellow light, as if the sinking sun were granting them its last beams. The couple was surrounded by quiet and peace throughout the night. If love could be seen, you'd see it in that bed.

Addiction is a craving for life, he said, and smoked forty cigarettes a day. He had Lena bring him his first cup of coffee in bed to wake him up, and he drank his last mug before he fell asleep at night. He hoarded books because he never stopped to discover what he didn't know of the world and of men. Lena carried the books back to his room when they began to creep through the rest of the house like ant trails. They piled up in the hallways, on the edge of the bathtub, next to the pots in the kitchen, on the stairs to the second floor, and in the basement. He read Seneca, Aristotle, Nietzsche, and Kant. He loved Brecht and Kafka; he knew Rilke by heart and sometimes recited his favorite poem to Lena like a goodnight prayer before they went to sleep: *I would like to sing someone to sleep, to sit beside someone and be there. I would like to rock you and sing softly, and go with you to and from sleep. I would like to be the one in the house who knew: The night was cold. And I would like to listen in and listen out into you, into the world, into the woods.* Karl Kraus's *The Torch* was dog-eared and worn. He read new books more quickly than the books that he already knew, which he nonetheless read over and over again, searching for ideas he might have overlooked. Canetti's *Crowds and Power* was his bible. He had stacks of books on fascism and war: novels and essays, reportage, documentaries, analyses. Memoirs by victims, notes by perpetrators. He was fascinated by psychology. Freud and Frankl, C. G. Jung, Erich Fromm, Melanie Klein, Alexander and Margarete Mitscherlich. In the Hungarian psychoanalyst Sándor Ferenczi's essay on the question of "Identification with the aggressor as a method of surviving violence," he'd underlined every word. Sometimes he just took it off the shelf to caress it.

For Heiner the book was a living thing – it had been written in Hungary and had Paul's face and Lassi's voice. *Father, father, take me with you.*

His books were full of green and red, blue, yellow, and white scraps of paper, and when the wind blew through the open door to the veranda, the bookshelf looked like a colorful field of flowers. He was happy with the neighborhood where he lived, but he hadn't yet reconciled himself with Germany. He avoided men of his own age; he bought medicine at a pharmacy owned by a young woman, even though it meant a half hour's drive. The pharmacist in town smoked a pipe. Like Klehr, who'd singled out naked men with its stem. The dentist was named Dirlewanger – how could anyone live with that name today? He was happy in marriage, but after five years with Heiner, Lena no longer knew who she was. A well-paid interpreter, a sought-after translator, a woman to whom others were drawn – but what else? I'm no longer five foot seven, she said during her first therapy session. In a few more years I'll be a dwarf. I don't laugh in his presence anymore – compared to his past, mine is just a string of banalities. As a child I fell off a swing and spent eight weeks in traction – but what is my swing compared to Boger's? He's a survivor, while I simply live. Sometimes I want to spend hours talking about lipstick and nail polish and movies that make you laugh so hard your stomach aches – but when he's around, something stops me. I have terrible fantasies. I want to bury the contents of his mustard jar in the garden and plant chives on top of it. Or tomatoes. I'd like to replace his burial object with sand from the playground and laugh over my trick the next time he sets it next to a guest's plate. *Look, what might this be?* I want to talk about recipes…

Why don't you? the therapist asked.

It's obscene.

Who says?

Me.

Lena left her session with homework, like a schoolchild.

I cut cooked waxy potatoes into medium-thick slices, while they are still warm, she explained to her cinema-friend Gesa in Heiner's presence, then I stir in a mixture of two egg yolks, white vinegar, and olive oil, and add finely chopped shallots cooked in vegetable broth until they're soft. My mother put chopped hard-boiled eggs in her potato salad and my grandmother added cucumbers and radishes.

And what do you serve with it? Gesa asked.

Meatballs, fried golden-brown, bratwurst, or fried eggs.

How did your husband react? asked the therapist.

He got hungry. That night he hugged me and said: Look, Lena, Auschwitz isn't the enemy of potato salad.

After thirty hours on the couch, Lena was able to separate the swing of her childhood from Boger's swing. After forty hours, she asked Gesa to order the silliest movie available, and two months later she admitted to the therapist that she didn't actually want to live without Heiner's "Look, Lena stories," which could be provoked by a sniffle, a cough, a sneeze, or a downpour, by fog, wind, a word, a cloud, a bird's cry, the first snowflake, or a stag at the edge of the woods. At her last session she said:

He is he and I am I – why did I need forty-two hours on the couch to figure that out?

When Lena was again standing five foot seven, she kept a shy distance from Heiner's photo albums and the blurred, fuzzy images that filled them – pictures captured with a stolen camera, taken by prisoners at the risk of their lives, drawings and sketches of the murderers and their victims, and of daily life in the camp, sketched in free moments with stolen pencils on scraps of paper.

While Heiner was out, Lena had taken the albums off the shelf and hadn't been able to shake the feeling of intruding on something intimate, like a diary. I'm ashamed by what I saw there, she said.

Ashamed? Why?

Lena saw herself sitting on the carpet in front of Heiner's bookshelf, leafing through the albums. There was a grainy photo of a man on the gallows. There was a photo of a prisoner who'd been shot by the Nazis as he tried to flee, and then propped in a wheelbarrow as a warning to others. They put a sign around his neck: Hurray, I'm back! And then there was the pencil drawing that she covered with her hands because she couldn't bear to look at it.

Describe the picture, the therapist said.

I can't.

Just try.

The picture hurts.

The therapist was silent. Lena lay on the couch and looked through the skylight at clouds drifting across the sky – the nicest possible companions for a therapy session. She saw the drawing in her head.

There's a woman lying on a whipping rack.

She paused for a long time after each sentence.

Two men are holding her arms.

Her arms are thin, like gnawed bones.

The woman is naked.

A man in uniform stands behind her.

His right arm is raised, and it's holding a club.

He's looking forward to hitting her. You can tell. The woman's face is frozen in fear or pain – you can't tell how many times he's already hit her.

Her mouth is open wide.

The woman is so gaunt it looks like she might break.

Maybe she won't survive the torture.

Next to the picture, in Heiner's handwriting it says: *My poor, poor Zofia.*

He must have known her, Lena said, maybe even loved her.

The therapist was silent.

Maybe he had to watch?

What do the words make you feel?

Pain. My skin burns. My back hurts.

Jealousy?

Are you crazy? Lena sat up, indignant. Of that poor woman? I couldn't be!

Or won't you allow yourself to be?

At the next session, Lena said: I will never touch a person's soul as deeply as the woman on the whipping board touched the man who wrote: my poor, poor Zofia. That's sad, isn't it?

Why? You're his joy.

Pain forms a stronger bond than joy.

Who says?

The picture.

There were times when Lena was tortured by questions, and years when Lena could handle Heiner, the mustard jar, and his games of Halma with confidence. They celebrated their tenth wedding anniversary at Schloss Tulbing near Vienna, a castle that belonged to his comrade Salomon, a typist in the infirmary, prisoner number 63 140, Heiner's friend – one of four survivors from his transport. Lena often looked at the album of anniversary photos. She couldn't get enough of the elegant couple on the dance floor. Heiner's hair had turned white, it still fell in curls to his shoulders. He wore a white suit and Lena a long, black dress. My black guardian angel, he called her. Heiner's friends came from Austria and Poland, bringing funny songs, toasts, and loud laughter. Heiner was a superlative host. He made sure no one was lonely, introduced everyone, brought Lena's colorfully dressed friends to meet his comrades, so that they could talk, dance, and drink together. As they opened the party with a Viennese waltz, Heiner's friends clapped, while Lena detected skepticism in the eyes of her friends. She saw the question no one would voice: What do they see in each other? What's the secret? Does she love him or pity him? Even Gesa, who knew Heiner, had asked on one of their cozy film nights: What is it about him? The way he kisses your hand is adorable and his charm is bewitching, he's good-looking, clever – but honestly, Lena, doesn't it drive you up the wall to be with a man who's retired at fifty-five?

Good question. Heiner was a retiree, and not a healthy man. In Vienna he'd taught printing, and he was let go because he was absent more often than the truants. He found work as a book-keeper for a publishing house, but after half a year he had to admit that he couldn't manage eight-hour days without a nap now and then. He tried taking quick naps in the bathroom, but once asleep, it wasn't easy for him to wake up. In Germany he took a part-time job, which went well until he was fired for not declaring his arrest in Vienna on his application, and his employer saw him as a fraud. Heiner had wanted to leave Germany after that – right away, I can't live here, he said, the experiment is a failure. Lena fought with her husband for a week before he agreed to give her country a second chance. He didn't wait for his written notice, he wrote it himself. *We are letting Herr Rosseck go because he suppressed information of his time in prison in order to gain employment with this firm. We do not work with former inmates, nor with Communists, which Herr Rosseck should certainly have known. We wish him well in his further endeavors.* He'd meant it as a malicious joke, but his boss signed it, and Heiner had proof. But of what? Not that this was the way everyone in Germany thought, but for Heiner, one person was one too many. He sent application after application. *My skills include leadership, good general education, polite behavior, I have good handwriting and am particularly good at typing – I can type fast and without error. I am hardworking and neat. Above all, I am honest. I was arrested by the Nazis and was a prisoner at Auschwitz.* Ten applications, ten replies. *Dear Herr Rosseck, We regret that we will not be able to hire you, as we have filled the position internally.* When Lena realized that he was provoking the rejections, she took his future into her own hands, and then it was only a matter of withstanding the deluge of documents and paperwork that confronted them in applying for disability benefit. He went to Vienna and spent hours and days at various offices. Everyone was very sorry, everyone wanted to help, everyone said: My God, arrested by the Gestapo! My God, Auschwitz! Only documents with a stamp and a signature counted. It took a year for them to recognize his 224 weeks of imprisonment. He let the official medical examiners and independent doctors turn him inside-out. Hop for us, bend at the waist, pedal on this bicycle. He had to prove that he was no malingerer, that he wasn't trying to commit pension fraud. In the camp he had survived spotted fever, typhus, and tuberculosis – but in the camp no one was ever officially sick or officially well. In the end, they certified that he had uncurable ailments: he'd had his gallbladder removed, and he suffered from circulatory disorders, a weak heart as the result of two coronaries, untreatable physical weakness leading to frequent chills, arterial damage in both legs, and chronic emphysema-bronchitis, leading to deterioration of the alveoli, shortness of breath, and asthma. You smoke too much, the medical examiner said – you should stop that. Then came the verdict: Heiner's "Employment Impair-ment Level" was one hundred percent, which meant that he was eligible to receive 410 Marks compensation for wrongful impris-onment fourteen times a year for the rest of his life. That added up to 2 Marks per week in Auschwitz, or 28 Pfennigs per day. In addition, he received a government pension of 300 Marks; Lena earned the remainder of their living. When her father died, she sold the house in Zurich and paid off the house in the village where the parents, the children, and the trees were all young.

OK, Gesa said. You married a sick man. Explain it to me – if it's not pity, what is it?

You can't explain love.

Try.

Love is like air, Lena said. You can't see it, but you breathe it in. When you hold it, you have nothing in your hand.

That's not much.

Love is an exploration. We want to get to know each other, but it only works if we allow ourselves to be known.

Gesa looked baffled.

He let me into his life, Lena said. He made room for me. Whenever he thinks of his life, he sees me as part of it. If you could take an X-ray of love, you'd see it spread throughout the whole body like alveoli are in the lungs.

Alveoli? That's it?

Gesa liked love in the movies. In real life she found it too taxing. In the cinema she liked to see passion, hatred, separation, and reconciliation, but in real life she avoided men who were serious about her. Gesa loved complicated films, but to her complicated relationships – like Heiner and Lena's marriage – were as risky as roulette. Don't you ever fight?

They fought. And how. They fought about things other couples could never dream of. The anniversary album had incited one such incident. Heiner had put it on the right-hand side of the bottom shelf, next to the albums with the photos and drawings from Auschwitz. Albums with albums, photos with photos – so you could find what you were looking for. It was that easy. Not so for Lena. As soon as she passed the bookshelf, she got a funny feeling in her stomach. She tried to get to the bottom of the feeling by purposely standing in front of the shelf and looking at the albums. When the queasiness returned, she said, as if to herself: How odd. I can't understand it. Heiner was reading on the sofa.

What are you looking for, dear?

Nothing.

What can't you understand?

I'm not quite sure. I think I don't want it to be there.

He didn't understand what she meant. What don't you want to be there?

The wedding anniversary album.

Where else should it be?

Somewhere else. Not there.

He put the book down. He looked at her, perplexed. Why?

It doesn't belong there.

It took him a few seconds to understand what she meant by "there."

The photos from our anniversary are part of my life, he said.

And mine too.

And?

It was the sharpness of his tone that gave her vague discomfort a focus.

Down there – she pointed to the bottom shelf – down there, our tenth anniversary turns into an episode from Auschwitz.

His face was completely still. He looked as if he'd been hit. Then he sprang from the sofa as if it had caught fire. His lips trembled. What did you say? he whispered. On my bookshelf our wedding anniversary becomes an episode from the camp? My albums are contagious, like a disease? Is that what you're trying to say?

I hadn't thought of it that way, but now that you mention it...

You mean – his voice was sardonic – you think at night the people in the albums mingle, secretly, while we're sleeping?

He looked through Lena as if picturing what he'd just said. He fell back on the sofa.

You think, he said softly, emphasizing every word, you really think that when we're not watching, the Klehr from my album asks the Lena from the anniversary album to dance? Heiner's face was white, his laugh was hysterical.

More likely he asks you, Lena said. You know each other so well.

She slammed the door behind her. She shut herself in her room and heard Heiner screaming: The album stays here!

She opened the door and screamed: You're crazy!

Me, he cried, I'm the crazy one?

Lena lay down on the couch. Her heart pounded as if she'd done fifty knee bends. She took deep breaths, then got a bottle of wine from the cellar and drank the whole thing. She didn't sleep next to Heiner that night. She stayed in her study, and heard from his steps that he didn't sleep in the bedroom either. He's right, she thought before she fell asleep. I'm the crazy one – but only because no one can live with this man and remain sane.

When Lena was long-since asleep, Heiner sat in the kitchen and poured himself too much whiskey. Lena was right – he was deranged, in the truest sense of the word. Just as one can rearrange furniture in a house, things in his head were not arranged the way they were in other peoples' minds. He listened differently, saw differently, felt differently. Why had he insisted on keeping their anniversary album with the albums that contained only gallows and hanged men, whipping racks and torturers, trains and chimneys – why? Why did Lena's request set him off? He drank and smoked, and couldn't find the answer. Why hadn't he said: My treasure, our anniversary isn't an episode from Auschwitz, of course not. Put the album wherever it doesn't give you a stomach-ache – in the kitchen, in the cellar, put it with the books that begin with "A," for album, between Ahrendt and Anders – just tell me where you'd like it, between Hesse and Hochhuth, I won't mind. Instead, he'd exploded. She'd hit a nerve, but which one? He listened at her door. He tried the knob, but the door was locked.

Lena?

There was only silence.

Lena, my treasure, open the door.

He went back to the living room, took a writing pad from the desk and wrote a long letter to Leszek, his friend and comrade in Poland. Dear friend – tonight my head is whirling like a carousel, and it's driving me crazy. Shaken, he described the fight over the photo album. What Lena had said, what he'd said. Exit Lena, exit Heiner – a scene from a play. As he wrote he began to understand what was bothering him. Dear friend – which has more power over our thoughts, feelings, and actions – the present or the past? Are there findings on this, essays, books? Or is it a decision that everyone has to make for themselves? You seem to have made a proper grave for our past, a grave that you can visit, care for, and then leave. You commute between then and now, while I, to carry the metaphor further, walk around arm in arm with a ghost that I frighten people with. I can't find a grave for this ghost, and, to be honest, I don't actually want to bury it. Maybe sometimes I should hide it. Or disguise it. The past will always be closer to me than it is to you, my friend, but at the same time, I don't want to grant it the power to destroy my present with Lena.

By morning, he had ten densely written pages in front of him. Exhausted, he wrapped himself in the wool blanket and fell asleep fully clothed on the sofa. At noon he wrote Leszek's address on the envelope, but when he stood before the mailbox on his evening stroll, he tore up the letter.

After a week of near silence he said: Take the album, dear, and put it in your room if that will make you feel better. No need, Lena said. She'd made copies of the photos and made herself another album.

Gesa was right, their marriage was complicated. Lena treated the huge book, the monstrosity her husband plunged into at night, with a mixture of awe, curiosity, and fury. This book didn't stand closely bordered, wedged in, comfortingly motionless on the bookshelf like the other books – it wandered from the windowsill to the carpet, from the carpet to the coffee table, from there to the sofa – it had even been found once on Lena's rocking chair. A book as heavy as lead. When Heiner woke up and couldn't go back to sleep, he'd get up, wrap himself in the velveteen bathrobe, put the blue Holland blanket over his legs, and open the book at random, leaf through and read and get lost in its pages until Lena found him there at dawn. His face would be pale, but his eyes wide and alert behind his glasses. His body was nearly invisible through the haze of cigarette smoke. Then Lena would open the door to the terrace and call his name, annoyed – why annoyed? her therapist had asked once – and watch the gray fumes float hesitantly away from her husband. Then she'd go to the kitchen and make coffee. It makes me angry to see him torturing himself like that. She cursed the book and sometimes also the man, who couldn't explain to her why he embarked on these nocturnal journeys. There was one question that the therapist asked that Lena wouldn't answer: Do you want him to take you with him on his journeys?

One night when Heiner was visiting friends in Vienna, Lena heard a noise on the terrace. She got up, slowly descended the stairs from the bedroom to the ground floor, turned on the outside light, and saw two small shadows jump from the table and skitter off. They were squirrels, who'd knocked the abandoned bread basket off the table and now were nimbly ascending the trunk of a pine tree like little brown elevators.

Lena cast a glance at the kitchen, where dirty dishes were starting to pile up. Wrinkled clothes lay in the laundry room; her study reminded her of an approaching deadline. The living room was Heiner's room, where she'd never been alone at night before. He'd folded the blue blanket carefully at one end of the sofa and placed the big book on top of it. She stood in the doorway, undecided. It was quiet there, quieter than in the other rooms. The place felt abandoned. She turned on the floor lamp and closed the curtains. The light fell on the indentations in the sofa. The bigger one was where Heiner sat, the smaller one was from his head when he slept. This was how the sofa would look when he was no longer around. Quickly, Lena went into the bathroom, put on his bathrobe and sat down in the middle of the sofa. She wrapped the blue blanket over her knees. As long as she kept his place warm, nothing could happen to him. She set the big book on her lap. *Auschwitz Chronicle 1939–1945* by Danuta Czech. Seven years, a thousand pages. Meticulously compiled facts from two thousand days. She leafed through. Dates, names, brief sentences, gray photos, sober captions: On the way to the crematorium. Selection. Ramp. Admission Building. Main Camp. Forest Crematorium. Prisoners at work. Train with deportees on Platform 3. Numbers. Dates. Names. The whole history, from idea to implementation. August 22, 1939 – the day Hitler told the commanders of the Wehrmacht: *Our strength consists in our speed and in our brutality; Ghengis Khan led millions of women and children to slaughter – with premeditation and a happy heart. History sees in him solely the founder of a state...*

Lena was engrossed. Nocturnal expeditions through a collection of murderous data – why did he do this to himself? He screamed when he dreamt of Auschwitz. Maybe that was it: When he journeyed through Auschwitz awake, he remained master of his dreams, could choose his path with open eyes, instead of being at the mercy of his nightmares, which seized him uncontrollably in his sleep. Lena opened to the year 1942 – the year Heiner came to Auschwitz. Numbers, dates, facts, day-by-day records of what happened. Who was admitted. Who got what number. Who escaped. Who was shot between January 1 and December 31, 1942. She read:

On January 6 a group transport arrived, on January 8 numbers 25 272 through 25 332 were assigned to sixty prisoners. On January 15 the Gestapo sent 135 prisoners from Prague. At 16:50 on January 16, SS

Officer Stadler, who was on duty in tower L, shot a Russian prisoner of war. On January 17, the Polish prisoner Franciszek Batek committed suicide in the bunker of Block 11.

Were his nocturnal journeys hours of remembrance for his dead comrades? Did he ask their forgiveness for his survival? *Between January 25 and 29, 266 prisoners died from the effects of hunger, hard work, sickness, and mistreatment. In February, prisoners arrived from Kraków, Brno, and Warsaw. On February 15, 1942, the first transport of Jews from Bytom arrived. On the ramp they were…their bags were…they were taken to the gas chamber and…with Zyklon B. The management of the German National Railway sued for payment for the delivery of 143 000 people. Between May 5 and 11, 1942, 5 200 Polish Jews from the ghettos of Dąbrowa Górnicza, Będzin, Warthenau, and Gliwice lost their lives.*

Why did he do this to himself? Was he punishing himself for the luck, the coincidence, the shrewdness, the strength of surviving?

On September 11, 1942, numbers 63 246 through 63 393 were assigned to 148 male prisoners. Lena knew number 63 387. That was Heiner.

From September 12 on, the transports arrived daily.

On December 24, female prisoners from Poland placed candles on a fir branch, sang Christmas songs, and wished for freedom in the coming year.

Lena closed the book. There were 696 more pages until the last entry on January 27, 1945. She made strong coffee, filled the thermos and sat on the porch swing on the terrace, Heiner's summer sofa. Could it be that he submerged himself in this book at night, because in the morning, it set him free and allowed him to live? Could it be that he emerged from the book not despondent, but happy, because he had escaped from what he read in its pages?

The woods were a black wall. No bird sang, no branch cracked under a stag's hoof. There was a melody in the woods at night that you couldn't hear during the day. It was composed of a bit of wind, a few pinecones falling on the ground like heavy raindrops, the wing beats of an owl, and the even rustling of hungry armies of ants in search of spiders, flies, and caterpillars. They'd visited the house twice and stood indecisively on this terrace. On their third visit the stag came out of the woods and Heiner had turned pale. She could hear his voice, his intonation as he said: Look, Lena, when we sit here again, I'll tell you about the most terrifying night of my life. She rocked on the porch swing and drank the hot coffee slowly, without sugar or milk, the way Heiner drank it.

He hadn't been freed from Auschwitz by the Russians. He'd been sent on a death march to the Slovak-Hungarian border. From there he'd run away to Austria, four months before the end of the war. He joined the partisans, where he met up with Martha. They were eleven men and four women – they raided police stations, stole weapons and ammunition, hunted Nazis and held them captive. Their prison was a cave in the mountains – a damp labyrinth, a stinking pen for sheep and goats. And then came the night he couldn't forget as long as he lived – the most terrifying night of his life.

He was standing in front of the cave alone, a pistol in each pocket. His comrades had left him to stand guard while they went ahead to find the Americans to whom they were going to deliver the prisoners. Imagine, Heiner said on a mild evening out on the terrace, after they heard another crackling in the woods, a cellar full of Nazis – and me.

They were men who had been with the Gestapo in Vienna, would-be defectors. Latvian, Estonian, and Hungarian fascists who had fought on the side of the Nazis. Over a hundred men.

Ortsgruppenleiter, and a mayor who had forced his prisoners to eat out of bowls on all fours like dogs. The biggest fish was Kaltenbrunner, an Austrian that Heiner called rotten to the core. Doctorate of law, Head of the Sicherheitsdienst, Eichmann's superior, responsible for deporting Jews from every corner of Europe. A coward, who'd denied his own signature at Nürnberg. Imagine – that creature was my prisoner!

They had barricaded the cave with heavy beams – but he was sure the door would have toppled if all the prisoners had decided to throw themselves against it at the same time. That night his teeth chattered so fiercely he was surprised they didn't break. There had never been a worse night in all his life. It was black, cold, and starless. At one point the moon emerged from the clouds, and what he saw terrified him more than the Nazis in the cave. There, bathed in chalk-white light, not thirty feet away, was a stag with huge antlers. A messenger from another world. Motionless, with its head raised, it looked at Heiner as if it wanted to tell him something – but what? Heiner didn't believe in other worlds – the world he had just escaped from was strange enough. The stag was eerie, but in the end it was only an animal in the moonlight and so, he tried to convince himself, frightening, but meaningless.

The clouds covered the moon, the night grew black again, and Heiner concentrated on the rustlings and grumblings in the rocky prison, which sounded as if it was full of snakes and mice. The Nazis whined for bread and cigarettes, they promised him the moon and the stars if he would only set them free. Do you know how often I dreamed of revenge in the camp, he asked Lena, do you have any idea? Red-hot hatred, every night. Shooting would be far too quick a death. I wanted their agony never to end. I wanted them to feel the fear of death. He wanted to chop them into bits. Or hang them, and watch them beg for their lives as the noose tightened around their necks. None of them would have the grace to die with dignity like the men and women whose death on the gallows he'd had to watch. And now he was standing with two pistols in his pockets in front of a cellar filled with over a hundred Nazi criminals, and in the morning he had to admit that he was incapable of laying his hands on anyone. He couldn't have so much as slapped Kaltenbrunner. He denied the Nazis cigarettes while he smoked himself, over a hundred in that one night. He blew the smoke through the cracks in the door, but he did no more than that.

When he told Martha about the stag later, she crossed herself: God appeared to you! He laughed at her. God? Who's he? But Martha, the Communist, believed in the legend of Placidus, the Roman general who was out hunting when a mighty stag appeared. A big, magnificent animal, like the one Heiner had seen. Placidus raised his weapon, but when he saw the image of Jesus on the cross in the stag's antlers, he dropped it in terror. Placidus, the stag said, wherefore followest thou me hither? I am Jesus Christ that formed heaven and earth. Placidus dashed home and did not tell his wife of his encounter – but that very same night she awoke screaming from her sleep – because she too had seen Jesus in a stag's antlers. The next morning Placidus was baptized, along with his wife and sons, and from then on he was called Eustace. The stag had prophesied that the couple's faith would be sorely tested, and indeed, they faced a series of trials. Eustace's servants, maids, and animals were killed by a plague. His house was plundered by thieves, his family was torn apart. They found each other again, but then they were tortured to death by the emperor Hadrian. Martha was a partisan and an atheist, but still: the stag that had appeared to her fiancé was the son of God, and it foretold suffering and trials. Heiner had laughed at her. To him a cross in antlers meant only a herb liqueur, which they'd called Göring-Schnapps after Herrmann Göring was made Reichsjägermeister in 1934.

It was February 1945. The sun rose around eight in the morning. A ball, dark-red like fire, as if the earth was being swallowed by a huge oven. Slowly, his bones warmed, and his comrades returned. He saw them coming along the narrow road that led from the valley to the cave. They brought Americans with them, who gave them cigarettes, chewing gum, and oranges, and loaded the prisoners onto their truck. A new day began, and with it a new era – Heiner's era, the beginning of a better world. What a bunch of loonies we were, he said to Lena when he heard the crackling in the underbrush and thought of the stag.

Lena, since when do you sleep outside?

Lena opened her eyes. There was Gesa, standing in front of the porch swing with a bag of rolls. Breakfast, she said. Is everything ok?

Tell me, Gesa, do you know how much of the past a person can stand?

II

Your organs, the doctor said, are much older than you are.

Heiner laughed. They haven't had it easy.

The doctor looked at him severely. Your heart is weak, your kidneys don't function as they should, you wheeze, you have poor circulation, and you yourself know what your cough sounds like. You need to take care of yourself, Herr Rosseck.

Take care of myself? For whom? For when?

For later, the doctor said. Or don't you want to live a long life?

Heiner smiled. Later is a vague promise.

The doctor was concerned. I'd like to send you away for treatment – I know a good place on the North Sea that's known for its special treatments for asthmatics.

Heiner liked the doctor. He was a friendly, understanding man with plenty of time for his patients. When were you born? Heiner asked.

November 1, 1942.

You were only ten days old when I first heard the term special treatment. Since then I've given it a wide berth.

Despite the doctor's worries about his organs, the rest of Heiner was doing well. He no longer had nightmares; he woke up early and drove the scooter to the bakery – two poppyseed, two caraway – and woke Lena for breakfast. Then he'd sit down at his desk and write appeals for donations, as if he'd been doing it all his life. He gave interviews and spoke eloquently – even over the radio, his pleasant, deep voice wasn't easy to forget. *There were no birds in Auschwitz.* He spoke at events.

1 860 people arrived on my transport, and by the end there were only 4 of us. He shocked reporters who came to see him at home with his nonchalance. Have some of Lena's plum cake – Auschwitz and

| 123 |

food belong together. Look, a jar filled with sand, what might this be? The stamp on my ID: R.U. Do you know what that means? He visited department stores, supermarkets, doctor's offices, and pharmacies, and founded a society with Lena that they called AAF: Auschwitzers and Friends. In front of the house stood a bright red truck, a donation from the head of a shipping company who had seen Heiner on television.

He turned the cellar into a storeroom: in four months they had packed three hundred boxes, and bundled up fifty sacks of clothing. The drug that made him younger than his organs was martial law in Poland. Seven hundred thousand people on strike. In the factories, the coal mines, the shipyards, rage was simmering over endless price increases, and in the streets people knelt before signs that said "Hunger." Solidarność had nine million members, and more were joining every day. General Jaruzelski threatened that the Russians would invade, and the Poles warned their powerful neighbor with leaflets: *Ivan, stay where you are – you won't win THIS war.* They had one powerful protector. The former Polish miner Karol Wojtyla came back to visit his homeland as Pope John Paul II. Wherever he spoke to his countrymen – in churches and marketplaces, in big cities and small towns – the people rejoiced: Sto lat! Sto lat! May you live a hundred years! They cried: Stay with us! Stay here! The Pope gave a homily in Warsaw's Victory Square, and each word was a message. *Lord, Let your spirit descend, and renew the face of the earth,* – the Pope paused for a long time before finishing the sentence – *and the face of this land.* The people went wild. Sto lat, sto lat, help us, stay here. The world is holding its breath, wrote the newspapers, will the Pope call for revolution? Two years later, on Sunday, December 13, 1981, the head of the Polish government declared martial law. Heiner sat in front of the television. He lept from the sofa. Lena, he cried, I know these images, this is how civil war begins. The day before, on Saturday, December 12, 1981, just before midnight, General Jaruzelski had deployed 70 000 soldiers,

30 000 police, and 2 000 tanks. The military took over radio and television stations and installed men in uniform behind the microphones. Jaruzelski's speech was played on constant loop, day and night. *Citizens of Poland, today I address myself to you as a soldier and as the head of the Polish government. Our homeland is at the edge of an abyss. Chaos and moral decline have reached catastrophic levels.* The general's voice hammered away without pause: *The nation is on the verge of a psychological breakdown. Enough is enough! We must handcuff the troublemakers before they plunge this country into civil war. At midnight, the National Council declared martial law throughout the country.* To Heiner, the General was nothing more than a cold scowl in a uniform. The Poles learned to fear the Zomos, the militia's most savage band of thugs. Signs on houses read Zomo = Gestapo. Poland hadn't forgotten.

Heiner thought of his friends: Leszek and Aunt Zofia, Tomasz, Tadeusz, Stanislaw, Mietek, and "the Eagle," his comrades from the camp who meant more to him than his daughter, his mother, his sisters. The Poles needed clothing, medicine; they had no butter, no oil, no coffee, no tea. The stores were as empty as they had been in Vienna in the days when Heiner sat in doorways seeing red whorls of hunger. Lena saw in her husband's face that of the radical boy from Vienna who couldn't be held back. His face was stubborn as he said: I have to go. Good, Lena replied, let's go.

The night before they left, they were as excited as children on Christmas morning. Heiner sprinkled the car's tires with vodka, poured vodka on the hood, sprinkled the tarp, the seats, the steering wheel, the gear shift, and even the spare tire. A drop for the clutch, a drop for the gas pedal and the brake. Before the bottle was empty, Lena gave the truck a name. "Czerwony": The Red. It had taken them a whole day to pack.

Their arms were as heavy as potato sacks, and a thousand needles stabbed their lower backs. They'd expected to sink into sleep like stones into the sea, but when they closed their eyes, a crazed ballet of powdered milk and coffee, tea, chocolate, and cocoa frolicked through their heads. They saw cans of peas and carrots, beans, lentils, and soup. They were attacked by rice and sugar and noodles, by canned fish, scouring powder and dish detergent, soaps and bottles of lotion, toilet paper and light bulbs. When they opened their eyes, the ballet withdrew in fright. Let's get up, Heiner said. There are worse things than a night without sleep.

Heiner drove, while Lena gave directions, the map spread across her knees: Friedberg, Alsfeld, Bad Hersfeld, Herleshausen – and then she unpacked the food basket. She had calculated provisions for the journey with the same logic she'd used when shopping, stocking up goods, and packing boxes. She divided the length of the drive – including the wait at the borders – by the size of their hunger and arrived at twenty sausage sandwiches, twelve cheese sandwiches, and ten hard-boiled eggs. She'd taken into account her thirst and Heiner's addiction to coffee. She'd tucked away two cartons of cigarettes in the storage compartment.

Where did you learn to drive a truck?

In the war.

And where will I learn?

From me, Heiner said.

If people are meant for certain times, Heiner was meant for times of upheaval, of danger, times that required strength and courage, times that compelled him from the sofa and quickened his imagination. If he wasn't needed at home, he went where trouble was brewing.

Four hours to Herleshausen. The guards at the West German border were friendly. They inspected passports and export documents. The couple didn't want to go to the GDR, their destination was Poland, so the guards weren't interested. And so the border to the GDR marked the end of the first, easy part of the journey. Twenty trucks stood in front of them, and they watched as the customs officials unpacked every shipment. Five hours later, every movement was familiar. The quick, imperative gesture towards the truck bed meant: Open up. The guards held mirrors under the trucks, as if anyone would have wanted to smuggle himself into the country. They barked orders and enjoyed the inspectees' helplessness. Heiner hated borders and border guards.

Open up. He untied the tarp.

Number of boxes?

Three hundred.

Contents?

Tea, coffee, and cocoa, peas, beans, lentils, sugar, and chocolate, salt. Lena droned out the list of contents, trying to look naïve. With pleasure, she listed the items that she hoped would embarrass the young guard: sanitary pads, tampons, condoms.

He pointed to a box in the top row: Open up. He wanted to see a box in the second row on the left; he had her dump out a bag of clothes. He wanted to see the contents of a box in the fifth row on the right. You see, Heiner said, we're going to Poland to visit people who, as I...

The customs official turned and left. Because what he said as he left sounded like: pack up, they brought order back to the chaos on the truck bed. Lena sat behind the wheel and closed the door. The gate lifted; they were released. Slowly, she got used to the feel of the seven-and-a-half-ton truck. Don't forget how long it is, Heiner said, or you'll scrape trees and streetlamps on the curves.

As they drove over a bad road toward Görlitz, Lena admitted to pasting dollar bills behind the labels of every can of peas, beans, or lentils. Heiner's face hardened. You've endangered the trip, Heiner said sternly. He stared at the road in silence. He smoked, his face angry. It took him three cigarettes to realize what Lena had done for his friends.

Dollars behind the labels – really? Welcome to the world of smuggling, Lena. He too had hid money in the well-secured bags of clothing.

They drove on to the next border – the end of the GDR. Görlitz was like Herleshausen. Where despotism is allowed, despotism will reign. Where snarling is not forbidden, snarling becomes the norm. Those who are given the right to harass will harass. The border guards rooted through their suitcases as if their contents were garbage. They pointed to the truck – unpack. They didn't need to speak in full sentences. They shone huge flashlights between the boxes.

We're going to Poland, he said, but he was paid no more mind than a mouse squeaking under the truck.

Explain who we're visiting, Lena said. Heiner declined to do so. I'm not explaining anything; we'll just put up with it. Four hours later they were dispatched, when the guards pointed to the gate and Lena drove the "Czerwony" a few meters further, to where Görlitz was called Zgorzelec. They hoped for friendly guards – but the officials here acted as if they didn't exist. Heiner chain-smoked. Over the hours at the border, the wrinkles in his face had grown sharper. In the white light of the streetlamps, he looked like an old man. Just when they began to think that the guards would make them sit there overnight before tearing everything apart in the morning, a patrolwoman emerged from the barracks and wordlessly stamped their passports.

Get in, treasure, Lena said, we'll manage the rest too. The rest was a good hour's drive to a place with an unpronounceable name with lots of sibilants. Lena took directions out of her purse, which were clearly meant to be read in daylight. How were they supposed to find the seventh linden tree after the crossroads, or the light-colored house in the field near the church, when the streets were unlit? At one point Heiner screamed: Lena, watch out! She had been heading for a tractor that stood with its lights off on the side of the road. They were wide-awake and dead-tired, heavy as lead and light as a feather at the same time. They hadn't slept in twenty-five hours. Another border and I'll go berserk, Lena said. Heiner smiled: Don't lose steam. If the directions are right, we're almost there.

In the pale dawn of a new day, they turned into the courtyard of a grey apartment block. In the only window that was still lit, they saw a man who waved fiercely and then, as if he'd flown, stood before them. It was Leszek. Heiner's friend, his comrade. For two years they'd lain beside each other on the same pallet. Leszek's feet at Heiner's head. Belly and chest at Heiner's legs. Leszek's head at his feet. And the other way around. Heiner's head at Leszek's feet. Chest and belly at his legs. Heiner's feet at Leszek's head. They were stuck together at night like a bizarre insect with two heads and eight feelers.

Leszek had big ears that stuck out. He wore a baggy flat cap. Heiner sprang from the truck as if he hadn't been nearly unconscious with weariness only a moment before. The men approached each other slowly, as if this small delay made the reunion even more precious. Heiner threw his arms around Leszek and Leszek lay his head against Heiner's chest. They stood there, still and intimate, their eyes closed. The one man tall and thin, the other a full head shorter and much squarer. Lena felt herself choking up as she looked at them. She had never been embraced with such devotion by any girlfriend or man; neither her mother nor Heiner had held her like that. Can one earn such an embrace? How? By doing what? By risking your life for a friend? Sharing hunger, beatings, the fear of death with a person – was that the price? Did she want to pay it? Was she jealous of their past? What an absurd thought.

Welcome to the madhouse, Leszek said, and kissed Lena's hand.

It's an honor to meet you, Lena said in her best Polish.

At the kitchen table Leszek filled three glasses with *bimber*, his homemade vodka – there was no better sleeping potion. He had cleaned out the broom closet for them: a long room with two hooks on the wall, a few coat hangers, a chair, a chest of drawers, two thick mattresses set on top of each other, and a window that looked out on the courtyard. Can you sleep like this? Leszek asked. Heiner let himself fall onto the bed. No lice, no bedbugs, no stinking straw. My friend, this is luxury.

Czerwony, the Red, was parked in the courtyard. Dogs circled the truck like a carousel of pale ghosts. They panted, skinny and starving – they wanted to get inside, to where they could smell food. They peed on the tires and tried to jump up on the tarp. When they failed to reach their goal, they bit the tires and growled. We're related, Lena thought. I too remain a dog, allowed only to snuffle around the edges of Heiner's world.

Leszek had put a lamp on the ground so that his friend could have a nightlight. Lena felt the truck in her every pore; there was still a droning in her head. When she closed her eyes she saw headlights coming toward her, and the shadow that had turned out to be a tractor. She opened her eyes – they really were lying in a broom closet. A naked bulb hung from the ceiling, and the nails on which their jackets and pants now hung had only a few days before held scrubbers, feather dusters, and cleaning rags. Was it right to have come with Heiner on this journey? I'm warning you, he'd said, in Poland I'll be a different person than the man you know. She thought of Gesa, and of how clearly she'd described her love for Heiner to her. Love is the desire to know, the craving to explore. What if she didn't like the "Polish Heiner," who, with his tenderness for his friend, was a stranger to her? She heard the dogs scratching, she heard a window slamming shut. There are worse things than a night without sleep. Leszek rumbled around in the bathroom; she heard the toilet flush, his steps in the hall. For a while the apartment was quiet, and then she heard a peculiar noise: quiet at first, then growing louder.

Heiner, Lena whispered. Do you hear what I hear?

He breathed deeply.

Heiner, it's eerie.

It was a voice. It sounded like the drone of an endless Our Father. The voice seemed to be coming from inside Leszek's apartment. She sat up. It wasn't Polish. The melody of the sentences was German. Now I've really lost it, thought Lena.

The hungry dogs continued to circle the truck, but more slowly than they had at night, exhausted from their futile attempts to reach the goods inside. The men sat in the kitchen, Lena could hear them laughing. She marveled. The Polish Heiner could laugh in the morning.

There were hard-boiled eggs and old sausage sandwiches on the table – the rest of the journey's provisions. To this Leszek had added cabbage and pasta salads, and had made coffee; he wore the baggy flat cap even inside the apartment. Two boxes from the truck sat on the windowsill, along with five tins of Nescafé that Heiner had packed for his friend.

The apartment consisted of two small rooms, a narrow kitchen, the broom closet, and a bathroom with no tub or shower. Dig in, Lena, Leszek said. Camp rule: No one can steal what you have in your belly. Heiner acted out the border scenes for his friend.

That one and that one and that one – open them!

Yes sir, Rottenführer.

Contents?

I respectfully report: Carrots, Carrottenführer, sir.

He was in high spirits; he looked terrific – no trace of the old man from the border.

In a brief moment of quiet in the kitchen, Lena heard the monotone singing, the Our Father that she'd heard as she fell asleep. She hadn't lost it, the voice was real. It was close, as it had been in the night, and it belonged to a woman. Who's praying? Lena asked. Leszek looked at Heiner, who nodded. Tell her.

The whole story – does she want to hear it?

She does, Lena said. No opowiedz! Let's hear it.

After the German invasion, Leszek had joined a student

organization. The boys – the youngest was twelve – were used as messengers. They had to remember street names, house numbers, floors, first and last names: their job was to say a sentence that they didn't understand to a person they didn't know. *The sky has a pink roof in the morning and evening.* Leszek had forgotten none of those sentences. *Keep the goat in the stall, she's not hungry.* He was proud of his work. *I don't have a garden – visit me there when it snows.* His father was in the Resistance, as was his mother, his two uncles, his grandfather, and now he was too. *Hide the sunflower in the coal cellar.*

Then came the day when his luck ran out. It was Thursday, March 20, 1941. He was supposed to ring Teresa Tabor's door early in the morning and say: *Fearless that it will rebound, soft's the nightingale's sound.* He looked around, the coast was clear. He opened the door to the stairwell and saw them: two Gestapo waiting for him. He greeted them – running away would have been suspicious. At first they were friendly. What's your name, my boy? Where do you live, my boy? He told them his name. Who are you going to see? No one, I just stepped in for a moment because it's raining. Oh, our little lad doesn't want to get wet! Then the smaller of the two, who spoke Polish, hit him so hard in the face that his head crashed against the wall and he sank to the floor. The sound my skull made, Leszek said, haunts me to this day. It sounded hollow, like a coconut falling from a tree.

They kicked his back, his kidneys, between his legs, and particularly his ears, while the mysterious message he was supposed to convey kept running through his head: *Fearless that it will rebound, soft's the nightingale's sound.* Did that mean someone had "sung"? Was it a warning? Who sent you? screamed the man who spoke Polish. Leszek was no hero. The reason he betrayed no one was that he couldn't speak from the pain, but they already knew who he was going to see. Tereza Tabor had long since been taken away. They hauled Leszek out to the street and threw him into the back of a pickup truck that they'd hidden behind the entrance, as if he were nothing more than a sack of potatoes. He cried; he heard himself whimpering: Mama, Mama, Mama. Then he heard a voice, as weak as a mouse's: Congratulations, friend. He knew the voice, and opened one eye cautiously. It was Karol, a friend from school. Congratulations to you too, he whispered. You look like a monster. Leszek nodded: So do you. It was Thursday, March 20, 1941. It was his fifteenth birthday.

They knew the Nazis made no distinction between children and adults. Big or small, they were enemies of the German people and would be shot by the side of the road or brought to Gestapo headquarters for interrogation, which, according to Leszek's uncle, was worse than death. The truck drove off. There were three Nazis in the cab, they knew the boys in the back weren't going to budge anytime soon. Karol's lips moved and Leszek understood that running was their only chance – they knew the courtyards and back alleys of Kraków better than the Germans. When the truck braked before a sharp curve, they jumped out and landed at the feet of a man who pulled them into a building as if he'd just been waiting for two boys to tumble out of a passing vehicle. He led them into the courtyard and showed them the way to a tunnel whose exit lay in another part of town.

Leszek put on water for the fourth pot of coffee. He gulped down the coffee as greedily as Heiner did. It had to be boiling hot, bitter, and strong. He never let the level in the cup sink below half-full before hurriedly topping it off. Reproachfully, he said: Lena, there's nothing on your plate. Did you forget? Camp rule: No one can steal what you have in your belly. Lena wasn't squeamish, but how could she chew, chomp down, sample the pasta salad – did

Leszek think she had no imagination? Was this journey meant to toughen her up? To teach her to keep her appetite even in the face of such memories? Leszek, she said firmly, it's insulting to eat during a story like this.

To whom? Heiner asked.

To Leszek.

Leszek will only be insulted if his cabbage salad gets soggy.

I'm supposed to eat while he's talking?

It's a long story, Heiner said. You might starve.

The men found it amusing to laugh at the hunger that could have killed them in the camp. Leszek said: Look at it this way. The world is nicer when stories are accompanied by food as dancing is by music.

Lena put two eggs and a crust of bread on her plate and nibbled the end of a sausage.

We knew we couldn't go home, Leszek said, the Gestapo would be waiting for us. You were so damned efficient, you Germans. The speed with which you brought the city under control, the quickness with which you ferreted out familial relationships and circles of friends.

Heiner is Viennese, Lena said, I was born in Danzig and raised in Switzerland – but fine, call it "you".

Karol hid out with his girlfriend's grandmother, who lived in a little garden shed at the edge of the city. Leszek tried to think whether his parents had any friends they had lost contact with. His head was pounding and his ears bled. He had no friends with garden sheds, his grandmother lived in Łódź; he had only an aunt – the pious Zofia, who played the organ and sang in church. Once he had been sent to bring her flowers, and had been given chocolate with nuts in return – he'd been ten, and his aunt seemed to him like some sprite from a fairy-tale. She had long blond hair and dressed differently than the women he knew. He remembered a colorful dress that reached the floor. She wasn't close to the rest of the family – they thought she was bit peculiar – and she lived in a ground-floor apartment on Szerokastraße, where not even his parents would think to look for him.

The litany in the next room now sounded like the complacent babbling of an infant.

Who is that? Lena asked.

Aunt Zofia, Leszek answered. That's what this is all about. My story isn't important. He lay his hand on his head. I can live with this German souvenir under my hat.

Zofia had rubbed the boy's sprained joints, bandaged his bloody knees, iced his swollen face, examined his head and ears, and made hot chocolate for her nephew. She put him in the back room that opened onto the garden and gave him stern instructions. Every sentence was a command. Onto the sofa with you! Sleep, if you can! Keep the door open! Don't undress! Keep your shoes on! If you hear me shout "Watch out," you zoom into the garden like a German grenade. Understand? He fell asleep immediately. He didn't see his beautiful aunt standing in the dark living room for hours, looking out into the street. When at dawn the car she'd been expecting arrived, she screamed: Watch out! And Leszek fled into the garden. Zofia was interrogated for five weeks and then put on a transport. It was the first time she'd heard the name of the camp: Auschwitz. A work camp, she thought – any work is better than being interrogated by the Gestapo in Pomorkistraße.

Everyone had been wrong about Zofia – Leszek's father, his mother – the whole family had thought of her as the pious aunt who lived on the other side of the city, pretty and crazy, a bit too otherworldly for her age. No one knew whether there was a man in her life. No one knew that she had been part of the Resistance since the first day of the war. She should have sent away the boy who came knocking at her door. He was the guide the Nazis had been waiting for.

Lena understood that Aunt Zofia lived in the room next to the broom closet. She listened hard, but didn't hear any more sounds. Heiner lit a cigarette, Leszek boiled more water for coffee and said: Lena, I don't see your plate getting emptier.

Zofia was lucky. She was delicate, but not weak. She wasn't sent straight from the ramp to "the showers." Instead, she got a number and was marched to work in the main camp. There she took walks with Leszek and Heiner along the camp road on Sundays when they didn't have to work. Heiner fell in love with the woman who looked like a magic fairy, even emaciated and shorn. Then came the day when four women were publically beaten. *My poor, poor Zofia.* Her thin arms, her gaunt back. Watching a beating is worse than being beaten yourself. Later Leszek's aunt was put in an Arbeitskommando in Birkenau where even a tough person couldn't last two weeks. Twenty women shoveled gravel fourteen hours a day from the ice-cold Soła River. Often they stood in water up to their waists while the Kapo hounded them: Faster, faster, dalli, dalli. They were beaten. At night they were bitten by fleas and couldn't sleep. Every morning there were women who couldn't be roused from bed even with clubs, because they'd starved to death during the night.

When a female prisoner from this Arbeitskommando disappeared one foggy afternoon, all of the women were transferred. Work in the quarry was a death sentence too. Women who collapsed under the weight of the stones were beaten to death while the Kapo bellowed: This is no sanatorium, this is a German penal company. He pointed to individual women with his whip: Where are we? Woe to the poor Polish, Russian, or Czech woman who couldn't repeat the sentence because she didn't understand it. After two months only one hundred and eight of the original four hundred women were still alive. Leszek's aunt got typhus, the deadly illness that saved her life. A doctor from Kraków who had good contacts in the camp got her morphine and she grew healthy again, if there was such a thing as health in the camp. She was allowed to stay in the typhus block and to work carrying the corpses. Anyone who had indoor work was lucky.

Heiner smoked. Leszek made more coffee. Both urged Lena to eat what was on the table. Eggs, bacon, cabbage salad – did they think the story would be easier to hear on a full stomach?

One evening Zofia sang her favorite Bach cantata softly for the women in her barrack: *Who knows how near my end is? It is known to dear God alone, whether my pilgrimage on the earth...*She faltered. An SS Unterscharführerin approached the group with the whip that she never put down; it was as if it had grown into her hand. In a place where you could die for the wrong kind of look, a cantata too could mean your end. Keep singing, she ordered: *Who knows how near my end is? It is known to dear God alone, whether my pilgrimage on the earth might be short or longer. Time runs out, death approaches.*

You speak German? Zofia nodded: A little.

The guard's name was Erdmute. She could choose to use the whip or not. She could destroy life or preserve it. Today one way, tomorrow the other. She could send Zofia to the quarry or offer her a job in the guards' barrack. Why? There was no why. There were good moods and bad moods and that day Erdmute was in a good mood, so Aunt Zofia was allowed to scrub the barrack until it shone. If Erdmute discovered a grain of sand, she kicked over the bucket and the scubbing started all over again. What seemed like bullying actually saved Zofia's life. She was only allowed to scrub when there was something to scrub. Once a week Zofia was allowed to shower, because the Unterscharführerin had a hysterical fear of fleas and lice. Lucky Zofia.

In January 1945 they heard the thundering of cannons that they'd been longing for. Every day a little louder, a little closer. The Russian army was advancing, and the Nazis began frantically destroying documents, killing witnesses, burning barracks – there was no time to be systematic. In January 1945, Aunt Zofia was sent on a death march into the "Reich" along with seven thousand other women, and on April 30, 1945, they were freed from Ravensbrück by soldiers of the Red Army. She weighed seventy-five pounds and headed for Kraków with five other women, and swore by the holy mother of God never again in her life to come anywhere near any of those cursed places.

But as often happens with vows, Leszek said, that same year, Zofia went to Auschwitz with her mother, who refused to believe what the daughter told her. Zofia showed her Birkenau. The railroad tracks. The ramp. The birch grove. The lake with the cuckooflowers. The women's camp. Her barrack in section B1a. Her bed. She found a bug-infested blanket and stroked it in memory of the women who had lain under it. She showed her mother the barrack that the prisoners called "Canada" after the far-away dreamland that had everything. The German Canada had been a place of unthinkable wealth. Money and gold. Watches and jewelry. Fur coats, shoes, and silken bedding. Toys for the children, and warm blue blankets that the Jews from Holland had with them when they were unloaded. Ham from France, tinned meat from Belgium, Danish cheese, chocolate, wine, tobacco and cigarettes – "Canada" was full of everything people pack when they think they're going to have to start a new life in a new land. "Canada" was filled to the ceiling with things that had been stolen from people before they were sent to the gas chambers. And now the camp was dead, but not for Zofia. She could still hear the constant buzzing of a hundred thousand prisoners' voices, and the wheezing of trains as they pulled up to the ramp. She saw the mud and felt winter in her bones, she felt the fleas, the clubs, and the whips. Not a millimeter of distance had grown between her and that place. Perhaps sometime later, perhaps one day, perhaps never. Zofia didn't let her mother out of her sight. She was the first visitor – what would she do? She tested out one of the beds. Four women in a tiny box like this, really? People froze to death in the night? She measured out the length of the barracks, she counted her steps. A thousand people in a stall like this – was it possible? She walked around like the prosecuting attorneys would twenty years later on their visit to the scene of the crime, or as the tourists would, much later – sticking rusted spoons in their pockets as souvenirs. Zofia understood. That was the future. Spoon collectors. Skeptics. Re-calculators. And none of them could see, hear, or feel how it really was – how was such a thing to be endured?

Until that trip her body had held itself together. Afterwards, it exploded as if it wanted revenge for everything that had been done to it. She always got better, Leszek said, but when the confusion set in, it was as if this was just the ailment she'd been waiting for. She didn't fight it. She threw herself into it as into the arms of a lover. Sometimes she would still go to the cathedral, sit down at the organ, and improvise. When she played, people would come in from the street to listen. She made wonderful music. She sang like an angel. When she could no longer find her way to the church, I brought her to live with me.

Leszek stood up. Come with me, he said, she loves having visitors. He'd piled a mountain of colorful pillows at his aunt's back. She sat upright in her bed. Her head was no bigger than a child's, and her skin was taut, almost unwrinkled. Leszek had braided her hair in two plaits. She wore a lilac-colored nightgown – she looked pretty, gentle as a fairy. Her heart is stubborn, Leszek said, it just keeps beating. Bumbum, bumbum, bumbum.

The room was small. A closet, a bed, and a little table next to it. Three of the walls were white, and the one across from Zofia was painted. A flat landscape that began at the foot of her bed and rose to a distant horizon. Thirteen feet wide, ten feet tall. At the right of the scene, a birch grove and a lake with cuckooflowers growing on its banks. Horizontal brown strokes and vertical red ones that reached into the sky. Railroad tracks divided the green landscape. It was the first time Heiner had seen the picture. He wanted to laugh – but he stopped.

Leszek, you've lost your mind!

I tried flowers, Leszek said, I tried trees, mountains, the sea. She cried every time, and I had to paint over it. Then one night this idea came to me. Now she doesn't cry anymore.

My poor Zofia, Heiner said, this is where you feel at home? Slowly, mechanically, Zofia turned her head toward her visitors. Her grey eyes looked huge in her small face. She showed no astonishment, no surprise, no joy. Visits didn't belong in her world. She turned her head away and began to sing her mumbling song.

This close to the bed, Lena understood Aunt Zofia's Our Father. *This is no sanatorium, this is a German penal company… this is no sanatorium, this is a German penal company… this is no sanatorium, this is a German penal company…this is…*

How long has she been doing this? Lena asked. Leszek said: To me it seems like forever.

Dismal buildings with narrow apartments for families who drove to work every morning and came back only to sleep. Leszek taught architecture at the University of Technology in Wrocław. From their broom closet they could see the courtyard with the truck and the lurking dogs. Breakfast lasted till noon. For three days they'd been living in a housing development comprised of five-story apartment buildings somewhere between Görlitz and Wrocław. Leszek was using his vacation time to be with them.

Eat, Lena.

I know.

She looked at the framed picture on the kitchen cupboard. A pageboy haircut, small eyes, a cleft chin. Leszek's sister? His wife? She didn't want to ask – she didn't expect to hear cheerful stories. Heiner, who had followed her gaze, asked the question. How is Roza?

She's well, Leszek said. She moved in with friends in Wrocław before we drove each other crazy living together in this apartment.

And your love?

It's endured that too.

That was a smart move.

The highway passed outside the kitchen window, beyond which there was a landscape with fruit trees, shrubs, and small shacks. Come, Leszek said, I'll show you the garden.

They walked through the courtyards of the apartment blocks. Dismal playgrounds with sandless sandboxes and rusted slides. As if they'd been waiting for him, from each block, two or three people waved at Leszek through open windows. Remember the raspberry jam, they called out, the winter boots have come. Leszek, they called, the bicycle is here, and my mother has wool. In the housing estate, eggs were traded for carrots, nylon stockings for canned sausages, a warm coat for half a goose. Leszek had a new selection of wares from the packages Heiner and Lena had brought. Medicine had highest trade value. Pills for sore throats or the flu, cough syrup, aspirin and ibuprofen, ointment, eye drops, and all sizes of bandaids. Sugar was important. Without sugar, no schnapps. They traded tires for radios. Books for hand-knitted sweaters. The true value of things emerged naturally from scarcity and surplus. "Private socialist capitalism" was Leszek's name for the system, and Poland was "the world's biggest second-hand store."

His garden was a plot sown with beans and potatoes, onions and kohlrabi. A chicken coop stood at the far end. Leszek placed six eggs in a bowl and asked Lena to bring them to old Katarzyna, who was watching them through the window of a crooked hut in the neighboring garden. A colorful headscarf, a thousand deep wrinkles, and a sly look in her eyes. In exchange for the eggs, Leszek pumped a canister full of fresh water from her sixty-foot deep well. It was cold and tasted like iron.

Leszek placed a can of sausages on the garden table, along with a bottle of vodka and three glasses. The sun was shining, and he'd hung a hammock between two apple trees. Climb aboard, he said to Lena. She looked at the sky and let Leszek swing her as she said: I hear chickens clucking, and somewhere a pig is oinking. This isn't quite how I imagined martial law.

It's all around you.

Where?

See the man on the roof over there?

The roofer?

Describe him.

Medium-tall, Lena said. Husky. Round face, short hair. He's wearing a yellow and green plaid shirt and brown corduroy pants.

He has boots on, and in one hand he has a hammer that he's using to bang nails into tar paper.

That's Edward, Leszek said, he's an informer for the party. That roofer is a fake roofer.

You can tell, Heiner said.

What do you see that I'm not seeing?

He's hammering too many nails, Leszek said. He's been looking in this direction too often. He's watching us. I have a rock-solid instinct for feigned naturalness. The roofer-impersonator will report this evening: Leszek has foreign visitors.

Can he hurt you? Lena asked. Are we putting you in danger?

No one has any interest in your trip, Leszek said, and me they take for a harmless old concentration camp fool with a memento from Auschwitz under my cap.

Are you a harmless old camp fool?

Leszek laughed. You'll find out.

Heiner said: Back in the camp, we killed traitors.

It was after midnight when they lay down on the mattress and Heiner put his arms around Lena. They could hear Zofia, they understood her words. Now that they knew the text, they could no longer think of it as an Our Father. Lena whispered: I'm seeing the quarry – what are you seeing?

The whipping rack.

Were you in love with her?

I wouldn't call it that.

What then?

She was the magic fairy that reminded us that humans are capable of tenderness.

The sentence that she keeps murmuring – was it shouted, barked, or hissed?

Shouted.

How do you stand listening to her?

I think of a Viennese waltz.

You dance with her?

She felt him nod.

Her text is like a tapeworm, Lena said. It's eating into my mind. I have to think about something else or it will make me sick. Do you know what I'd like?

Tell me.

I'd like to make up a verse that I can use as a mantra. What rhymes with sanatorium?

Crematorium.

Good idea! What else?

Memoriam. Moratorium. Emporium. Auditorium. Baritone. Telephone. Marathon.

Auditorium is nice, Lena said. Pretend Zofia's saying: *This is an auditorium and there's a bass baritone.* But what rhymes with penal company?

Atrophy, Heiner suggested. Biography. Democracy. Fantasy. Prudery. Celery.

The murmuring had grown louder. I'm rewriting it, Lena said, I can't stand this – listen: *This is an auditorium, and there's a bass baritone. On my desk, a red telephone.*

And every good democracy has celery, Heiner said.

I see a peaceful Sunday morning in Kraków. What's the name of the street where she lived?

Szerokastraße.

Listen: On the day I'm imagining, there was no escaping boy. There was no Leszek hiding in the apartment, no car at dawn, no arrest, no interrogation, no war. The doves cooed and the church bells called people to prayer. Zofia gets up early and leaves the apartment around half past eight. She turns her face to the spring sunlight. She looks forward to the day ahead of her. She wears a blue skirt and a jacket with big buttons, and a hat whose brim bobs with her every step. She walks quickly and elegantly on her high heels. A man waits in front of the cathedral. He's big, with a white scarf around his neck. He goes to her and embraces her. They enter the church together and go up to the gallery; the pews are full, all the way to the last row. There's Bach on the program. Zofia sits down at the organ – no one can play this oratorio as movingly as she. The man joins her with his deep voice. *Well then, Your name alone shall be in my heart.*

Heiner said: That's just how it was, Lena. Just so.

The next day, when Lena returned from a stroll through the allotment gardens, she heard loud voices in the stairwell. She could make out every word – the men were fighting. Do you want her to drive through Poland without really seeing it? Do you want to cram her full of your concentration camp stories? Do you want her to suffocate? Is that what you want? Shouldn't she be allowed to get an idea of who's rising up against whom in this country and why? That was Leszek's voice. Lena stood outside the door and listened. She'd never heard Heiner yell before. You're endangering our journey. I don't care if they catch you – you know what awaits you – but keep Lena out of it. She opened the door. Are you quarreling?

Your husband, Leszek said, wants to keep me from giving you a tour of Poland. He wants to beat you to death with the one lousy piece of land he apparently can't live without. I'm driving to Wrocław and I thought you might come with me.

To find out if you're a harmless old fool?

That too.

Lena looked at Heiner. And you?

He'd propped his elbows on the table and wrapped his hands around his coffee cup to warm them.

Heiner, I'm talking to you.

He stared at the table like a stubborn child. Lena stood behind him and put her hands on his shoulders. They were stiff and unyielding.

Your friend wants to show me his homeland – what's wrong with that?

He was silent.

In Polish, Lena said: Leszek, when do we leave?

Zaraz. Right away. Bring your passport and toothbrush.

In the hallway he said, loud enough for Heiner to hear: Your husband never avoids danger. He's foolhardy. He risks his life for those he loves, but he's dying of fear when others put themselves in danger, and, he raised his voice and called into the kitchen: That's why I love him!

They heard the kitchen chair push back and then saw Heiner in the doorway. His face was no longer frozen; he had tears in his eyes. The men embraced. They didn't slap each other boyishly on the shoulders; they simply rested their bodies against each other. Intimate. Tender. As if they'd once been lovers.

He watched them from the kitchen window and waved until they couldn't see him anymore. Then he went into the hallway, took his coat from the hook, put the key in his pocket, and went out to where the garden plots were. He walked down a path, approaching the house where yesterday the man that Leszek had called a fake roofer had been. The man stood at the garden fence, smoking. He didn't look at Heiner – he was staring in the direction Leszek's car had gone. Heiner stood close to him, slowly lit a cigarette, and blew smoke in his eyes.

Edward?

The man took a step back, and very softly, Heiner said one of the only Polish words he knew: Szpicel. Then he continued in German, knowing that the man understood every word.

When they reached the main road, Leszek threaded the car into a long line of vehicles. The people of Wrocław were returning from their Sunday excursions.

Leszek, where are we going?

He steered around a pothole and looked in the rearview mirror. Instead of answering, he said: Lesson one. How do you tell if someone is following you?

She looked around. Aside from size and color, all the cars looked the same. The men sat behind the wheel, the women sat next to them; children sat in the back looking out the windows; there were grandmas, grandpas, or dogs. There were dolls on the back shelf, or stuffed animals – nothing unusual. Families driving home. This wasn't Lena's idea of what surveillance looked like. She said: I'd watch the cars that stay behind us for a long time in the rearview mirror, and if there's one that never passes us...

Leszek laughed. Clever, Lena! And what if it's a coincidence? What if the driver is simply going the same direction as us? Or what if there are three cars following us, or five, that keep switching? What do you do then?

I've never been followed.

He pointed to the glove compartment: Take out a pad and pencil.

Then he said: Pay attention – we're going to zigzag through Wrocław, then we'll leave the center of town and drive towards the quieter outskirts. If we have a tail, we'll discover him there more quickly than we will in the city.

He'll discover us more quickly there as well.

That's as it should be. We have to let him attach himself to us or we won't recognize him. We'll drive north, then west, then back north or south again, without a plan. Write down the license plate numbers and brands of cars that pass us, come towards us, or start right after we've driven by. Do that for half an hour.

Leszek, I don't know any brands of cars.

Doesn't matter. If you see numbers that appear repeatedly, you'll develop an eye for brands, even if you don't know what they're called.

He criss-crossed the inner city, then turned towards the outer districts where there was less traffic. Lena stared at license plates and wrote down what she could remember. She didn't get much. Her eyes were too slow. While she lowered her head to write down a number, four or five cars would pass them before she could even catch a glimpse of their plates.

Keep your eyes on the road, Leszek said, write blind.

In the next thirty minutes Lena compiled a long column of letters and numbers. She wanted to succeed, to be Leszek's prize pupil, but despite her efforts, she couldn't find any plates repeating.

Leszek, I can't do this, I'm too dumb. Or maybe no one's trailing us. He shook his head. Can't be. On a day like today, there must be. Keep trying.

She changed her method. She used her eyes like a camera, fixed the numbers in her mind as images, and said out loud what she saw: WCZ one, nine three, four, seven. OPL eight, nine, five, two. The longer she wrote, the faster she got. Soon no car passed without her noting it. And Leszek was right: certain combinations of letters and numbers kept popping up over and over again in front or behind them. DW 437. DBL 1463. WW 5698.

Leszek, she cried excitedly, there are three of them!

Having three surveillants from the secret police was a dangerous thing – but in the moment of discovery, Lena was as excited as a schoolchild learning the alphabet and writing her first words in a notebook: Cat, dog, sat, bat. DW 437. DBL 1463. WW 5698.

Well done, Lena. We're being followed by a big green Polish Fiat, a small brown Polish Fiat, and a blue Russian Lada, right?

Leszek didn't have to write down columns of numbers to figure out who was following them. He sat impassively behind the wheel. He knew the game. Surveillance was obviously part of his daily life. The broad brow under the flat cap, the stick-out ears, the strong chin – Leszek wasn't gentle, like Heiner, but he exuded the same promise: Nothing will happen to you while I'm around.

Leszek, can I ask you something?

Be my guest.

What was Heiner like – there?

He smiled. I'm glad he found you.

I found him. Tell me what he was like.

The Heiner from that place doesn't exist anymore. I think people like us have three lives. One from before "there," a second one "there," and a third life that's unimaginable without the second. When I first met him, I said to myself: Stay away from that one, he's a classic suicide case. If he hadn't managed to turn his hatred into an all-consuming mission, he would have lunged at Kaduk, Klehr, or Boger, which would have been an immediate death sentence. Everyone who didn't believe in God found a mission that gave them strength. Heiner's mission was: Stay alive. Be a witness. Stand in a court of law and say: I saw what happened there. But just as much as a mission gives strength, it requires energy. It was easier, more tempting, to give up, to touch the electric fence, to let them shoot you. If you're dead, you can't be cold, or hungry, or thirsty, or afraid. He laughed. Dead people have an easier life, if I may put it that way.

What drew you to him?

Not his charm – he left that in Vienna. He was…how you

say…faithful unto death. If you were his friend, it was for always. I was already on Klehr's list. I wouldn't be driving you through Wrocław today if your husband hadn't hidden me among the dead in the hospital.

He said you saved his life.

Could be. He saved me, I saved him, we saved each other.

And your mission?

A face.

A pageboy, small eyes, a cleft chin?

He nodded. We were already holding hands as schoolkids.

Leszek looked in the mirror. Hold on, he cried, and turned sharply into an alley without signaling, stepped on the gas, and sped the wrong way down a one-way street; they were lucky that no one happened to be coming towards them. In the mirror he watched the brown Fiat shoot past on the street where they'd just been driving. He turned the car into a farmyard and waited behind the barn until the green Fiat had also lost them. He decoyed the blue Lada's driver by parking quite visibly next to a church where the service was to begin at six.

Lesson two, Lena. Get out. Slowly.

They fell in with the people heading towards the church. By the time the young man in the leather jacket who had been following them arrived to look for them inside, they had already left through the crypt and were standing in the graveyard. Leszek pressed a knit cap with a pompom into Lena's hand.

Put it on.

With one quick movement he traded his grey flat cap for a red beret. For a moment his head was bare – a shiny skull with a wide scar. They strolled across the cemetery like mourners on their way to a grave.

You look pale, Lena, do you feel ok?

I'm fine.

He can't follow us, Leszek said. He's trapped in the crypt. The priest accidentally locked him in.

Lena's knees were weak, and there seemed to be some kind of crazy drummer in her chest where her heart usually was. Leszek was calm, almost amused.

Give me your hand, Lena.

Could one lose fear like a key, or a button? The secret policeman was in the crypt – Leszek must have planned the whole thing in advance.

Leszek, where are we going?

He put his arm around her. We're a pair of lovers on our way to a party.

They left the graveyard through a side entrance, took the tram, and got off at an avenue lined with tall trees. Leszek led Lena into a stairwell, through a bicycle storeroom, across a vegetable garden. Lesson three. In times like these, it takes a little longer to get where you're going. They entered the house where the "party" was taking place from the back, through a cellar door to which Leszek had a key. He knew the way. He bounded up the stairs in the dark and called: Katinka, Marian, it's me, Leszek. A woman's voice answered: We're in the music room, come on up. They climbed up a winding wooden staircase to the second floor. The wooden floor was grey and well trodden; plaster was flaking off the walls. The ceiling had stucco decorations in the shape of violins and grape leaves, which were no longer colorful. The faded stucco betrayed an elegant past.

Fifteen or so people were standing around a grand piano in the middle of the room. The curtains were closed and the room was lit by candlelight. A couple broke away from the group – Katinka and Marian. You must be Lena, they cried. Welcome to Poland!

Katinka, a wiry woman with short hair, took her arm and led her from one guest to another. Staszek – Lena from Germany. Krystyna – Lena. Ryszard, Jozef, Adam, Jacek, Antonia – Lena from Germany. They were young – in their late twenties, early thirties. Leszek could have been their grandfather. Katinka and Marian were older – forty, maybe. Lena was soon at the center of a storm of questions. Where are you from? Frankfurt? Do you know Rüsselsheim? I worked at the Opel factory there. I have relatives in Ingelheim – they work at Boehringer. Where do you work? Is this your first time in Poland? You were born in Danzig? They hugged Lena when they heard that she spoke Polish. How long are you staying? What are you doing here?

None of the guests moved more than a few yards from the piano, upon which stood a small portable radio. Every now and then they cast a glance at the dial, as if fearing it might move by itself. The needle stood between 68 and 71 megahertz, which was the frequency at which Radio Solidarność, the illegal station, would be speaking to them for the third time, at 9 pm. In two hours.

Katinka looked at the clock – everyone kept looking at the clock. On a Sunday like this, the clocks were read differently. It wasn't simply five, seven, or eight, it was four, two, or one hour before the magical number nine, the beginning of the broadcast. The women's faces had a special kind of beauty. Even when they laughed, they had the solemn gravity of people who have decided to be brave. They were risking beatings and imprisonment and being barred from their professions. For the last four months Marian had no longer worked as a physics professor; instead, he cleaned the streetcar tracks. Heiner was right, Lena thought, I'm endangering our trip. Was Leszek sure that no one had seen them entering the house? An informer could be lurking anywhere, like Edward in the garden colony. Did the young people here know what to do if the doorbell rang or the door was kicked in? If she were Polish, would she have been there?

Leszek, when do you know whether you're a coward or a brave person?

When you decide.

When does that happen?

When circumstances ask you where you belong.

And then?

You decide. Open your eyes or close them. Hide or fight. Fear or courage. No one wants to be a hero, but sometimes it's the only way.

One hour before the magic number nine, Leszek said: Come, let me show you something.

He led her to a terrace on the third floor. From there she had a good view of the street and the busy intersection at the end of the gardens. At first there were still people on the streets; ten minutes later, the streets were empty, and then a rumbling, deep and uncanny, announced the arrival of the tanks approaching the intersection slowly, guns swaying. Helicopters whirred over the roofs – an armada of vehicles were making a racket as if they were trying to drive the whole town mad. Helmeted men, with their visors down, tramped past the front gardens. Where had they all come from so suddenly? Where were they before? The military washed over the city like a malicious wave. Still thirty minutes to nine. Not only did everyone in this house know it, so did every informer in the country, as well as the police and the military, otherwise they wouldn't be out in the street. Leszek laughed. You know Lena, even an illegal broadcast has to be publicly announced in order to be heard.

The terrace doors opened at the house across the way, and Lena counted eleven young people staring down into the street.

For five months, a war has been raging, Leszek said, but the Poles can't believe what's happening before their very eyes. They're appalled, aghast, indignant. In the last thousand years, Poland has been carved up, reunited, attacked, occupied, reassembled and smashed up, over and over again. No people know its history better than we do. Kingdoms became duchies, duchies became occupied zones; there were wars against Sweden, the Ottoman Empire, Austria, and Prussia – you come from Danzig, you know the story. The Poles fought Stalin's Russia and Hitler's German Reich – terrible times – but the lines were always clear: Poland versus the rest of the world. That's what I wanted to show you, Lena. What's happening right outside the door now, Pole versus Pole – this is a war we can't understand.

A rumbling filled the air. It smelled like gasoline. Lena, do you understand why the radio is their worst enemy, why they hate it so much? Leszek asked. They have to haul all their toys out of the garage just for a few minutes of broadcast time.

They won't find the transmitter?

Of course they'll find it. Their helicopters are equipped with cutting edge direction finders, but it will still take them twenty minutes to figure out which part of town the broadcast is coming from. But the transmitter shuts off automatically after ten minutes. Then their buzzing locusts are left hanging in the air, not knowing where to look.

And then?

Another transmitter in a different part of town in another attic picks up the program. The same game. They search, they locate, they hightail it over to where they think the second transmitter is, and just before they find it, it turns off and a third transmitter turns on, hidden in a tool bag on a bicycle that's leaning against a tree somewhere. So they buzz through the air like angry hornets

– that's when the Zomos come. When they come, it's time to run. They know no boundaries: blind with rage, they'll kick down entrances and apartment doors, smash furniture and dishes and lash out against anything that moves. What do you think, Lena – can one see martial law?

A woman had come out on the terrace. She stood next to Leszek and he took her in his arms. A pageboy, small eyes, a cleft chin – Leszek's mission, his love. She hugged Lena as if she belonged with them, and for the first time Lena had the feeling that she was more to them than just Heiner's wife. She was a visitor from Germany, a woman who spoke Polish, a person who was there with them at this special hour.

Leszek looked at his watch. Five minutes to nine. The radio crackled and hissed, everyone stared at the second hand of their watches. Two minutes. Sixty seconds, thirty, twenty, ten. Lena held her breath; the tension was unbearable. It was quiet as a chapel in the music room; outside, the helicopters whirred. Nine, eight, seven, six, five. Four seconds, three, two, one, and then: eight clear tones – the beginning of a melody. Leszek whispered: an old song from the Resistance against the Nazis.

Nine o'clock. The radio's crackling grew louder, then came a woman's gentle voice:

Radio Solidarność. Walcząca. Wrocław. Radio fighting Solidarity. Wrocław.

The people in the room applauded. Their radio – it was broadcasting. The voice said: Dear ones, we are happy and moved to be able to speak to you, even if only for a short time. We see you sitting at your radios, listening to our words. The words that they want to imprison. This is our third broadcast. We turn now to all those who have a tape recorder. Record this broadcast. Why? It's not hard to imagine that the people who control the mass media will try to imitate our voices, to fool the public. We want you to know our voices better, so that you'll recognize us in future broadcasts. We will always present these programs together. With God's help, until the victorious end.

Marian walked to the window and pushed the curtain aside slightly. All hell is loose out there, he said, his face alight with David's joy at Goliath's misplaced blows. Though the streets of Wrocław belong to the military, the voice from the radio said, we lift up our heads, for the future belongs to us. The radio fell silent. There were tears in everyone's eyes. Lena crept away to bawl in the bathroom. She seemed to be more moved than the Poles, which made her ashamed of herself.

They didn't drive home after the "party" – no one went home. The nights after a Radio Solidarność broadcast could be deadly. They sat at Katinka's long kitchen table and ate and drank everything that had been brought. Soups, bread, cabbage salad, and vodka. No one seemed to get sleepy; only Lena's eyes began to close around four. Too many new things in one day, Leszek said. The tank is empty. Katinka brought Lena to the "guest sleeping hall," a room on the ground floor, big as a gymnasium – Katinka's yoga school. Twenty soft mats, a tower of wool blankets, a basket of pillows. When Lena woke up, she found herself lying between Leszek and Roza.

The next evening, she sat with Heiner and watched the deployment that she'd seen from the terrace replayed on television. The Polish news agency spoke of arrests, of ending the illicit underground broadcast once and for all. That Sunday was followed by another one, and another, and each time, Lena thought of the party where heads were bent over a radio that whirred and crackled, and of people who counted down seconds. Five, four, three, two, one – the second hand jumped to twelve. Nine p.m., eight clear tones, and a young voice: Radio Solidarność Walcząca. Radio fighting Solidarity here. Good evening, dear ones. This is already our fifth broadcast…

Early in the morning, Heiner knocked on Zofia's door, listened, then entered the room tentatively, as one would a sickroom. Zofia lay on her mountain of pillows and looked at the landscape that began at her feet and ended where it met the sky. She looked calm and pensive, as if she were going for a stroll on a pretty day. He sat next to Zofia on the bed and stroked her hands until her murmuring ceased. Let me make you pretty, my magic fairy, he said, brushing her hair strand by strand and braiding it into two long white plaits. Leszek and Lena watched.

What do you think of when you see the two of them?

Of the middle finger of the woman in Szerokastraße, Leszek said, of the woman who dabbed the blood off a blubbering young boy's knees forty years ago. The boy stared at the blood, and since he wouldn't stop whimpering, she said: Don't look at your knee – look at my ring instead. I focused on the ring that she wore on the middle finger of her left hand. I'd never seen a ring like that before – instead of a stone, it had a coin engraved with a greenish-black beetle with blade-like pincers. It wasn't a pretty animal, but I was captivated by it because it looked powerful. She told me it was a sacred scarab beetle. Its wing-cases shone like gold. It reminded the people of ancient Egypt of their god Ra, Aunt Zofia said, who glides across the sky in a sun barque. I didn't know what a barque was, but to this day I'd still be able to draw the beetle and the pretty hand that pressed two big bandaids on my knee. The scarab is a good-luck charm, Zofia explained. You lay it on a dead man's chest so that he'll rise again.

Look at Heiner, Lena said. Look how tenderly he's brushing her hair.

Don't worry about it – anyone who's ever had his head shaved is entranced by long hair.

There was no "good bye," no embrace, no "be well," when they left; Heiner simply turned abruptly from his friend and jumped into the truck. With every foot they drove, Leszek grew smaller, until all they could see in the mirror was two hands fluttering near a flat cap. Heiner unfolded the map and gave directions: Turn onto the E 22 towards Gliwice just before Wrocław, then take the E 221 towards Katowice – Oświęcim lies between Katowice and Kraków. He estimated the drive at five hours. The food basket stood between them, filled with salads and eggs, bread, and water from old Katarzyna's well; the neighbors had brought sausages and a roast chicken. *Eat, Lena – no one can steal what you have in your belly.* The streets were empty – they'd already driven six miles when they saw the first tank. The long gun swung in their direction as if it had been looking for them. Don't stop, Leszek had said. Don't swerve. Keep driving, stay calm. Only stop if they signal you to do so, and then hand out chocolate and cigarettes. Don't be scared: tanks are just big cars filled with a bunch of children they call recruits.

The street was grey and straight as an arrow. The sun fought with the clouds and lost; it was a bleak day. Drive faster, Heiner urged, or it will be dark when we arrive. Lena drove the seven-and-a-half-tonner not one mile faster than the potholes allowed.

Leszek is a great guy.

Didn't I say so? He saved my life.

He says you saved his.

He saved me, I saved him, we saved each other – who can really say?

Heiner reached into the basked and peeled two eggs. In Gliwice he took the wheel. He refused Lena's request that they stop for half an hour to walk in a field and stretch their stiff legs. He was too close. The current was tugging him onward. He drove too fast. They found a gas pump and a shack in the middle of a barren landscape. They needed gas, and they needed to check the tires for air. A thin man emerged from the shack, yawned, and rubbed his eyes.

Nice nap? Lena asked.

The man seemed to have been dragging his right foot for so long that he'd made a little ditch between the shack and the gas pump. He glanced at the German license plate and then cried: Come in, come in, as if selling circus tickets, and pointed behind the shack with his thumb. He wanted them to fill up illegally behind the hut, where no one could see, and pay with dollars. After stuffing the bills into his pocket, he said to Heiner: German-man good man, German-man perfect. German-man come back, march through Poland, one-two, one-two, one-two-three. Zackzack.

For heaven's sake – why?

Make Jaruzelski kaput, then get out again, dalli, dalli.

I see, Lena said. Blitzkrieg, right? And then to Heiner, who'd sat down behind the wheel again: I'll drive.

You're tired.

She gobbled down a chocolate bar; Heiner climbed into the passenger seat and smoked. A barren landscape – he liked it. A tree in a field, a bush by the side of the road, little farms with a goose in the garden, statues of the virgin Mary under little roofs, and finally a sign: Oświęcim.

I'm scared, Lena said.

Don't be scared. This place holds no fear.

For whom?

Tour buses were leaving; the parking lot in front of the museum was almost empty. Heiner threw open the door and jumped out before the truck had even come to a stop. Lena drove up to the administrative building; they were planning to drop off a large portion of the clothing and boxes here. She turned off the motor, put the truck in reverse, put on her sun-yellow straw hat, powdered her face, and touched up her lipstick. She was hungry for hot soup and thirsty for a beer. Heiner ran, his arms wide, towards a man with white hair. Lena locked up the truck.

Heiner didn't want to rest, didn't even want to drink coffee. He left his suitcase in the truck, smoked, was restless, hurried Lena – he had to get to the camp. Look, Lena, look. The red barracks of the main camp, the wide camp road, the tall trees, the evening sun on the roofs: they could have been arriving in a quaint village. He entered the grounds through the wrought iron gate. He could never have explained the cold fever that came over him when he tread this ground. He was at home here. He had to touch everything, as after a long separation. No place on earth would ever enthrall him the way this one did. His first steps on this ground – like a lord of the manor who had long been abroad and had let out his house and land, then returned to discover everything at sixes and sevens. Look, Lena. The gallows. Back then it was polished, cared for, cleaned till it shone in the sun like silver. Heiner scratched the surface with his fingernail: rust. It was no longer his gallows, but a neglected museum piece.

Look, Lena – the roof of the kitchen building is rotted out. Back then there had been tiles with beautiful old-fashioned gothic inscriptions, gleaming-white: There is only one path to freedom. Its milestones are: Obedience, Diligence, Order, Honesty, Cleanliness, Truthfulness, Sacrifice and: Love of the Fatherland. Woe to the poor soul who couldn't recite the milestones in flawless German. Look, Lena – and now rain and snow, heat and cold have washed the milestones away.

Would you want the writing to be restored?

Absolutely. How can you understand my Auschwitz if it's no longer as it once was? Look at the camp road! It used to shine like a mirror – not one speck of dust, not a single grain of sand, you could have eaten off it. Prisoners, harnessed like oxen to a plow, pulled the multi-ton roller over the street from morning till evening. Back and forth. First tar, then the roller. He would never be able to shuffle down these streets like the tourists. He had seen stumbling comrades lose their lives under the roller, and now gravel crunched under tourists' shoes as if they were walking an untended hiking trail. Look, Lena, it's a betrayal of the dead.

They walked beside each other, but they were no longer in the same place. He didn't see the young Chinese woman who sat on the steps of Block 7 with a bottle of beer clamped between her knees. He saw no tourists, no school groups. He saw the pretty gardens in front of the Blocks, gardens visible to no one but him. Artistically designed, meticulously cared for, each blade of grass stood as straight as a German soldier. Which Block had he lived in, when the Red Cross Committee visited to verify that the accommodations were clean and well kept, that the prisoners were healthy and receiving good medical care and were being treated humanely? Was it Block 9, or was he then already in Block 21? Either way, he'd already been slipping up to the attic. What an insane hope they'd attached to that visit. They'll see everything, everything. The lice-infested beds, the ramp, the chimneys – they'll tell the world what's going on here. And then they came, the people who'd been sent in from beyond the barbed wire, and they marveled at the flower beds and the wrought iron lamps over the doors of the blocks and were delighted by the murals the Kapos had forced the artists among the prisoners to paint. The inspectors saw the Rembrandt they'd painted in the hallway, the van Dyck on another wall – but the thirty thousand striped ghosts living in the main camp – no one saw them. They'd been forbidden to go outside, or were being mistreated somewhere outside the camp, or, like Heiner, they'd slipped illegally up to the attic to witness the outrage when a member of the Committee spontaneously opened a door that wasn't part of the scheduled tour. They have to feel it, he thought. Why don't they feel all the eyes following their every step, why don't they feel the prisoners' thudding hearts as they approach the Gestapo's dungeon, why don't they hear our prayers – more fervent prayers have never been said: Go inside, go inside, please go inside. When they came to Block 28 – Dear God, if you exist, send them down to the cellar where stinking corpses are piled up to the ceiling because the crematoriums are overwhelmed with work. Damn it, God damn it, dear God, why are they just standing there, why are they letting the Nazis lure them away to a nice convivial lunch? Dear God, please strike them down before they can go home and say: It was nice over there in Poland. A lovely sanatorium.

Heiner touched a concrete post, took hold of a bit of barbed wire. He wiped a grimy pane with a handkerchief, and turned the knob of Block 21 – his Block, the HKB, for *Häftlingskrankenbau*: prisoner's infirmary. Tenderly, he stroked the black wall between Blocks 11 and 12, as if his touch could reach the comrades that were killed there. Treated humanely. He didn't see Lena knotting her hands behind her back. Nothing in the world could have brought her to touch anything here. These things were not dead.

They settled into the double room they'd reserved at the camp hotel. Heiner unpacked his suitcase and walked comfortably over the creaking boards of the former SS-barracks, like a man finally reaching his vacation destination after a long day of travel. He was looking forward to dinner. He opened the window and looked out on the camp. The employees were gone for the evening, and the tourists had left on buses for their next destination. He breathed in the fresh air and said: Listen, Lena, the birds are singing so beautifully. In those days no birds sang at Auschwitz. A delicate veil of mist drifted over the roofs of the Blocks. Heiner showered and changed. Look, Lena, my stories are nothing more than drops in the ocean of Auschwitz.

At around ten o'clock, they sat alone in the big cafeteria. The camp hotel's guests had left the dining room, but Heiner didn't look like he wanted to get up yet. The kitchen worker wiped the tables, the cleaning woman swept the floor, the cook put the last dishes in the dishwasher and wished everyone a good night. Heiner asked the worker for a fresh glass and a bottle of beer.

Go to bed, Lena, you look tired.

And you?

With his index finger he scraped a dried splotch of soup off the table. It was the same motion he'd used to scrape rust off the gallows.

I'm going back, he said.

To the camp? In the dark?

The entrance. And over the entrance, the sign with the upside-down "b." Four million square feet of familiar ground. During the day, when the sky is blue and the sun shines, the watchtowers, the gallows, and the barbed wire are museum pieces, but now, with the pale moon turning everything big and eerie, he's in the camp of his nightmares, where he knows his way around. To Lena, it was a mild night in May 1982; to Heiner it was an icy morning in September, forty years earlier. His first day with the name 63 387.

He sits down on the steps of Block 9. They'd spent the first night here, herded in like livestock, four to each lice-riddled pallet. He listens to the camp. Wind sweeps through the woods. It's quiet here, far too quiet, a peaceful place, where only five hours ago tourists had been roaming with their sunhats, bottles of beer and water – peaceful visitors who tried hard to feel a trace of what had once existed there.

He jumps up, walks quickly to the middle of the camp road, stops, turns abruptly, tilts his head up, thrusts his chest out, clicks his heels, stands tall and calls out his name: 63 387. He takes off his cap and claps it against the seam of his trousers, his eyes frozen and unblinking. Muster at half past four in the morning. Prisoners in front of him, behind him, next to him, a thousand, two thousand, ten thousand – he hadn't counted – outside in thin rags at twenty-two below. He points to the left, towards the exit, where Rapportführer Kaduk is goose-stepping towards them with the list. He straightens up. Legs spread wide, he's showing off. Bellows: Five hundred men to the road-building Arbeitskommando! Count off! They count, man by man, to five hundred.

Fall into rows of ten!

Everyone runs and no one knows where he's supposed to go.

It's muddled disarray. How do you make rows of ten? The Kapos know it and they hit the men until they stand stiff as tin soldiers. They march towards the camp gate – can you see them, Lena? The prisoners freezing, their panicked fear of the man with the list. Stand up, Lena, come here, stand next to me.

Lena doesn't move. Heiner, you can't be serious.

Come on!

Hesitantly, she gets up and stands next to him. I can't do this, Heiner, she says, I can't relive your time here.

You have to try!

Heiner, I wasn't there. I've never feared for my life. I don't know what it feels like to be beaten with a club.

Look to the left, there's Kaduk.

For you, Heiner, not for me.

God damn it, why not?

They stand in the camp in the middle of the night, pondering why it isn't possible to transfer memories like a book. Heiner is distraught.

What do you see when I speak? Nothing? You just hear words?

I see images, but they're not the ones you see.

What are they, if they're not the ones I see?

I see pictures that my mind knows because I've seen them before somewhere – in books, films, or photographs. I'll never see what you see – is that bad?

It's a catastrophe.

She takes his hand. During my last year at school we did *Danton's Death*. I played Julie, his wife. At the beginning of the play I ask Danton: *Do you trust me?* Danton says: *How can I tell? We're lumbering, thick-skinned animals. Our hands reach out to touch, to feel, but the strain's pointless. All we can do is blunder around, rubbing our leathery hides up against each other. We're very much alone.*

If images can't be passed on, what about sounds? Heiner hears sirens. The way they wail when an attempted escape is discovered. He hears commands: bellowed, barked from men's throats. He hears thousands of wooden clogs hitting asphalt, and the music of the camp orchestra. The songs of prisoners marching; he hears dogs yapping, he hears their excited panting before they're let off their leashes.

Lena, what do you hear?

The wind. And you. You want to bring the dead camp to life. What are you trying to find here?

Prisoner 63 387.

Does he still exist? What do you want from him?

I want to make sure that he doesn't die.

Why do you keep nursing him?

One time he had gotten in line with the people who stood waiting to buy a ticket to enter the camp. Inch by inch he advanced patiently, one among many, indistinguishable from the other museum patrons. It was summer, peak season – he waited for an hour to reach the ticket counter. When he was asked how many tickets he needed, or if he was alone, he'd turned around in horror and run away. He couldn't buy tickets, it was impossible – he wasn't a visitor. Entry had been free for prisoners, and it ought to remain so.

They sit back down on the steps of the Block. It's quiet in the camp. The birds are asleep; somewhere rats or mice are rustling. There are Blocks that no one has been in for years, whose inner walls have all collapsed. Heiner lights a cigarette. He's not a nervous smoker – he enjoys every drag as if it's his last one. He draws the smoke deep into his belly, holds it there, and then slowly lets it out again. Look, Lena, the road-building Arbeitskommando. Average survival time: fourteen days. Three weeks, if you're lucky.

On his first "workday," he'd pushed a wheelbarrow full of sand back and forth across the grounds for sixteen hours straight. The Kapo screamed commands at his back. Go, go, you lazy pig, dalli, dalli. He had to fill the wheelbarrow to the brim with heavy wet sand. Why the rush? he whispered to his neighbor. They have a thousand years. That first day he was still able to make jokes. He didn't touch his soup at lunch, though hunger was devouring him. The soup was foul – it stank of cabbage and shit.

Look, Lena, the Kapo of the road-building Kommando – I'm not sure if the man had a shred of humanity in him. Jupp, he was called. Jupp Krankemann from Cologne; we called him "the fat pig." He was a giant. Jupp came to Auschwitz as a common thief. They made him a Kapo, and he voluntarily did the SS's dirty work for them – he killed ten men a day, sometimes fifteen. Poles, Russians, Germans, Jews, Christians – it didn't matter, only the numbers mattered. Never fewer than ten. Jupp crept up behind them, raised his spade over their heads, turned it vertical, and struck. Heiner jumps up, raises his arms, which grip an invisible handle, swings it over his head, sneaks forward a few hunched steps, shoots up, and lets his hands hurtle down. Can you see it, Lena?

Stop it, I feel sick.

Then you see it! Jupp could cleave skulls with his spade – his technique was perfect. He hit them right in the middle of their heads. On my first day, he stood behind me and screamed: Why isn't your wheelbarrow full, you lazy pig, and out of the corner of my eye, I saw him lifting his spade…and then suddenly you have the strength, because you want to live, and you run with your full wheelbarrow, even if you don't think your legs will carry you one more foot.

She puts her arm around him. Why are you torturing yourself like this?

I don't think, he says, that Jupp killed for the pleasure of it. It was greed: he got more bread for each person he killed. Ten dead men, ten slices of bread. It wasn't hunger, either – not even the fat pig could eat that much bread, but bread was the currency of the camp, you could get anything with bread. Cigarettes, jewelry, chocolate, watches – whatever you wanted. The camp was a school, you see. Anyone who didn't learn quickly was dead, and I had learned. Day one, lesson one: Prisoners kill prisoners. Lesson two: Remember the words of the songs – your life depends on it. Lesson three: You're part of the system; whether you want to be or not, you belong to it. Do as you're told; do it quickly and well, and don't attract attention. And never look any of them in the eye. They don't like that, it can cost you your life.

His voice, his gestures. He acts out the camp, and Lena sees more than she wants to. Look, Lena, in the evening they carried the dead into the camp on their shoulders. March in step, the Kapo screamed, one, two, three, four: They sang *On the heath there blooms a little flower, and it's called: Eeeerika. Eagerly doted on by a hundred thousand bees: Eeeerika.* They bellowed until they reached the gate of the camp. *For her heart is full of sweetness, a tender scent escapes her dress of blossoms.* At the entrance, the Kapo screamed: Road-building Arbeitskommando – halt! Then Kaduk came out of the Rapportführer's office and counted up the living and the dead. Five hundred men minus fifteen dead made four hundred and eighty-five, if no one had escaped. If it added up, work was done, and he could retreat to his private pleasures. He crept through the singing rows like a dog sniffing. He stared at the men. He had a sixth sense for bread that didn't come from the camp. It was as if he could smell it. Bread from outside means death, but – Lesson four: you can die for less. Because an SS man doesn't like your nose, because you remind him of someone he doesn't like, because he's in a bad mood, because his wife has stopped writing to him, because he doesn't want to be at Auschwitz either. Keep your eyes open, learn the structure, learn to read the signs. When the smoke that curled out of the chimneys at Birkenau was thin and white, the crematorium wasn't busy. When it was thick and black, it was best not to think about it.

Heiner turns his head toward the camp gate, as if Oswald Kaduk was still standing there. Everyone had a specialty, he says. Kaduk did it with a club. Any man he found with bread, he'd knock down. Then he'd lay his club on the man's adam's apple and seesaw it back and forth. Kaduk was a strong man, you see. That's how he killed people.

While four hundred and eighty-five people watched.

I was one of them, Heiner says.

And you had to just bear it.

You want to jump in, you want to tear the club from his hands, you want to beat Kaduk to death, you want to scream, you want, you want, you want – but do you want to die? You don't. You're happy that it's not you lying there. His death means your life. You stare through everything, you don't lift a hand, you see everything and sing *Eeeerika*. And you're ashamed of it for the rest of your life.

You didn't kill him.

That's not an acquittal, Lena. I allowed it to happen and I watched it happen. It's my fault that I'm alive.

Only a living person can be a witness.

Oh, Lena, but at what price?

Heiner raises his head. Do you hear what I hear?

I don't hear anything.

It's a kind of whimpering, he says, I'm going to go look. He crosses the camp road – he knows every nook and cranny, he doesn't need sunshine or a flashlight. He disappears between Blocks 19 and 20 and leaves a little gray cloud of cigarette smoke on the camp road behind him. His steps depart across the gravel; they grow softer, and then Lena can't hear them anymore. The wind has gone to sleep. It's still. Still as death. You have to watch your words here – they take on a new weight.

She waits five minutes, then ten. She doesn't trust herself to call out to Heiner, and certainly not to look for him between the dark Blocks. She wouldn't have moved from her spot for anything in the world. If he doesn't come back, she thinks, I'll just stay here until the sun rises. She props her arms on her knees and rubs her eyes to erase the image of Kapo Jupp and Rapportführer Kaduk from her mind. She's tired and would have fallen asleep, if she hadn't heard crunching, then steps approaching. It's not Heiner – his steps are faster, less tentative, and the sound isn't coming from the direction he left in. It's behind her, at her back, then right next to the Block where she's sitting. Her heart is in her mouth. She spins abruptly. Her voice is shrill.

Heiner, is that you?

Who else would it be?

He's carrying a tiny cat that he strokes as he walks. Poor kitty, he says, she got lost. The cat opens her little mouth and yawns. Heiner, Lena says, I almost died of fear.

Fear? he asked. Who would harm you here?

Some crazy murderer.

He sets the cat in her lap, and looks at her like a child who's talking nonsense: No one has ever been murdered here.

He thinks about the words he's just spoken, and then laughs like no one has ever laughed in this place before.

For thirty-five years, Heiner's white-haired friend had been living in a room in the former SS headquarters. A hundred and seventy square feet packed floor-to-ceiling with books and files – more archive than living room. There's an immersion heater on the stool, and space for two hot plates on the dresser. He clears a stack of blueprints off the table, sets them on the bed and takes cups and saucers from a cabinet that also holds books. He sets out bread and butter and a jar of apple compote that he made himself. Are the apples from here? Lena asks.

Why do you ask?

Just because.

Do you want five-minute eggs, or four-and-a-half? The chickens are from here too – does that bother you?

There are 43 353 numbers between Tadeusz and Heiner. Szymanski came to Auschwitz in August 1941, and Heiner arrived in September of the next year. So Tadeusz, whom Heiner calls Tadek, had suffered thirteen months longer, and between them, that counted for a lot. In a place where ten thousand people can be killed in one night, thirteen months of survival is a major achievement. Or a miracle. It took Lena many more encounters with Heiner's friends to understand the complex calculations that determined camp nobility and hierarchy. The first thirty prisoners, Nos. 1 to 30, brought to Auschwitz on May 20, 1940, were German criminals. Called "functionary prisoners," they were SS stooges. Lena had understood that numbers were important, but she never guessed that at Heiner's side she would develop such bizarre specialist knowledge. Once learned, prisoner numbers could be read like labels. September 1, 1939 was the invasion of Poland – on June 14, 1940, the first political prisoners were brought to Auschwitz from the jail in Tarnów. They were young men, practically children. They were given the numbers 31 to 758. Polish schoolboys, students, and boy scouts who had taken part in the fight against the Nazis. Often Heiner would say reverentially: Look, Lena, that man is eighty-four. He would introduce his friend and say: Talk to him. He has more stories to tell than I, he's 248. Prisoners with numbers in the eleven and twelve thousands were Polish Resistance fighters, having arrived between June 1940 and March 1941. Once the war with Russia began, the number of prisoners increased rapidly. In October 1941, numbers up to 25 000 were assigned – those were for Russian prisoners of war. The men from the Terezín ghetto, Theresienstadt, got numbers starting from 98 153, and the women got numbers from 33 252 on. The Greek Jews from Salonica started at 116 000. Numbers over 180 000 didn't impress Heiner – those were beginners, people at the bottom of the hierarchy, who arrived only a year before the end of the war, when he already had two years behind him.

Tadek had three numbers. He'd been prisoner 20 034 in Auschwitz, prisoner 77 236 in Gross-Rosen, and prisoner 128 031 in Buchenwald; he had come to Auschwitz at age twenty-four. He was Polish, since his parents had been Poles, even though in 1917, the year of his birth, the maps had shown no country called Poland. At that time, his homeland had been part of the Austro-Hungarian Empire, and his village lay in the mountains that belonged to Bosnia. Ask him to tell you his story, Heiner says. It's an interesting one.

Ask him. If only it were that simple. Lena is married to a former prisoner, but Heiner talks without being asked. Look, Lena – and he's off on a story. Heiner's friends, too, don't wait to be asked, they talk when they're in the mood. Ask him – about what? How should she begin, with what words? How is she supposed to know if he feels like being asked this morning? And anyway, after the night in the camp, she'd just as soon keep silent. She's had enough camp stories for the time being, and Tadek doesn't look like he's waiting for Lena to ask. *The chickens are from here too*, he'd said, knowing exactly what she was thinking. We might as well keep being direct, Lena thinks, and says: Do you know what I thought when I saw you yesterday? What is Curt Jurgens doing at Auschwitz?

He likes the comparison. He'd seen Curt Jurgens in Vienna in the mid-sixties in *Everyman*, and he had been impressed with his powerful stage presence. I'll never forget it, he says – the part where the woman calls him: Eeeeeeeverymaaaan. And so, by way of Everyman, God, Death, and the devil, they come directly to Tadek's story.

After the camp was liberated, he'd gone home, vowing never again to set foot on this godforsaken piece of earth. At home people had looked at him mistrustfully: How come you're still alive? We thought there was only one way to freedom at Auschwitz: through the chimney. Their eyes asked: What did you do? Were you a Nazi stooge? At whose cost did you survive? If only they had asked him directly. He found their secretive looks repugnant.

Twelve months later, on the way home from a convalescence treatment for former prisoners, he stopped at the place he'd sworn never to return to. It was curiosity, no more. Just take a quick look to see what's still there, and then: leave, forever. But the camp wasn't empty, as he'd expected it to be. He was greeted by Baca, the friend with whom he'd survived a death march and a perilous escape. Baca said: I'm staying here. Baca said: Will you help us? We're turning the world's biggest graveyard into a memorial.

You were excited, I'm sure, Lena says.

And how. It was a suggestion to set up house inside my nightmares.

That night he stood at the open window in his pajamas. The air was icy cold, it was raining – the weather couldn't have been more typical for the region. He lay in bed, got up, thought of Baca. For Baca, the decision was easy, he didn't have to think about it. For Baca there were no ifs or buts – thought and action were the same. But Tadek didn't just have nightmares, he had dreams too. He wanted to study, travel, see the world – he wanted to bury the nightmares, or the night attacks, as he called them, under a full and colorful life. He lay down, stood up, lay down, and then at some point he stood fully dressed at the door, as if his clothes had put themselves on him without his help. I could work on a trial basis, he thought, and if it doesn't work, I can say to Baca: I'm getting out of here. At that point he could have gone back to bed, but then he looked at the clock. Just before midnight. The witching hour. A good time to walk to Birkenau. It was a dark night, windy; he felt as if he were being whipped by the drizzle, which pleased him. One can't make such a decision in bed, in a warm room, or in a conversation weighing pros and cons. Some inner authority has to decide – but does he have one? And where is it? Does it know what he wants of it? It had never spoken to him before. He set out, and listened to the voices that spoke during his walk through Birkenau. There were many. They mocked: Tadeusz, you stupid dog, what are you doing here? They warned: Run away, Tadek, hurry! They admonished: You're nuts, Szymanski – do you want to be married to ghosts? One of the voices played itself off as the cool, reasonable, moral one. Tadeusz Szymanski, it said in the voice of a stern governess, there have to be people who make sure that nothing that happened here is ever forgotten. You're right, he said. But can you tell me why it should be me, of all people? The voice was silent. Coward! he cried. Do it yourself!

There he was, standing in the middle of Birkenau's uncanny

landscape, and he might well have turned around, had he not seen a shadow in the distance, rocking back and forth, slow and steady, back and forth. The Jews in his village had moved like that when praying. Don't be afraid, Szymanski, he reassured himself, go on, look, there's no such thing as ghosts, even at midnight in Birkenau. Carefully, he approached the black shadow. The idea that a Jew was praying here appealed to him – two sleepless crackpots out in the rain – that would have been an interesting encounter. Then he realized that the praying Jew was only a bush, rocked by the wind.

The nightmares stopped when he moved into SS headquarters. He'd come to meet them, so the bad dreams no longer had any reason to pursue him. At first they were just eighteen crazy people, and everyone did everything. Later, he was in charge of the memorial's art and publicity department. He'd been retired for five years now: he cooked five-minute eggs and had no paying job any more but plenty to do. He opened exhibitions in New York, Brussels, and Berlin, and gave lectures in Paris, Hamburg, Warsaw, Vienna – wherever he was needed. He knew about everything that had been drawn, sketched, painted, photographed, carved, or written by prisoners at Auschwitz, then hidden and buried, and he'd gotten used to people asking in astonishment how he could possibly live there. It was part of every tour of Auschwitz. Bewildered head-shaking. Szymanski, Szymanski, how can you live in the world's biggest graveyard! As you can see: I can.

When he leans out the window, he can see the flat roof of the building that the prisoners called the "little death factory" – the first crematorium, the "rehearsal room" for Birkenau. To his right, behind the garden, stands Höss's former villa, now crumbling. But really, how can you live here? Lena asks. Curt Jurgens smiles. It's an exquisite location. Very reasonable accommodations. Fresh air. Plenty of sky, and outside my door: just peace and quiet.

He doesn't lead tours anymore, he says. He can't stand to listen to himself any longer – it is as if his voice has become independent of him when he explains the camp. He doesn't like this voice; it turns around and around inside him like a record. But if you want, he says, you can accompany me on my afternoon stroll. Around three, OK? I won't talk much. Heiner nods. He's giving Lena permission – the invitation wasn't directed at him.

At three, Tadek sets a black beret on his white mane, folds his hands behind his back, and walks the nearly two miles from the main camp to Birkenau with the steady gait of a hiker. Lena is at his side. As he walks ahead of her over the narrow footpath on the bridge over the Soła, she suddenly knows what it is that marks Heiner and his friends. They're surrounded by what's lost, as by an invisible cape. It had surrounded the witness from Vienna when he collapsed in the courthouse hallway. It surrounds Tadek as he walks before her over the bridge.

Tadeusz stops inside the big gate as if entering a cathedral. The sight of this landscape still gets to him, even though he knows every stone on the premises. Barracks, all the way to the horizon. The mind fills in the places where they've decayed or been cleared away, where only naked red chimneys loom towards the sky. Ten million square feet. A landscape of enslavement. Flat. Barren. Boundless. It doesn't even end where sky and earth collide. The sun is warm. It smells like grass. Crows sit atop the red chimneys, dozing.

Lena adjusts her pace to Tadek's. When he walks fast, she walks fast, she stops when he stops, tries to see what Tadek sees, and knows that it will never be possible. They're alone in Birkenau, aside from two men who are roaming unusually quickly over the grounds. Each holds a video camera. They film the paths, the tracks, the barracks; they pan up to the sky, trace the chimneys and barbed wire with their viewfinders; they capture Lena and Tadek too. Two fat men with round heads. Their shirts are open, exposing the hair on their bellies. They're wearing white cable-knit knee socks, sandals, and shorts; they look like father and son.

What are you looking for, Tadek asks in Polish, English, and German. We are Hungary-people, the father says. Where did Hungary-people live? There? He points to the left. No, Tadek says. That's section B1a, that was the women's camp. The Hungarians were…wait a minute…they were over there…B2c. He points to a small path. That can't be, the son says. We looked over there, but my father couldn't find the house where he lived then.

How could your father recognize his barrack, Tadek says, when they all look alike, and most of them no longer consist of any more than the chimney?

Tadek shakes the father's hand. He introduces himself. Tadeusz Szymanski, 20 034. How long were you here? The man shrugs. Don't know. Month one, month two – then away, another camp. He gestures into the distance. Tadek lays his hands on the man's shoulders. Be glad, comrade – you were very lucky. The two switch their cameras back on and go back to searching for the father's barrack, their devices whirring. Szymanski walks on. *Couldn't find the house where his father lived.*

Ask him. How? Where was your house, Szymanski? Where did you survive? Which Arbeitskommando did they put you in? Tadek's steps are resolute. He walks through the camp in silence. He doesn't look around; he's not looking for anything. He's just going for a stroll. As the Hungarians cross their path again he says, without preface: My friend Igor was in the Sonderkommando. One night he said: The rumors are bad – they're exterminating the Hungarian Jews. He was right. The first transports came on May 15. We heard the wheezing of the trains night and day for twenty-five days, eleven months before the end of the war. Tadek links arms with Lena. Each train had thirty, forty, fifty stock cars. An endless mass of people streamed out of the trains and were herded to the crematoriums. Mothers pushing strollers, old people, young men supporting frail grandparents, half-dead of thirst, half-starved; very few were admitted to the camp as workers like the Hungarian whose son was looking for the "house." The Nazis put open cars full of wooden beams on each train, and the Hungarians thought it was wood for the lodgings they were meant to build. No normal mind could imagine that the wood was for their own cremation. The men of the Sonderkommando went mad, they had to fill quotas, day and night, and there were only two ways to avoid this work: suicide or escape, which was the same thing. Twelve gas chambers. Thirty-eight ovens. In only a few weeks, 438 000 Hungarian Jews were killed. Tadek stares into the ruins of the crematorium as if unable to believe what he's saying.

Once he'd heard one of the few survivors of the Sonderkommando speak – but – "speak," Lena! What Henryk Mandelbaum did here can't be called speaking. He stood as if the place belonged to him, like a farmer in his field, in "his" crematorium. What did he care for the rubble, the "no trespassing" signs? Here was his life, his place, his work, his martyrdom, no sign had any power over him here. He talked urgently, impatiently, without distance. He didn't wait for translation, he wasn't in an auditorium, this wasn't a lecture. He was in the gas chamber. He spoke quickly, breathlessly, in Polish with bits of German thrown in, using whatever words came to him. Now and then he'd look up and stare into one of his listeners' faces, and when he said "understand," it wasn't a question, but a command. I'm explaining my job, understand! He led women, men, old people, and children into what they thought was a harmless "shower." He made them feel safe before they were sent into the gas. It was his job to build trust, to calm them, to dispel their panic – and he acted this out for the visitors. Watch, all of you!

He went to the "shower," looked to the side, almost lovingly, as if he were speaking to someone next to him allaying the invisible comrade's fear and mistrust. Come, brother, let's walk together – all will be well. Mandelbaum stooped and showed his horrified audience – really, Lena – how much strength it had taken to pull the dead out of the gas chamber afterward. They were twisted and knotted together; they'd clung to each other in their panic. He spared the visitors nothing. Absolutely nothing. He explained the most effective incineration technique. While he spoke and gestured, he was digging like a frantic miner, tunneling through all those years, until he arrived at the place where he was now once again standing. He didn't make it easy for anyone, least of all for himself. He wanted to demonstrate the perversion of the word "work" by insisting that this job too demanded competence and expertise, and that everyone who worked here was a special-ist. He screamed into the faces of the speechless people that fat people burn better than skinny ones. He explained how to make a mixture that would burn well, stooped to lift invisible corpses from the ground – big ones and small ones, and piled them on skids that were shoved into the oven. He was doing something unthinkable, and I stood there howling with rage, because he was recklessly tearing down the wall between then and now. No one who experienced his "talk" will ever forget it. You carry this man with you like a burden. Henryk Mandelbaum, Tadek says, was a wild, sad, strong, deeply wounded man.

As the evening sun drenches the grounds in glowing orange, they see the two Hungarians once more. Resolutely, as if he's had this in mind from the beginning, the son climbs up on the hunks of rubble that once were the crematorium. The father films him. They take Kippahs from their pockets and put them on. The son turns his head towards the place where they'd looked for the father's barrack, takes a few deep breaths, and then sings the first words of the Kaddish, his voice strong, savoring every syllable: Yit-gaddal veyitqaddash shmeh rabba. He hesitates, looks at his father. Without putting the camera down, he sings the words that his son doesn't know, repeating them until he no longer needs help. The Hungarians' voices accompany Tadek and Lena all the way to the exit. If I hadn't decided to stay a long time ago, Tadeusz Szymanski says, then a moment like this would have convinced me.

After their stroll, Lena saw Tadek only one more time. He called to ask if she might want to have ice cream with a tired Curt Jurgens. He was no longer the strong man with the white hair, he'd grown thin and looked almost transparent. They took the same path along the Main that Lena had walked with Heiner after the trial.

Tell me, Lena – what's it like to live with one of us?

What do you think it's like? It's like living with a singer who can't stop singing the song of his life. He sings it in the morning, he sings it at noon and in the afternoon, evening, and night. It has many verses. You have to like the song, or you'll go crazy.

Tadek laughed. At least there's some consolation. One day the singer will forget the song of his life, and then he'll stop singing. It sounded like a confession, when he told her that daily life running the museum had robbed him of his memory for sounds. It was loud at Birkenau, he said – it hummed and buzzed like a thousand flies trapped in a small jar. Now when I walk through Birkenau, I hear the wind, the crows, the voices of visitors, but no longer the camp.

He stopped, looked at the Main, listened to a tugboat chugging, and to the waves slapping the banks. He put his arm around Lena. The sounds have left me, and with the sounds, the images have gone as well. They've faded, I can't recognize them anymore. At Birkenau I see what every visitor sees. Chimneys. Barracks. The remains of walls. My history has dissolved.

Can you live without it?

No. It's time to leave the world.

He looked so sad that Lena could think of no better comfort than to give him a long kiss.

Heiner was powerless against the old "auntie Fear". At every goodbye she whispered into his ear: This is for always. He avoided goodbyes. He wanted to simply leave, without a kiss, without an embrace, without waving, without even turning around. The melancholy gesture of a last look seemed to harbor the secret fear that he'd never see the other person again. "Take care of yourself" was anathema to him, as was come back, be well, see you soon, see you tomorrow, see you next week, next year, see you at Christmas, Easter, see you next birthday, go with God, God bless you – no, he wanted none of that: simply close the door and go. Death is the twin of the moment when one says good bye. That morning he didn't want to hug Tadek or promise him anything; he didn't want to make any plans, so as not to have to admit the thought of their ultimate parting. He climbed into the truck, cast no second glance at the camp or at his friend who stood at the entrance. It wasn't just the big farewells that he hated, but the small ones as well. Death was everywhere: on the street, on airplanes; it could fall as a tile from a roof or lay in wait at the supermarket as he reached out to grab a jar of his favorite pickles. No goodbye – no thoughts of death. Isn't our goodnight kiss a goodbye, Lena asked, or the goodnight poem, doesn't that scare you? Death takes many people while they sleep. He didn't want to do without the kiss, nor without the poem. When we hold each other tight, he said, we're one being with two heads, and death is scared to approach a monster like that, just ask Leszek.

There was yellowish-white fog on the road the morning of their departure, as if some packages of powdered milk had slipped off the truck during the night. I can see treetops, Lena said – but where's the road? Somewhere in between, Heiner said, stuffing his jacket behind his head and closing his eyes so as not to see Tadek waving, while Lena cheerfully steered "Czerwony," the "Red," out of the parking lot, waving and calling "na razie," see you soon. Lena thrived at times that forced her to try something new. Like this morning, when she drove the truck through a wall of fog that became thick as semolina pudding as they left Oświęcim. Stay here, Tadek had said, wait for nice weather, but Lena wanted to prove that she could drive even when it wasn't sunny. You would have survived Auschwitz, too, Heiner said, and fell asleep.

Two hours later the fog had risen. She saw no treetops and no sky, but she could see the road and the ditches alongside it, and houses with no roofs. When they reached the outskirts of Kraków and Heiner was still sleeping, she shook him awake. Tell me, who are we going to see? He yawned. First Kosta, then Mietek – they're good guys and fine comrades. Lena had expected nothing less.

There were eight hundred survivors in Kraków, and for the thirty who were faring particularly badly, Heiner had made special packages. In addition to food and medicine, they contained scarves and hats, coats, mittens, warm sweaters and shoes. The survivors' clubhouse was a flat building in the courtyard of an old half-timbered building. Lena turned vigorously into the narrow entrance and heard a grating screech of metal, but kept driving and stopped only when she came to the clubhouse. Heiner gave out a long cry, sprang down from the seat and traced the scratch like a man possessed, as if trying to remove it. His face was white. His eyes were wide and full of panic. Lena tried to calm him. Don't get upset, my treasure, I'll pay for the damage. He didn't hear her. His hands trembled. Calm down, she said, we didn't explode, we're not in a ditch, no one is hurt, no one is dead. He moaned, cried, didn't look at her, rubbed the scratch like a wound. Heiner, she screamed, shaking him. It's only the metal that's scraped. Metal, do you hear me? He didn't react. Lena grabbed his hands, pulled him across the courtyard like a stubborn child, and sat him down on a bench under a large chestnut tree. She sat on his lap and held him tight until his trembling lessened.

Heiner, what's wrong?

Nothing.

He watched indifferently as the packages were unloaded. Should I get the doctor? the caretaker asked. Heiner shook his head.

A glass of water?

He nodded.

The truck had long since been secured, the helpers had gone home, and the meeting house was closed until they were to meet with Kosta. They still sat under the chestnut tree, Lena irritated, Heiner as exhausted as if he'd carried a hundred packages all alone. When his hands were warm again, he blew his nose and said, as if he'd just survived a harmless fever: Let's go have some cake at Café Florian, what do you think?

First of all we cancel our meeting with Kosta.

She couldn't have made a worse suggestion. Heiner was wild with excitement about seeing him. Kosta was his friend, a big shot in the writers' guild, he'd been part of the Resistance at the camp, they called him "the Eagle." Before they left the café, Heiner said: be nice to him, Lena – he's earned it.

Why wouldn't I be nice to him?

He's not easy.

Neither are you, Lena said.

Kosta was a strong man, bigger than Heiner. He stood in front of the clubhouse like a column, clapped Heiner on the back several times in greeting, kissed Lena's hand, and looked at her briefly, without curiosity. He led them into a green meeting room with bare walls, no books, no carpet – drab as an empty aquarium. Their voices echoed in a way that made the encounter feel slightly artificial.

The table was long, the chairs were spaced far apart. "The Eagle" sat at the head as if leading a discussion. Heiner sat next to him; there were three empty chairs between him and Lena. Heiner said that he was glad his friend wanted to inform them about the current state of affairs in Poland – no one could do that better than a comrade in his position. A young man set Nescafé and hot water on the table; Lena asked for sugar and milk. He brought sugar, but there was no milk. Once they each had a mug of coffee in front of them, the Eagle began his report, as if sitting before not two people but two hundred. This didn't seem to bother Heiner – he patiently accepted the fact that their reunion was more formal than he had envisioned.

Kosta's first sentence was: I hate war. His German was perfect. By the second sentence, he was defending martial law as the only thing Jaruzelski could have done, given the circumstances. The circumstances, as he explained them, were the explosion in Solidarność's membership, and the extremely dangerous path the trade union was treading towards confusing itself with a political party. The result was chaos and moral decline, which could be seen on every corner of every Polish city, in every town square. It was the same speech Jaruzelski had given on television, practically verbatim – nor did Kosta leave out the threat that the Russians would use the situation in Poland as an excuse to invade, as they had in Prague.

Heiner stared into his cup. His friend was on Jaruzelski's side – how could it be? They'd called him "the Eagle" because of his powerful bald head, sharp nose, and small, sharp eyes. He wasn't the soul of the Resistance, but its head and spine, and that was what mattered. If Heiner had had to make the decisions that the Eagle made, he would have tried again and again to save people who couldn't be saved. You can't fight a death-machine with your heart, the Eagle had said. Heiner warmed his hands on his mug. He looked for subtext. Maybe the Eagle was playing the committed patriot because he knew the place was bugged – but if that were the case, they could have met in a café. Kosta's hands were motionless on the table; he didn't use them to assist his speech nor to contradict it. There was no hint of irony in his eyes – he meant what he said. Heiner shot Lena a quick glance. She was stirring her coffee, her spoon clinked against the side of the cup, the coffee was a carousel. Heiner began to trace the cracks in the table. Had they been friends at Auschwitz? Or just comrades? But they were the same thing – so why wasn't there any warmth in his friend's eyes? No signal: You and I, remember back then, remember how it was? The Eagle spoke to them like tourists from the West, as if they had no shared history.

The young people on the barricades, the Eagle said, are troublemakers, dreamers at best, but mostly stupid, deluded revolutionaries, anarchists, led astray by capitalist propaganda. Heiner raised his head – he couldn't stand the coldness between them any longer. Oh Kosta, he said, as if expressing his heart's desire, let's not talk politics. How are you, my friend? Are you healthy? I just want to know whether you're happy. The Eagle continued his report. Heiner lowered his eyes and fingered the crack in the table again. Yes, they'd all been Stalinists, but hadn't they learned something, hadn't the gulags destroyed the dream of Communism with a human face? Twice the Eagle had helped him to hide Paul Szende, his Hungarian friend, from Selection. He'd kept Paul's son Lassi from certain death when the boy raved on the camp road, crazy with despair over the loss of his father. *Father, father, take me with you.* He'd roared in the boy's face like the worst Kapo, and when that didn't help, he'd slapped him and dragged him to the next Block before some exasperated SS man could say: Climb aboard, my boy, you can go with your father.

If we don't deal harshly with the troublemakers, Kosta said, if we don't expose and quash the infiltrators and spies as quickly as possible, this country will plunge into the abyss.

Lena was no longer listening. She was standing in a music room, listening to the crackling of a radio, a woman's gentle voice: Dear ones, we are happy and moved to be able to speak to you… we see you sitting at your radios, listening to our words. The words that they want to imprison…we come into your living rooms to bring you comfort…Solidarność lives, Solidarność will live on… my dear ones, we lift up our heads, for the future belongs to us.

Without looking at her husband, Lena said in Polish: Stalin is dead, Comrade Kosta. Look at your friend's face. Do you see how he looks? The Eagle stared at her, dumbfounded. She could see what he was thinking: This uppity German woman, why is she speaking Polish? He looked from Heiner to Lena. He'd lost his stride, and he stood up. Heiner didn't move. He clutched his cup and searched for words to appease his friend. The Eagle pushed his chair under the table, lay his hand on Heiner's shoulder for a second, as if he pitied him his impudent wife. He left the room slowly, and uncannily quietly.

For heaven's sake, Lena, what did you say?

I told him to be nice to you.

Is he coming back?

I don't think so.

Why not?

He's not a nice person.

Over the rest of the journey through Poland, they fought repeatedly over their meeting with the Eagle. Heiner was angry – his wife had no right to alienate his friend. She'd broken the cardinal rule: No criticizing Kosta, no criticizing Leszek, no criticizing any comrade whose selfless courage had proven his worth for all time. I understand, Lena said, but do I have to listen to your comrade's bullshit, just because he was at Auschwitz?

What did you say?

The "just" appalled him. It made it sound as if his friend had been vacationing there. Heiner ended every argument with a sentence that was like a dogma: Kosta is my friend. And I'd rather not imagine, Lena said, what would happen if you were his prisoner and he was interrogating you. They were silent, abandoned the subject, and then the fight would start all over again. She'd said *just*. It was that word that troubled him. Just because he was at Auschwitz. After endless debates, Lena lost her patience. Heiner, my dear, she said sharply, let me enlighten you on the word that's bothering you so much. *Just* is a small, embittered word with a difficult life. It has to push its way into sentences, even those where it isn't absolutely necessary, and imbue them with new meaning. First: The *just* in my sentence is meant in the sense of "although," and does not diminish your friend's suffering. What I wanted to say was: *Although* he was at Auschwitz back then, I don't have to accept it when he talks nonsense today. Secondly: When I write to Olga: It was *just* a crazy coincidence that I met Heiner, it's not to belittle our meeting, it just means that without the assistance of chance, we wouldn't have met. Thirdly: When I say: The book *just* costs five Marks, I think it's very reasonable. Fourthly: When I say: The old woman remembers nothing, *just* that one summer day, *just* means something like "solely" or "exclusively," as in the phrase "I made this just for you." *Just* is a chameleon. It changes its meaning from sentence to sentence. Fifthly: When I tell you of some horrifying experience and at the end I say: but I *just* dreamt it all, it doesn't mean "solely," or "exclusively," but rather: It wasn't so bad, it was *just* a dream. Sixthly: When I say: Tomorrow, tomorrow, *just* not today, or: *Just* hold still – I mean it in the sense of "merely," and seventhly: When you take the drill out of my hand and say: *Just* let me do it, it doesn't mean that you want to do the job exclusively, nor that the job is unimportant, but rather: Let me do it, I want to help you. *Just* is an enigmatic character among all the words – capricious and demanding. In some sentences, in order not to be misunderstood, it requires a particular emphasis. When I say: Today I *just* read, that could mean: I allowed myself to be lazy today. If I stress the *just* and stretch it out, I'm declaring that I've worked hard today, since I've *juuuuust* read. Eighthly: *Just* why am I getting so upset?

Because I love "the Eagle," *just* differently than I love you. *Just* in the sense of "but," – did I understand correctly? They could laugh again. Nonetheless, the encounter with the Eagle plagued Heiner. In the camp, Kosta had already been a fierce Stalinist. He'd tried to save comrades who were important for the Resistance – sympathy and friendship didn't come into it. That's how it was back then. And now? What would have happened if Heiner lived in Poland today and was one of the people the Eagle had called infiltrators and spies? Would Kosta persecute Heiner, have him locked up and tortured, because his comrade had become an enemy? Or would he protect him, because friendship is more important than political views? What would he himself have been capable of, he, Heiner, if his comrades in Austria had been victorious? Prison, torture, and camps for the enemies of the working class, because desperate times called for desperate measures? Were there people who could never be perpetrators, on either side of the barricade? Was he one of them? Would he have been the victim of his own comrades, which was even sadder than being the victim of the Nazis? He pushed the thought aside. What would have happened if – hadn't he himself once called that question point-less and dumb?

The sun was struggling over Nowa Huta – it had to fight for its beams to reach the earth. The city hadn't been planned as a regular highrise complex after the war, Nowa Huta had a mission: it was supposed to be a bulwark of proletarian socialism against the intellectualism of Kraków, which would never dream of bowing to Russian socialism. Nowa Huta was defiant, with wide avenues, laid out in a way that was easy to understand and control, as if even those who planned it had had their doubts about the friendship between workers and those in power. A quarter of a million people lived there, including Heiner's friend Mietek. The ramshackle ironworks, the "new steel mill" that gave the city its name, had turned the whole place black in only a few years. Black facades, black window frames, black roofs, leaves that hung on the trees like briquettes of charcoal. In the evening, the inhabitants wrote the first letters of their names on the street with white chalk, because every night in true socialist fashion, the sticky black soot covered everything that stood or grew or parked here. Next to Mietek's car was an "M." The car in front said "O," and the one behind, "P." Every day some optimist tied a balloon to a tree – sometimes it was red, sometimes green, sometimes yellow, white, or blue. It was a reminder: Don't forget, friends – the world can be a colorful place.

Heiner's description of Mietek was brief. Prisoner number 662. First transport. Camp nobility, younger than he, not yet sixty. He looked forward to seeing Mietek in a different way than he'd looked forward to seeing "the Eagle." Without awe, but with a twinkle in his eye. He laughed when he thought of him: a real nutcase, you'll see. Mietek was a surgeon at the biggest clinic in Kraków, but he only worked there because it had a swimming pool, and there was a park next to it.

What a greeting! They fell into each other's arms, let go, balled their fists and exchanged playful blows on the chest and shoulders, embraced again, balled their fists and circled each other joyfully, like boxers in a ring. Mietek was stocky – a rectangle made of muscles. He'd hugged Lena like an old friend. His chest and belly were hard as concrete. Even his hands were muscular – she could easily imagine them holding a scalpel.

Where did you learn to speak German so well?

Lena would never again ask that question of a Polish person Mietek's age. She'd asked out of politeness, to fill a brief silence during dinner. But for Mietek they were the magic words he'd been waiting for. He set the cutlery on the table and commanded an invisible crew: One, two, three, four! He jumped up, clapped his hands against the seams of his trousers, stared straight ahead and sang in a deep voice: In Auschwitz camp is where I was/Holleries and Holleras!/But thinking of dear ones far away/makes me feel so glad and gay!/Every morning with the sun/is our hard day's work begun/Driv'n by work or even sport/A happy song is our report/Yet we know there'll come the day/when from Schutzhaft we'll away/Then happ'ly we'll go to our homes/Ne'er again from there to roam!

Heiner looked at Lena, unsure how she was taking his friend. Since she'd ended their meeting with the Eagle so abruptly, he no longer felt there was any guarantee of harmony between her and his comrades. Cautiously, he asked: Mietek's a funny one, huh?

As she listened to the man singing, Lena's eyes filled with tears. Mietek had no idea how lonely he looked, and Heiner didn't notice it either, because he looked the same.

And the milestones, remember them? Heiner asked his friend.

There is only one path to freedom, Mietek cried smartly, its milestones are: Obaydience –

Obedience, Heiner corrected.

Obedience, Mietek repeated, Diligence, Order, Honesty, Cleanness – Cleanliness, Heiner corrected.

Cleanliness, Truthfulness, Saycrifice –

Sacrifice, Heiner corrected, and: Love of the Fatherland!

In Poland I'll be a different person, Heiner had said, and in that moment Lena was sure that if she weren't there he would have been laughing uproariously. But if she weren't there, Mietek wouldn't have sung – or would he? Or would he and Heiner have sung together?

You know, Lena, Mietek said, when the Kapo suspected a Pole, a Russian, a Greek, Czech, or Rumanian of just silently opening and closing his mouth like a fish, he'd put his ear right up to the man's mouth and woe to him if no German words came out!

One, two, three, four, he commanded: Girl with a bob! With arms spread wide like an opera singer, Mietek stood in the kitchen and belted: Oh I climbed up the mountain, to see a pretty little maden –

Maiden, Heiner corrected

– little maiden, and I was glad. She had two beautiful blue ayes –

Eyes, Heiner corrected

She had two beautiful blue eyes and her hair in a bob and she looked good.

The songs turned Heiner's stomach, Lena knew, but when Mietek was able to sing them and laugh, everything seemed to be OK. If you want to impress Lena, Heiner said, sing *Once a boy a Rosebud spied*.

Mietek pounded his chest proudly. Four-year German intensive course, he said. There's no better way to learn a language so quickly and inexpensively. With every whack of the club, bam, you learn a new word. Boy. Bam. Rosebud. Bam. Where's the rosebud? On the heath! You wonder: Is heath the singular form of heather? No, Goethe. New words stick in your head with terrified firmness, they cling tightly so as not to get lost. The maid's name is Dirndelein. Your tongue stumbles over the black-brown hazelnut. But if you survive, then later you can sing Goethe: *Now the cruel boy must pick Heathrose fair and tender; Rosebud did her best to prick – Vain 'twas 'gainst her fate to kick – She must needs surrender.*

Mietek looked at Lena. Have you heard about the speaking tree? Didn't your husband ever tell you about the speaking tree? German for beginners. Pay attention – this is how it was. When you ran into an SS man, you had to take off your hat, slap it against your thigh and cry: Number 662 respectfully reporting. But many of the comrades had long numbers – 134 276 – tongues that had never before spoken a word of German would get all twisted, and that was where the tutoring tree, that was supposed to help us learn German, came in. Your language must have been invented by a German shepherd – to us it sounded like growling and yapping. Imagine: Chased by vicious dogs, ten or twelve men who couldn't cope with this German barking, ran to the speaking tree and climbed up its branches – the higher you went, the safer you were. The dogs, the Nazis screaming with laughter, the crackling and breaking of the branches, the screams of the men who'd fallen down and were being attacked by the dogs, can you imagine it? A tree full of panicked birds bellowing out their numbers: 5 432. 20 311, 662. And underneath you, the branches were cracking. He savored his own words. He was seeing the tree.

Tell me, Lena, in which tree did you learn Polish?

In the summer, under a chestnut tree in the garden. In winter, in my father's library. Always on Sundays, between eleven and one. There was tea with cream. The teacher came from Warsaw and stayed for lunch. Her hands smelled of rosewater.

They'd brought Mietek a silver-gray jogging suit – the fabric was soft and comfortable.

In 1945, when Mietek's legs and arms were skinnier than the speaking tree's skinniest branches, he'd invented a regimen he called the triple sport. In the lake behind the school, he swam his first strokes. First two, then four, then six – two more each day. Then he got on a dented old bicycle, rode to the end of the street, rested, biked back, and then tried to run a few meters. He never missed a day of this program. Wherever he was, he swam, biked, ran. No night was too dark, no morning too early, no wind too cold, no soot too black. His arms grew stronger and muscles filled out his legs – to this day, Mietek doesn't go to bed before he's run half a marathon. Only when he's completely exhausted is he able to fall so deep into sleep that the dreams can't reach him.

After dinner he wrapped a long scarf around his neck and promised a maygical surprise at midnight. Magical, Heiner corrected. Mietek laughed – one, two, three, four: Dear Lola! – and slammed the door behind him. They heard him springing through the stairwell singing: *Dear Lola, stop your crying/Please dear don't you cry/Often he thinks of his dear Lola/When the moon is high.* Heiner said: When we sang that song, we all thought of those we loved, and cried inside. When they could no longer hear Mietek, Heiner said: Look, Lena, exercise at Auschwitz…

Lena put on Mietek's apron and began washing plates and cups.

Are you listening?

She put glasses for vodka on the table. I'm listening, but let me clean up, I need to move.

Look, Lena, once upon a time Mietek and I were among the Nazi's favorite victims for sports practice. We were hungry, we could have killed for a crumb of bread, and then along comes an SS-man and says: You lazy bastards! Sports are a great way to strengthen your muscles! And with malicious excitement he'd point at any prisoners that happened to be in the vicinity: You and you and you and you. We were ordered to exercise, you have to understand, when it was forty below and when it was boiling hot. First: Knee-bends. Up, down, up, down, twenty, thirty, fifty, a hundred times. You get dizzy, you stagger, you're at your limit, and then: push-ups. Up and down, up and down, not so slowly you stinking pigs, you disgusting intellectuals, fifty pushups and then: bunny hops. Bend your knees, arms outstretched: Hop, bunny, hop. They waited for you to lose your balance and fall on your back. Then they beat you like an exhausted beetle. You know, Mietek was a champion of the double ironman, once the exercise that he'd invented just for himself became a real sport. 4.9 miles swimming, 223.6 miles biking, 52.2 miles running. No break. No one can kill Mietek with exercise anymore.

He opened the bottle of vodka. Mietek is one of a kind. So are you, Lena said.

At a quarter of an hour before midnight, Mietek flung open the door and called: Turn out the light and go to the window – the maygical surprise is beginning.

He ran from the bathroom to the bedroom, from the bedroom to the living room, from there to the kitchen – he was check-ing every clock in the apartment. Heiner and Lena stood at the kitchen window. The housing complex was black as soot. A city without light. As if dead. Mietek counted the seconds to mid-night. Five, four, three, two, one, and at zero he turned on the harsh ball-shaped lamp that stood on the bedroom windowsill. At that second, precisely at midnight, the neighborhood turned bright – but in a different way than before. In some apartments only the kitchen light was on, in others only the light in the bathrooms, living rooms, or stairwells. Mietek hopped with pleasure like a giddy child. He clapped his hands, crying: Funkcjonowa! Funkcjonowa! Heiner whispered: Magic, magic. On the front of every highrise, from the roof to the cellar, was a letter made of light:

"S."

Mietek kissed Heiner and Lena. Men, women, and children hung out of the windows that were left dark, waving and chanting: Solidarność! Solidarność! Nowa Huta was no bulwark against the eggheads in Kraków. The black city, where the workers and students lived, declared war on martial law with a single letter:

"S."

As police helicopters flew over the houses, the lights went off and on, off and on. The helicopters descended, flying deeper and deeper through the complex of buildings, flapping dangerously close to the windows.

"S."

Thirty minutes of terror. Then the grey locusts swung westward, back in the direction from which they'd come, towards Kraków, and when only their black tails were still visible, doors were flung open on every floor. Na zdrowie! What an operation! What logistics! Na zdrowie, the neighbors cried; Mietek has guests from Germany, and Heiner and Lena could count neither the number of hugs nor the glasses of vodka that were pressed upon them. Heiner drank until he couldn't stand up any longer. He listened to the story of the operation again and again. The idea – fantastic! The planning – perfect! The transformation – gigantic! No traitors! Modern terror gives birth to modern resistance, and the fact that he was there to experience it – Heiner cried for joy. He imagined a huge W made of light in all the windows of

Vienna: War on Fascism. Before he went to bed around three, he clung to Mietek and murmured Funkcjonowa, Funkcjonowa. I'm totally drinked, Mietek said. Tomorrow in the OR I'm going to cutlet a big "S" into everyone's bellies.

Heiner tossed his summer jacket over his shoulders. He wanted to weave one carefree day into his life: a day without heavy thoughts, just holding Lena's hand, the sun on his face, wandering aimlessly through the streets of Kraków. To start the day, he'd lifted his blood pressure out of the cellar with three double espressos.

They walked through a market hall where there was nothing to buy. They sat in a church, where there was a surplus of things that weren't for sale: songs and prayers. The eyes that met theirs welcomed them: Look at what's happening here. Tell the world. They picked up a pamphlet that the wind had swept across their path. The text consisted of only a few lines in big letters: See, Lord, how your country weeps. Strengthen the fighters, the prisoners, the oppressed, and bless Solidarność.

The big "S" with the anchor, the symbol of the military branch of the Polish Resistance, was emblazoned on street signs, sprayed quickly in red paint. The postcards they bought came from a time when the shops were full, when there were colorful window displays and the streets were packed with tourists. They would happily have bought postcards of martial law, but those didn't exist.

A group of young people were standing in front of a gallery. Ask them what's going on, Heiner said.

Dzień dobry, Lena said, hello, may I ask what you're waiting for?

We're not waiting, we're protecting the exhibition.

They pointed to two large-format photographs on an easel. The first photograph showed a man's face. His eyes were swollen and blue-black-purple, his nose was broken. The second photo showed the same man's back. It was lacerated and full of bloody welts.

Underneath was the slogan of the exhibition: Punk po Polska – Punk in Poland. My God, Lena said. The gallery owner must be tired of living. Or undaunted by death, Heiner said.

They stopped in front of a butcher shop that didn't have even the smallest piece of sausage. The white tiles gleamed, but the cases under the counter were empty. The door to the storeroom stood open so that everyone could see the empty shelves. The display window held a piece of cardboard illuminated by two naked lightbulbs. A single word was written on the sign: Nic. Nothing. It's like in Vienna. Back in the days when I was seeing red hunger-whorls.

They sat on a bench next to the Vistula. Across the river was a factory with a red chimney, from which thin white smoke was puffing into the sky. They're not very busy, otherwise the smoke would be thick and black.

Silently they watched a woman walking a dog on the bank of the Vistula. The woman picked up a stick, brought her arm far back, and flung it towards the river. For a moment they raced – stick and poodle. Then the dog stopped, watched the stick fall into the water, and didn't even consider jumping in after it. He turned to the woman, barking indignantly. She tried thin branches, thick ones, short ones – always with the same result. The stick fell in the water, and the dog sat on the bank and yapped. Smart dog, Heiner said – look how fast the Vistula's flowing. If he jumps in, it will whisk him away. Lena said: What if that's the point?

The wicked idea seemed to please him. He had no time for dogs, not even for small ones. Cats couldn't have chased Mietek into the speaking tree.

Heiner, Lena said. What was going on with the scratch on the truck?

He answered with a question: What do you hear right now?

The dog. The Vistula. Cars. An airplane. I hear you smoking.

Sounds are sneakier than words, Heiner said. Did you know that? If words remind you of something, you can ignore them or quickly push them away. But a sound you're not prepared for is a landmine. You explode – there's no protection.

I was the cause of your panic?

Look, Lena, it's a long story. It begins with my leaving Auschwitz in an SS uniform. Do you have any idea how that could have happened?

Attempted escape in a Nazi uniform?

No.

Then perhaps you became a Nazi, my treasure.

He nodded. She stared at him.

The evening before their departure, they piled ten packages in Mietek's hallway: two for him, and eight for the hospital ward where people like Zofia were taken care of when they retreated beyond the reach of the world. They needed shoes and coats, pants and sweaters, canned vegetables, coffee, tea, and honey; above all they needed painkillers and antidepressants, which were unaffordable in Poland. The dollars that Heiner and Lena had hidden in the cargo would be used to pay for additional nurses and caretakers.

On the night of their departure, Mietek brought nine potatoes and six eggs from the hospital kitchen, plus an onion, which he cut into tiny cubes. Lena peeled the potatoes and fried them – a specialty of one of her aunts from Danzig. Heiner set the table. The dish was served in tall glasses. A fried egg went on the bottom, topped by fried potatoes and onions, with the second egg sitting on top like a cover. Mietek and Heiner stabbed their forks through the eggs and potatoes and stirred until everything turned into a mushy yellow pulp. Lena stared at the table during dinner. Mietek ate like Heiner, grinding and smacking his lips: two prisoners obliviously sucking every bit of nourishment from their food.

Lena, why aren't you eating?

She pushed her glass towards the two of them. The men smashed up the pretty layers of egg and potato and shared the mush. When it got dark, Mietek dressed to go jogging, and Heiner went for a walk: the pitch-black streets were calling him. An "S" made of light on the building, and not a single snitch – what a wonderful Resistance. And the letters written next to the cars – did they carry secret messages, only understood by those in the complex? And Mietek's running in the evening, the scuffling of his shoes announcing his presence long before he was visible – was that a signal, a message, or did he really just go running because he couldn't sleep without completely exhausting himself? Punk po Polska – what a country. Welts on the man's back and a broken nose – and he, Heiner, brought packages to Poland, while his friend Mietek stood to lose his job, if not his life.

What do you think, Lena – if we lived in Poland, would I be with the people who made the big "S"?

You'd be in the first row, where else?

He poured vodka into two glasses, tossed his back like medicine, and shuddered. He lit a cigarette and searched distractedly inside himself for the story he wanted to tell, never guessing that it was the one Lena feared above all. Heiner in an SS uniform? Unthinkable. Absurd. On the other hand – after all she'd heard, what was unthinkable?

Look, Lena: Dirlewanger. It all started with a rumor that filtered into the camp from outside. It was said that they were going to transfer political prisoners from the concentration camps to the special "Dirlewanger" brigade. Dirlewanger, we thought then, it can't get worse than that. The special brigade, the Sonderregiment, you have to understand, was comprised of criminal SS men, who were sent on parole to the most dangerous fronts, and since no one survived long, the unit had to be replenished with another kind of "criminal": Prisoners who were Aryan citizens of the Reich.

Two months after the rumors started, Heiner received a red slip of paper with his number: 63 387, a date: Tuesday, November 7, 1944, and a command: Five o'clock, at the camp gate! How often he'd dreamed of being freed, of how he'd leave the camp forever with his head held high. The dream was so graphic that he could feel the camp road under his shoes. And then there he was, standing with a hundred and fifty men in the icy wind at the camp gate, a Schutzhäftling with two letters: R.U. The commandant stood before them. Men, this is your chance! You can repair the damage you've done to the fatherland. You're all volunteers – no one will be forced, and whoever doesn't want to take this opportunity – the commander took his pistol out of the holster and held it pointed diagonally towards the ground, a gesture they knew well: a shot in the back of the head. No one came forward. They marched smartly from the camp to where the SS uniforms were stored. There, Heiner had to take off the hated prisoner's uniform, never imagining that he would soon long for his favorite suit! He put on the uniform of his tormentors – it burned, like a suit of barbed wire on his bare skin.

Dirlewanger – what did they know about Dirlewanger back then? That he was a dyed-in-the-wool Nazi, an officer, a member of the Waffen-SS, that he'd been sent to jail for shooting a superior officer in a fight. They didn't know the worst of it.

After the war, Heiner collected everything that had been written about the man. When the war began, Dirlewanger wasn't yet forty. He'd studied political science, gotten a doctorate, and then was sent to jail for two years for raping a thirteen year-old girl. During the war he devised his own "pleasures." He threw parties and had people beaten to death in front of his guests. He gave female prisoners strychnine and invited his guests to watch their death throes. In Belarus he burned seven hundred villages to the ground and prevented the inhabitants from fleeing. He used men, women, and children as mine-detectors. He was a highly decorated officer. He was given the "German Cross in Gold" for his valiance in the fight against the partisans.

Heiner poured more vodka and said: Drink with me, Lena. It's just water with extra flavor.

In the winter of 1944, one hundred and fifty Aryan German prisoners were taken from Auschwitz to the Dirlewanger special brigade. Destination: death. A train took them to Kraków for a brief military training, then they were transferred to northern Slovakia. From there, the disguised prisoners marched to the Hungarian-Slovakian border – about thirty miles a day. At first glance: One hundred and sixty Nazis. The difference was only obvious when you looked closely. The men stumbling and vomiting in their uniforms were Nazi impersonators. The uniformed men shooting the weakest in the column were the real Nazis.

Hold on. Stay alive. He'd promised Martha – he'd sworn three holy oaths: Hold on. Stay alive. Come back. Franz, a German from Hungary who spoke Czech, marched next to Heiner. At the Slovakian-Hungarian border they were led up a 6 500-foot mountain. Shovels were pressed into their hands and the order given was: Dig! Once they were down in the holes, guns were handed out – a glorious feeling, Lena, can you imagine? Joy tingling through every finger. Karabiner 98k's. Shapely cartridges shimmering in the chamber, index fingers crooked on the trigger – power in our hands, finally. Look, Lena – We looked around, Franz and I, we looked around carefully. Before us we saw meadows with big snowdrifts, to our right was a small forest. We heard machine-gun fire, and shells exploding in the distance; we were there to fight Slovakian partisans. Franz and I thought: Our chance is coming. After a few days in the holes, the commander said: We need a reconnaissance team – Volunteers come forward. Franz and I shot out of our holes like rockets. One SS man came along to guard us. At the first sound of the partisans, Franz yelled in Czech: Don't shoot! We're coming! We're prisoners from Auschwitz! We have an SS man with us! Sturmbannführer Kruse had no choice – we would have killed him if he hadn't come with us. The partisans took him away and we never saw him again. They interrogated us for hours. Why are you wearing Nazi uniforms? Yes, why? Long story. Why don't you have numbers on your arms? Aryan German prisoners don't get tattooed. Where did you get the weapons? From the Nazis. What do you mean, from the Nazis? Where are your pay books? We showed them. Are you Jews? No, Communists. What's the name of our partisan leader? Tito. First name? Josip Broz.

They were given bread and cheese, and the same questions were asked again: Where did you get the uniforms? And the weapons? Show us your arms – where's the number? German prisoners, Schutzhäftlinge, don't get tattooed. What's a Schutzhäftling? You don't have numbers? On the contrary. 63 378 and 52 419. Good. They were assigned to a troop of five partisans charged with tracking down the Dirlewanger brigade. With the partisans, Heiner was no longer afraid of death.

They heard the apartment door, Mietek panting and spluttering under the shower; he came into the kitchen and sat down with Heiner and Lena. Don't mind me. No opowiedz. Go on with the story.

One afternoon in March 1944, the troop approached a valley where the Dirlewanger brigade had been sighted. The air was cold and clear. A dog howled, they heard the soft tinkling of sheep bells, and then there was another sound: a screeching noise that stopped suddenly, began again, then stopped. To Heiner it sounded like a carpenter at work. Fearing an ambush, they hid behind trees and entered the clearing only when no more light came from the valley. They watched the workshop through binoculars. No one left the building and no one entered it; all the houses in the valley appeared deserted – they heard only the dog and the sheep. They approached the workshop with guns cocked. Something sinister lurked in the building, Heiner could feel it with every step he took. It seemed like even the leaves were holding their breath – as if the whole valley was in shock. When they got to the workshop, the leader of the partisans pointed at Franz: You. Tentatively, he opened the door, took a few steps inside, then rushed back out screaming and heaving, unable to utter a word. The leader, a stoic man who had never quite trusted the two Germans, pointed to Heiner. Now you.

He entered the building as if it were a minefield. It was dim inside the workshop; he stood in the entrance, allowing his eyes to get used to the half-light. A bit of light fell on the floor through two hatches in the roof, and he saw an icon that had been split in two. He still remembered it as clearly as if he'd spent a whole day looking at it, instead of a few seconds. The top half consisted of a round face with black eyes, a long, straight nose, and puckered, childlike lips. A halo surrounded the head. On the lower part of the icon, he saw a bright red garment from whose wide sleeves slender arms protruded, the hands folded in prayer. The most remarkable part, however, was that swords were growing out of the hands: three from the right hand, four from the left. The image stayed with him. Many years later he had the meaning explained to him. The swords symbolized the seven sorrows of Mary, mother of God. The flight into Egypt. The search for Jesus, lost in the desert. His capture. The way to the cross. The crucifixion, the descent from the cross, and the entombment. Heiner wished he could have stayed there looking at the icon, in order not to have to see what Franz had seen, though he'd already smelled it – the dull sweetness had already crept into his nose. He took two steps into the workshop and looked to the right – then rushed out screaming and vomiting as Franz had before him.

Look, Lena, Heiner said. When I hear something that reminds

me of the sawing noise in the valley, the images attack me like hyenas. He lit a cigarette and watched the smoke rising towards the lamp. Words I can keep at arm's length, Lena, but not sounds.

Mietek broke the silence: There's cottage cheese and plum jam – something sweet can't hurt. He knew the story. He finished the story between the living room and the kitchen to spare his friend: The carpenter, his wife, two children, and the assistants – they'd been killed and sawed up.

Quickly, Heiner explained how Oscar Dirlewanger had met his end: prisoner of war in France. Recognized by prisoners and killed. Buried in Germany. Rumors: Dirlewanger was Nasser's bodyguard in Egypt. Disinterment and examination of the corpse in 1960. It was him. That was good news.

Lena steered the "Red" to the side of the road. Time for a break. They stretched, bent their knees – they felt the truck in every bone. Heiner pointed to the valley below – what a nice little town. Lena took out the guidebook: Nowy Targ. German name: Neumarkt. County seat, 30 000 inhabitants. Between 1251 and 1254, Bolesław V allowed the Cistercians to settle here. City destroyed in the Polish-Swedish war. Plague in 1710, visit by Pope John Paul II on June 8, 1979. The furriers of Nowy Targ make the best fur coats and leather jackets in Poland. Do you know Radevormwald?

Why?

Nowy Targ's sister city, Lena read, is the German town of Radevormwald. Where's that?

Between Herbeck and Uelfe.

How do you know that?

That's where Kaduk is supposed to have lived after he was released.

Heiner looked dreamily out over the little town in the valley. You know what? Let's drive to Nowy Targ and buy leather jackets! Lena said: You're nuts. They rummaged through all the jackets the stores had to offer, discussed size and color and price, argued over smooth leather and suede, tried on twenty different jackets – they were in high spirits, carefree. Smooth and black were out of the question for Heiner – no Nazi jackets, not in Poland. Lena found red too flashy, green too noxious, blue too cold, yellow too clownish, and for Heiner's sake she rejected black as well. They chose two soft brown leather jackets, which they named "Stag-Jesus Jackets" in honor of Heiner's uncanny encounter. In German, that gave them the initials HJ, like Hitler Jugend – they had to keep a sense of humor. They wore the HJ jackets in summer and winter, and it always made them think of the valley and the nice little town of Nowy Targ.

The sun shone into the cab of the truck, the landscape was gentle and powerful at the same time, the air was mild like good wheat vodka. They rolled down the windows and stuck their arms into the warm wind. Why vacation in the South Pacific when the sun shines in Poland, too?

The event began at eight. The Polish boy scout association had invited Heiner's friend and comrade to speak, in honor of the association of German boy scouts, and his name was written in big letters on the flyer. Stanislaw Piontek, 23 153. Lena understood. Camp nobility. Second or third transport, December 1941 – approximately three years at Auschwitz. But in a place where one could lose one's life at any moment, approximate calculations don't suffice. Stan Piontek had survived 1 136 days in Auschwitz.

The stage of the parish hall was lined with black velvet, and was far too large for the dainty table, the spartan chair, the reading lamp – the furniture looked as if it belonged in a dollhouse. The hall, as well, was too big for the sixty scouts and their chaperones – every third chair was empty. Heiner and Lena sat in the first row. Heiner looked forward to his comrade's performance – he was proud of this friendship. Stan was 40 225 numbers ahead of him. The boy scouts seemed cheerful until the lights went out and suddenly a man appeared on the stage – no one had seen him enter, he'd come quietly through a hidden door. His body threw a long shadow across the stage, and the audience was scared into silence.

Stanislaw Piontek was a stocky man with wild white curly hair. In his right hand he carried a battered briefcase, like an employee on his way to the office. He bowed, and the young people clapped. What are you applauding for? he said harshly, freezing their hands in mid-air. He took a microphone out of the briefcase and checked the sound: One-two, one-two, one-two-three. Then he pointedly tipped the chair against the table. He would not be doing the show from a seated position.

Dear audience!

As you hear, I speak German. I use microphone because I am hoarse always. You want to know how I learned German? I tell you: through singing.

German songs, Lena thought. They were part of their lives as much as being kicked and beaten.

Stan Piontek took a step back from the table and stood alone in the middle of the big stage. With the strength of a whole chorus, he sang: In Auschwitz camp is where I was/Holleries and Holleras!/But thinking of dear ones far away!/Makes me feel so glad and gay/Every morning with the sun/is our hard day's work begun/Driv'n by work or even sport/a happy song is our report/ Yet we know there'll come the day/when from Schutzhaft we'll away/Then happ'ly we'll go to our homes/ne'er again from there to roam!

Dear audience!

For a moment Lena worried that he would force the audience to sing the song with him. But he just began walking slowly from one side of the stage to the other. Sixty-five feet there, sixty-five feet back – a human pendulum.

I want to tell, he said, what can happen when a person in Auschwitz run away from his Arbeitskommando. Understand? He didn't wait for an answer. When a person flee, he said, the Kapo roars: Company fall in! Everybody throws tools away and runs to muster.

Lena didn't know how often Heiner's friend had performed here before. He knew how to make the most of the creepy space, he used it perfectly. When he wandered to the farthest part of the stage, he was almost invisible – swallowed up by the velvet curtains. Then it was just white hair crossing the stage, accompanied by his voice.

Dear audience!

When somebody run away, whole landscape, every shrub, every bush, every ditch is checked. The Blockführer and Lagerälteste call name and number of missing one for minutes on end. In the story I tell, Lagerkommant Höss appears personally, which cannot be good. Silently, standing stiff at attention, we wait for the bad thing that will happen. Höss orders his flunkies choose from people in our Arbeitskommando: You and you and you and you, randomly, no matter who it is. They haul six comrades in Block 1. Poor comrades. SS men open windows, we're supposed to hear. Have to listen to the whistling of the bull whip and the shrill cries of people being hit. It goes on for an hour. Dear audience, imagine it: Being hit for an hour with a bull whip!

Look at your watches!

It was an order, and everyone in the hall obeyed. Those who didn't have a watch looked at his neighbor's. Stan Piontek walked down to the very front of the stage and opened his pocket watch. He let the audience stare at his watch for sixty endless seconds. Then he resumed his pacing back and forth across the stage.

Dear audience, that was only a minute – imagine sixty. Then the torturers come out looking tired and satisfied and have new plan. They ask, cool and mischievous: Who slept in same room as man who ran away? Two people raise their hands. An old man and a boy my age – eighteen, maybe. They're beaten half to death before our eyes but can't confess anything, because they know nothing from escape. Then comes the Kommandant again and threatens: If someone doesn't come forward soon who knew about the escape, every tenth person gets it. He takes out his revolver and holds it pointed diagonally at the ground, bang, shot in the back of the head. German language is nice language, dear audience.

Gets it! Like a prize!

When Höss threatens to shoot, you don't have doubt, you can believe, it will come true. We stand stiff as tree trunks for seven hours at muster. No water, no food. Muscles fail, legs swell. Anyone who goes in his pants gets an extra beating. Then night comes and we look longingly at stars and moon. They are our stars, it is our moon. It is our earth, where they are torturing us. What did we do? Why do they do this? As morning dawns, more and more men lose consciousness. We stand for sixteen hours. Suddenly Höss changes plan. No one will be shot, torture is over. But the eight prisoners suspected of helping the escapee will go starvation bunker of Block 11, whether they're guilty or not – no matter.

Sometimes Heiner's friend stopped in the middle of the stage and lifted his head, as if listening to something inside himself, as if checking to make sure he wasn't crazy, that he wasn't holding forth on some fever dream, that everything he was telling them had actually occurred. Several times he hit his forehead with the flat of his left hand, as if he couldn't believe the madness he was recounting. Once he leaned on the table. His hands lay under the light of the reading lamp as if the ten white fingers and microphone were the only things on stage.

Dear audience, do you want to know how it goes in a starvation bunker?

He waited. But for what? Were they supposed to nod? Say, "yes, please!"? Were they allowed to say "no"? He was going to tell the story – he'd prepared to tell them, and if Lena didn't want to hear it, she'd have to leave the hall. But a man like Stanislaw

Piontek was quite capable of calling across the room: Madam, am I boring you? And then? She'd have to say: It's not boredom, Herr Piontek, it's horror. If a cell is called the "starvation cell," you already know what happens there. Lena remained sitting, as did everyone, and by the end of the presentation, everyone knew that the words "starvation cell" didn't begin to convey what really happened there.

To Stan Piontek, silence meant consent. He continued wandering back and forth over the creaking stage.

Starvation cell has no window, he said. Is dark. We sit on the concrete floor and get used to the grey light. In the ceiling is little opening, where a bit of light comes through. We are three Poles. Two from Warsaw, me from Bydgoszcz. Two Czechs from Prague; I don't remember where the Russians are from. The German comes from Lüdenscheid, young guy, we call him Lüdenscheid because we find it funny. We are silent. There is not much for to say. This is the end of eight people, and you can believe it, if Höss said it. How long does starving take? Lüdenscheid asks. Five days? Six? Seven, eight? Thirst is worse, I say. Before we die we'll go crazy. Is there hope? asks one of the Russians. No one answers; there are no miracles in the camp. One of the Czechs ask: What can we do so they'll shoot us? I say: Nothing. Sentence is starvation, sentence is not death by shooting. My Polish comrade says: Let's kill each other. I ask: How? He says: Strangling. I say: And who strangles the last one? He says: He strangles himself. We laugh like crazy.

How long are we without eating, without drinking? Already sixteen hours standing at muster – and then come a grey endlessness without night or day. Lüdenscheid calls for his mommy. He's seventeen. I take him in my arms, dear audience, and while I rock him like a baby, I dream of fresh water, a huge roast, white bread with butter and ham. My pharynx spasms, my saliva thickens, my lips are cracking and hot as glow and I know it will get worse. At some point the older Czech begins to talk about his wife. Very quiet, very tender – he conjures an angel in the starvation bunker. His comrades fold their hands. He says long prayer I don't understand, but it's beautiful, like a song. Fever begins, thirst hurts, but now we are seized with the need to tell stories from our life, good stories of love and happiness.

Dear audience!

The first one to lose his nerve is the Russian who'd asked about hope. Suddenly he starts banging the door with his fists and calling the Kommandant. Höss! Höss! Höss! What do you want from Höss? Lüdenscheid asks. Kill him, screamed the Russian, kill everyone, put all of Germany in the gas chamber, shut the door and that's it for Auschwitz. You do that, Lüdenscheid says, but spare me, at least. We can still laugh a little. The Czech who had conjured the angel into cell has a black triangle on his jacket, not a red one like us Communists. He's an Aso, an Asocial prisoner, no one knows what Aso means for the Nazis. A sweet guy – maybe he'd just stolen a piece of bread. On the third night the Russian who'd wanted to kill all Germans spits blood. His body seizes and cramps.

The hall was still, as if everyone had forgotten to breathe.

Dear audience, I tell you end. My Polish countrymen tear shoes in pieces and make eight little piles. They've heard that you can extend your life by chewing leather. Everyone has heard it, but I don't believe it, I don't touch the piles. Little Lüdenscheid lies in a corner like a corpse, sees, feels nothing. It doesn't take long, then they vomit, the ones who chewed the leather. They have terrible pains, they scream and writhe like worms. That night my Polish friend dies in agony. Our first casualty. Then the Russian loses it. He hits his head against wall, foams at the mouth. My head whirls and roars, I can't tell who's alive, who's not. Always the grey light. I can feel death taking me into its arms. It's fine, I think, it should be this way – they sent the father to the gas before your very eyes, where the mother is, you don't know, should take me too, death, should bring me to my father. All is peaceful, all is still, I'm float-ing away, it's all over. Dying is beautiful.

Stan Piontek stopped in the middle of the stage. He looked out into the audience, letting his gaze sweep from the first row to the last, so that everyone had the feeling that he was looking at them personally, even Lena, though she told herself that the man on stage couldn't possibly make out a single face: the footlights blinded him.

Dear audience!

I was already up with my father in heaven when I heard familiar command. "Get up, dalli, dalli, you pigs, you dirty fucking Polish intelligentsia!" What horror: Is heaven full of Nazis too? No, only Gestapo visiting from Berlin. Dalli, dalli, the cellar must be clean. Visitors mustn't find bodies covered in their own vomit and shit in starvation cell. Kapos cleaned away our six dead quickly. Little Lüdenscheid and I were carried to our blocks like trophies, they cared for us like babies. We were a sensation! Two people who sur-vived the starvation bunker! Stan and Lüdenscheid. History must be rewritten – there are miracles in Auschwitz.

Stan Piontek put the microphone back in the briefcase. He said "any questions" in a way that did not invite questions. Before the silence in the hall grew too heavy, Heiner stood, introduced himself as prisoner 63 387, and said: Stan, my friend, tell us what you've done since the liberation.

Stanislaw Piontek looked out into the hall as if he had to consider the request, but he knew exactly what he wanted to say. He sat down on the chair, clicked open the briefcase, took the microphone back out and said, as if the sentence had just occurred to him: Dear audience, I'd like to introduce you to the five Stans.

The first one he introduced was twenty years old in 1945. He wandered for days through his hometown of Bydgoszcz before he dared to knock on his parents' door. He didn't expect to find anyone alive. But then he heard steps, a key in the lock, and was shocked by the face of the woman that greeted him. Treblinka. Bergen Belsen. Dachau. Ravensbrück. His mother had survived four concentration camps. She was a skeleton – just like the young man standing in front of her, a man she didn't recognize, a man who frightened her.

The second Stan was Stanislaw the schoolboy, who had already learned all the lessons there were to learn about life, but now studied old books to prepare for his exams. Geography. History. Geometry. Literature. Music. Sports.

The third Stan, the student, gave up his studies in disgust at twenty-one, because he found the questions of his chosen discipline, Philosophy – about the meaning of life, good and evil, right and wrong – just perverse.

The fourth Stan was between twenty-five and thirty: a gluttonous omnivore would couldn't get enough, who spent five years boozing and smoking and womanizing and wanted nothing more than to keep vomiting.

The fifth had had enough of life. He longed for a rope or a revolver, but before the end he wanted to eat and drink his fill. Because that required money, he'd applied to be an extra in the theatre – they were looking for people to play prisoners, and he thought he might try his hand. After the first rehearsal he knew that the stage was the paradise he'd been searching for. An angel today, a devil tomorrow, sometimes a king, sometimes a beggar.

He could be a different person every day, and when he really wanted to, he could perform his own text.

Stanislaw Piontek stood up. He put the microphone in the briefcase and closed it. He leaned the chair against the table. He took a bow.

Dear audience, thank you for listening.

A city made of wood is a living thing: it can breathe in and out, groan, moan, and sigh. When the night wind whistles through the valley, the houses draw in on themselves, freezing, and when the sun rises over the mountains in the morning, they stretch, relax, and sprawl. That night, Zakopane froze.

They walked the short way back to the hotel in silence: a man and a woman in stag-brown leather jackets, and a gentleman with a coat, hat, and briefcase. After the performance, Stan Piontek had turned gentle, leaving his armor in the props box. He was in as high spirits as if he'd just starred in a play. Heiner knew that after only a short pause, his friend could act the whole "play" again, in just the same way he'd done it the first time. In the same words, with the same controlled emotions, the same dramatic wandering across the stage, the same five Stans.

The plan was to end the evening with a "Wässerchen." Drink, Lena, Heiner said – show our friend what you've learned in Poland. Lena sipped at the glass. The "Wässerchen" wasn't sweet, as if made from molasses, nor heavy, as if from potatoes, nor quite as smooth and gentle as if from grapes – it was a good, full wheat vodka; Stan and Heiner drank coffee alongside. Lena had had enough for one evening; she didn't want to hear any more stories, she wanted to sleep. After the first glass she stood up and bade the men good night, but Stan stopped her with his seductive actor's voice: *And wilt thou, faithless one, then, leave me, with all thy magic phantasy, with all the thoughts that joy or grieve me, wilt thou with all forever fly?* He kissed her hand and sat her back down in her chair. Vodka, my little dove, cures stage fright and heartache. Above all, you need to hear how Heiner and I met. Do you want to hear? He didn't wait for her answer.

Heiner's friends were like Heiner. Charming, authoritarian, and used to getting their way. They wanted closeness, affection, attention, and time, and they used their painful past to demand their due: affection, closeness, attention, and time. Heiner, too, knew how to plead and beg: Lena, my treasure, stay a little while longer – there are worse things than a night without sleep. Two hours later they were still sitting around the coffee table, which now held two empty vodka bottles. The men couldn't find a good place to stop – nor could there be one, since every story had a prequel, which could only be understood if one also knew the story that came before that. For Heiner, Auschwitz was an ocean of stories, and that night Lena was bobbing on it like a paper boat. Stan raised his glass: Na zdrowie. Look, Lena, Heiner said, just one more pretty little goodnight story. He knew the allure of his voice and the power of his eyes. He didn't wait for Lena to answer – he gave his story a title that made it impossible for her to leave. Look, Lena: October '42.

Picture a beautiful Sunday. Free time at Auschwitz. In the Stammlager, the main camp, thirty thousand people are humming and buzzing around the blocks; the place has all the clamor and bustle of a fairground, and right in the thick of it I see a man I know from Vienna – Gustl, a friend from the underground. And he sees me: he laughs, he's happy, he opens his arms and cries: Ah, Heiner, how nice to see you! What are you doing here? I can't help but laugh and say: Oh, Gustl, what a dumb question – what am I doing here? The same as you. I'm going for a walk. When he finds out that I'm in the road-building Arbeitskommando, he's horrified: Holy shit, you won't last fourteen days there! How long have you been here? Thirteen, I say, and I learn what it means to have comrades in this place. Meet me in an hour, Gustl says, and runs away and…well…about an hour later he comes back and says: Look, I have a great idea. Can you type? No. Doesn't matter, Gustl says – at evening muster talk to Stani in the infirmary in Block 21. He's a nice Polish guy, Stani – a comrade from Bydgoszcz, he's practically a saint, he survived the starvation block – tell him Gustl from Vienna says hello and tell him that you can type.

Type? Type what?

Death notices, he says, it's not hard – and he disappears into the crowd.

And so from Stan, Heiner learned how to write on a black rattletrap called ORGA. At first his hands hung helplessly above the keys, his eyes scanned the letters, and when they found what they were looking for, he'd press the key down carefully with his index finger: Stan deemed his first attempts suicidally slow, and taught Heiner the "Prisoner beats Nazi" system. A quick circling over the keyboard, lightning-fast descent to the desired keys with at least two fingers at a time, shrewd distribution of labor: The left hand takes twenty three Nazis, the right twenty two, the thumbs take care of the space bar. If you want to survive here, said Stan, you have to type blind – you're typing for your life. By the end of the first shift Heiner's fingers understood that they had to shoot down at the keys with the force of an avenger, and after a week, Heiner's typewriter chattered away as if he'd been typing out quotas of death notices all his life. There are some places where one learns faster than elsewhere. Stan poured – I promise, Lena – one final Wässerchen, and Heiner smoked – I promise, Lena – one last cigarette.

Perhaps a Wässerchen can cure heartache and stage fright, but it has no power over stories from Stanislaw Piontek and Heiner Rosseck. Lena was as sober as if the vodka was made of water.

They'd been given the nicest room. A canopy bed fit for a king, a chandelier with fake candles, wine-red plush armchairs, and a mirrored wall that turned the room into a great hall and Lena into a red-eyed dwarf. She stood at the window and soaked in the cold night air. No lights burned, the city slept; the boy scouts had been picked up by bus after the performance. Snow lay on the mountains that surrounded Zakopane; a big "W" sparkled in the heavens. If you find Cassiopeia in the night sky, you get to make a wish. Lena said: Cassiopeia, grant Heiner and his friends a long life, and let them always have good vodka.

When she lay down, she was no longer tired.

Heiner?

He lay atop the covers, fully clothed and fast asleep. Heiner, Lena whispered, where inside you is the archive where you store your memories? She took his shoes off. You and your friends change the stories, you rewrite them, every time you tell them, they're different, do you know that? She unbuttoned his shirt. If a book makes me cry, and I read it ten times, it stops making me cry – is that why you change the stories? She took off his pants. Do you do it for yourselves, rather than for others? Are you trying to save your grief?

Heiner?

She took his socks off. The idea that Heiner and his friends would take the universe in their heads with them to the grave was monstrous. They wrote down what they remembered, they spoke into microphones, yet what they'd experienced was not the same as what could be read or heard later. Their memories ought to be made into vaccines, to prevent the illnesses that had caused them.

Heiner?

How would the world look if memories could be given as injections? He breathed deeply and calmly. She listened to his heartbeat until she, too, fell asleep.

Stan knew his friend, and his aversion to goodbyes; he opened his arms. *No word, not even the slightest, can keep the full blow from the heart; the hour is heavy, the coach stands ready.* Lena started the truck, Stan waved and called "See you later," until they could no longer hear his voice, though they still saw his mouth forming the words.

Always this damn "See you later," Heiner said. Where, my friend? In what country, beside whose grave?

III

When the birds grow restless and the day comes to an end, he takes out two tall glasses and makes the cocktail that Leszek brings to his aunt at the same time of day. "Zofia's Medicine" is made with a few drops of raspberry syrup, three tablespoons of crushed ice, a large fresh mint leaf, and a generous shot of vodka. When the ice crackles, he calls upstairs: Sundowner, my treasure. If he hears nothing, he calls again, louder, and waits until he hears Lena's assenting grumble from the study. The twilight between sunset and darkness has become their most intimate time of day. Fifty minutes of unwritten poetry, Lena says. Usually they're silent; sometimes they speak a sentence that needs no answer, since it's barely more than a thought said aloud. Heiner's favorite thing is to close his eyes and listen to the most beautiful music he can imagine. The plover's high voice and the cheeping of the oystercatcher, punctuated by the short calls of sheldrakes, mourning doves, and gray geese, the coloratura of the black-headed gulls and herring gulls, the yearning song of the gliding swans. He thinks of his friend in Poland. *Fearless that it will rebound, soft's the nightingale's sound.*

Whispering, Lena tests the sound of the translation she's working on. First in German, then in Polish, then again in German, she murmurs the beginning of the novel she knows by heart, this endless sentence with its peculiar, faraway sound, as if it's spoken from a faded memory:

"The story that I have to tell was first made known to me a good half-century ago in the house of my great-grandmother, old Mrs Feddersen, the senator's wife. I learned of it as I sat in my easy chair and busied myself with reading some old magazines that were bound in blue cardboard; I can't now remember whether they were issues of the Leipziger *or the* Hamburger Lesefrüchten…"

There's one sentence that comes up a lot: Look, this light. They'd discovered it in the springtime, but it's present in every season, in every kind of weather. The color of the rain changes when the night sneaks in, white mist turns gray – even the birds perceive the end of the sunset hour. They squeal like children who don't want to go to bed – that's Heiner's signal. The glasses are empty, he puts on his soft-soled shoes and leaves the house. Lena brings the glasses into the kitchen and goes to her study. As always, Heiner says: I'm not taking the keys – you'll be here, and begins his circuit, which he'd undertaken sullenly at first, like a slave, but now without a walk there's a hole in his day. Why don't you go the other way sometime, Lena had said during their first year there, go right instead of left, first to the mound and then to the water, or not to the mound or the water at all, but to the fish pond or along the canal – you're a free man, you're not taking laps around the prison yard.

He nods and goes to the right, along the lane through the fields that leads to the water, as always. Those who change their path too often don't see enough, he says. Only by walking on the same path every day can you understand where you really are. The sea draws him, yet remains alien. It changes its color and tempera- ment according to mood and whim, sometimes hourly. It's as tame as a puddle by the side of the road, it rumbles like heavy thunder, swings through every nuance in between, and sometimes it's not even there – then it's low tide. He finds the sea's diversity uncanny – you can't rely on the sea; nonetheless, it's always the first stop on his evening walk. He stands on the dike, face to the wind, and takes care to breath in deeply and out even more deeply, as Mietek ordered; he thinks of his lungs and of the large and small bronchia, and turns away from the water to walk along the arrow-straight path to the mound, where the changes don't force themselves upon him; here the changes have to be discovered – they're small and precious, like the ants in Olga's amber. Just as Olga sees the past in the delicate filaments of plants, Heiner can see the future in the present. He has never lost this way of seeing: Look closely, learn the structure, don't overlook the little changes – they can take on great importance. His head slightly down, his step as steady and patient as a hiker's, he takes the same path every day through the fresh air that Mietek prescribed for him. His hands are clasped behind his back – a message for Lena, in case she looks out the window: Look, empty hands, I'm not smoking.

The fact that he lives in the North, a place he never felt particularly drawn to, is the result of a birthday present that arrived unexpectedly, unwrapped, which gave everyone a shock – everyone except him. The gift was given to him by Mietek at Schloss Tulbing near Vienna, by the friend who'd come all the way from Nowa Huta, and really wanted nothing more than to raise a light-hearted glass to Heiner's seventieth birthday. The castle belonged to Heiner's friend and comrade Salomon, whose prisoner number – 63 140 – Heiner knew as well as his own. Salomon had worked with him in the typing room, and had arrived on the same transport; his Schutzhaftbefehl, too, contained the letters RU. In all this they were twins, sharing the crazy luck of having survived. Heiner and Lena had celebrated their tenth wedding anniversary at Salomon's castle, and they were again his guests for Heiner's seventieth birthday, because Heiner had saved Salomon's life, which Heiner denied, saying it was the other way around, which Salomon then denied. They celebrated Heiner's three lives. The "before" had lasted twenty-two years, the life "there" lasted forever, and the life "after" consisted on his seventieth birthday of forty-five years, twenty-five of them with Lena. Rose petals lay on the white tablecloths, tall candles stood in silver candelabra, Heiner wore a white suit and Lena a long, black dress. Lena's friends were there, including Olga, all the way from Gdańsk. Of Heiner's friends, only Kosta was missing; "the Eagle" had sent a brief note: Too much to do, the political situation – two excuses in one sentence. The band played a wild combination of Mozart, Strauss, and songs from the Polish Resistance. In his speech, Leszek called Heiner the most deadly serious and dead-funniest person he knew, and ended with a greeting from Aunt Zofia: *This is no sanatorium, this is a German penal company.* The Poles laughed – they knew Leszek's Aunt Zofia and the bedroom landscape that brought her peace. They clinked their vodka glasses. Na zdrowie. *This is no sanatorium...* Heiner noticed the bewildered faces of their German friends, but made no attempt to explain survivors' humor. There is a laughter nobody can join without having lived through what Heiner had. Mietek embedded his declaration of love to his friend in two camp songs. Dear Lola, he sang, and: One, two, three, four – "Girl with a bob." Tadek told of the praying bush that had kept him in Birkenau, and Stan took the microphone from his scuffed briefcase and recited Ringelnatz's "The Great Bird." He'd found the line that Leszek, as a young messenger in the Underground, was supposed to say to an unknown woman in an unknown stairwell, without knowing the poem it came from. *The nightingale – a captured bird/No longer could her song be heard/People threatened, tickled, bid/'Gale sang not/till she was hid in the darkest cellar without light/Locked in/Unheard, all alone, fearless that it will rebound, she sang/not/'Gale died softly, underground.*

That evening Lena discovered something that vexed her. The stories Heiner's friends told were beginning to unravel. They were starting to break free of the people they belonged to; they mingled and supplemented each other. One day Aunt Zofia would be in one of Stan's stories – Stan, who had never met Zofia, but would be convinced he'd been there when she was beaten. One day Heiner would tell of the starvation bunker as if he'd been there, and Leszek would speak of the speaking tree, as if he'd sat upon its cracking branch instead of Mietek, screaming his number to the skies. Was that theft? Were the stories owned jointly, so that none of them could ever be forgotten? They said "Auschwitz" less and less frequently. They called the place where they'd become friends simply "there."

Lena wanted to give a humorous account of her marriage to a man who lived in three worlds, but as she was considering when might be the best time, Heiner tapped his glass with a dessert spoon and stood. I'm not going to offer thanks for this party in a castle, he said. I want to remind us all that we would have died of laughter, if I'd said back there that I'd be inviting you to celebrate my seventieth birthday in Salomon's castle. I can hear the laugher: Salomon's going to have a castle? Where? A castle in the sky? If I had talked about a party in Vienna with living friends, you would have said I was crazy. They clapped, called out "RU!" and laughed. Salomon has a castle in the sky and a castle on the earth! Heiner took a sip of water and propped himself up on the table with both hands. He coughed.

Heiner, are you OK?

Lena saw Mietek get up. He was a doctor, he saw that the pause was too long.

I don't want, Heiner said, his voice strong again, I don't want to talk too long, and first of all I'd like to just – he smiled at the "just" and looked at Lena – just in the sense of solely, declare my love to this woman. She was my angel thirty years ago, when I sank to the floor in the courthouse hallway. Lena jumped up.

Heiner!

He wheezed, struggled for air, took gasping breaths in, but

barely any air came back out. Mietek gave the commands: Open the windows! Don't panic! No one smoke! He sat his friend down on a chair, positioned like a coachman, with his upper-body bent over. Salomon called a doctor.

Mietek, Lena cried, what's wrong with him?

It's a classic asthma attack – does this happen often?

Never this bad before.

Look at the dogs, Heiner whispered, they're laughing.

Yes, Mietek said, that's not unusual, they're always laughing.

Heiner clutched at his throat.

He stared through the open window into the night. The tree there – he ran toward the tree as fast as he could, he heard the dogs chuckling behind him, they were laughing at him, they were going to catch him, they didn't have to hurry, it was a game, their game, much more fun than fetching sticks for their master. Every dog has his day. Later he remembered thinking this stupid saying. A dog in boots stood at the camp gate, waving him through; the pack kept their distance, prolonging the game, and no wonder. The faster he ran, the farther away the tree was, as if it too were fleeing the dogs. Or was it fleeing him? Was the tree already occupied, or didn't it want to shelter anyone else? He stopped; he gave up. Why fight? At that very moment, Mietek's hand hurled him with incredible force up to the top of the tree. He wanted to call out his number, but he'd forgotten it, he yelled any numbers he could think of, and he heard Mietek's voice: Calm down, my friend, don't be scared, you can say your number later. The voice came from far away, and it was right. Everything was OK: Mietek had thrown him into the heavens; down below, the dogs were laughing, and above, they laughed until they cried at this unbounded, senseless landscape.

When he awoke, the sun was shining on the bedspread. Mietek sat on his right, Lena on his left. Mietek held Heiner's right hand, Lena held his left. Both wore white coats. Heiner smiled, once again almost scornfully.

What's this game called?

Before he could say anything else, Mietek said: You're going to take a break, Heiner Rosseck, listen to me carefully now, understand? Heiner looked at Lena. She was pale, and her eyes were small – in the white coat she looked like a tear-stained head doctor.

That was close, last night, Mietek said. That could have been the end.

You threw me up to heaven, why didn't we stay there?

You're not going to slip away like that, my friend. Not on your seventieth birthday, not without a speech, not without a declaration of love.

Didn't I give the speech?

You started, but then you lit a cigarette, stared at the table, wheezed and coughed and gasped for air, and then you collapsed like a limp balloon. That was only a moderate asthma attack, and not your first, am I right?

Heiner nodded.

Mietek began a severe lecture on breathing, on the lungs and their function. They're good for more than just taking deep drags. He described them as a tree, and called the windpipe the trunk and the bronchia the branches and twigs, which would wither and dry up if they didn't get enough oxygen. He talked of whistling breath, tightness in the chest, pain, lack of air, attacks of suffocation, and fainting spells, and recommended sea air.

But my heart is strong, Heiner said.

How many coronaries?

Three.

Four, Lena said.

How long has he had this cough?

As long as I've known him.

Coughing is the body's way of sending a message, Mietek said, a warning. How many cigarettes per day?

Twenty, Heiner said, sometimes fewer.

Forty, Lena said, sometimes more.

Everyone has to die of something, Heiner said.

So you're going to die of asthma?

If that's the plan.

The plan! Whose plan? Suffocation isn't a pretty way to die, my friend.

Then how do you want to die? Heiner asked.

As if he'd been waiting for the question, Mietek abandoned the doctorly demeanor and became again the friend and comrade.

How would I like to die? That I know exactly. As an ironman in Hawaii. On the podium. After swimming two point three nine miles, biking one hundred eleven, and running twenty-six point two one nine. And all that in under eight hours. I'd like to fall over on the victor's stand with the gold medal in my hand. And you? Are you sticking with asthma attack?

I want to die in Lena's arms. Awake, with no pain. I see a long goodbye, where we remember all we had that was good. Then she'll look at me, so I can take her look with me. Do you know how Stan wants to die? On stage, as a king…

Lena jumped up. Her voice poured out. You lunatics with your dreams of exquisite deaths! For your seventieth birthday, your friend gave you life, can we talk about that? Isn't that important? She pulled Mietek out of the sickroom, slammed the door, and cut Heiner off in the middle of his sentence. In the hallway she started to sob.

Mietek, how can one dream of death without thinking about those who will be left behind?

You can't take us seriously.

What did he say as we were leaving?

That I've already saved his life many times, that it's nothing special.

Nothing special? He said that!?

As Lena's tears turned into hysterical laughter, Mietek pressed her to him and held her tight with all of his ironman strength. He wound her hair around his hand like a bandage. She heard his heart. Heiner and Mietek – what a pair. Fifty years ago they were figures in stripes, young, wide-awake and overtired, they looked exactly alike, thin as a rail and half-starved, each saving the other's life, every hour, every day, clinging together at night, warming each other and praying for the strength to get up the next morning. Even if they told a thousand and one stories about laughing dogs and speaking trees, Lena would never truly understand all that was between them.

It's OK, Mietek, let me go. Suffocation isn't a pretty way to die, my friend.

See, he said, relieved, you can already make jokes again.

Lena blew her nose on Mietek's shirt. One has to be completely insane to stand you all.

Leaving the sea, he approaches the mound in a sweeping curve. Its forbidding solidity fascinates him each time he sees it. As soon as he's sure Lena can't see him, he takes his cigarette case out of the inside pocket of his coat.

Together they'd inspected the landscape that Mietek prescribed him: Lena with curiosity, Heiner with the feeling that he was surveying the land of his future exile, although to him exile – as long as it wasn't in Siberia – was hardly the worst punishment. Prison was worse; dungeons, torture, psychiatry, too. They hadn't gone in the summer, when even dilapidated barns were transfigured by the broad skies, but in winter, when houses look morose. Silently, they drove up the coast, rounded the Eiderstedt peninsula, and continued north. After staring mutely into the landscape for a long while, Heiner said: Let me tell you what I see. Lena nodded: Please do. He was silent. His silence continued for a long time. Then he said: A chicken. Then he was silent again. Lena drove through villages that looked like they'd been abandoned by their inhabitants. Heiner said: Five cows. In the afternoon, it snowed. When the sun broke through the clouds, the fields glittered like fireworks in the sky. The snow blanketed the sheep; they looked like shifting sand dunes. Pretty, Lena said – don't you think?

Heiner reported a hedge and two cows with black curly hair.

Galloways, Lena said. He nodded. Read what it says on the arrow pointing at them.

Sausage.

Compared to that, Heiner said, "Arbeit macht frei" is practically poetry.

Lena stopped the car. If you don't want to live here, we'll turn around.

He got out, looked at the landscape, seemed to measure it with his eyes. His gaze traveled from the toes of his shoes over the fields, the hedges and furrows, the pastures, the barbed wire. When his eyes came to the place where sky and earth met, Heiner said: A landscape for Zofia.

Further north, near the Danish border, he found hills that gave his eyes something to rest on. As they approached a particularly high ridge, with imposing farms clustered around a church, he said: Let's stop, Lena.

"Village community," read the sign, but the village looked more defiant than inviting – stand-offish, but pretty, nonetheless. Red brick paths led into the heart of the village, but Heiner and Lena weren't brave enough to follow them. A man was sawing wood. He greeted them, stooped, and looked at them questioningly. Can I help you? No, thank you. The place seemed too intimate for their tourist curiosity. They drove to the next town, bought a guide-book, ordered grog with rum at Café Wattenwurm, and learned that these hill settlements were called dwelling mounds, and that hundreds of years ago, they hadn't been part of the mainland, but had been holms, surrounded by sea. The houses had been built on hills to protect them from the direst of enemies: the sea, which attacks their land savagely when it is angry, sucking animals and people into the abyss. We'll fit in there, Heiner said, with the lunatics, the unyielding ones who understand that the disaster will always recur, the ones who keep fighting anyway, David versus Goliath. He ordered a second grog, and realized he could make peace with his exile, if this was the place they were to stay.

They looked at houses that were too big for them. They stood in huts with ceilings so low that their heads brushed the beams. They found a realtor who said a sentence they'd heard before: Take your time, the house has to suit you and you have to suit the house. They saw a farmhouse that told the tale of how people had been living for generations. In the tiny kitchen: an oven, a table, a bench. In the small bedroom, the wardrobe and a double bed, and next to the bed, a door that led to the barn – a life of much work and little sleep. Heiner opened the door and inspected the barn, as if measuring it. Bits of straw lay on the bare floor. Wooden signs with spirited inscriptions hung above each stall. Hanna, Frieda, and Karla, Anita, Dora, and Dina stood on the right; Ulla, Mara, and Maria were across from them. Slowly, as if trying to memorize the names, he walked through the stalls. Wienke, Trude, Elise. Do you like the barn? Lena asked. Do you want to keep cows?

There are no numbers in this barn, he said. They had proper names.

They saw houses with rotted roofs and cottages with musty walls. In old aunt Käthe's house, a water pipe burst when the realtor unlocked the door. They could have had the neighboring house for very little, if they'd been willing to take care of Arthur. Arthur was ninety: he looked at them like a child who wanted to be adopted. Wrong vintage, Heiner said. The realtor showed them the site where the RAD camp for dike workers had been during the war. Of course a Reichsarbeitdienst camp belonged in Zofia's landscape.

Stubbornly, Heiner circled the huge mound with the defiant houses, the church and the village square in the middle, where the animals are herded when storm surges come. Sixty inhabitants, fourteen farms: he could live near a mound like this.

They drove back to the house by the woods, and traveled north two more times before suddenly the house they'd been searching for stood before them, as if it had sprung up overnight. A thatched roof, a bright room for the couch, the wall of bookshelves, the television set, and the cuckoo clock. Two guest rooms on the second floor, a study for Lena, and a pantry next to the kitchen where Heiner could stock provisions up to the rafters. Why this house? the realtor asked. Lena said: Because it's been waiting for us.

The people on the mound have grown accustomed to the reticent man who adopted their greeting. Moin, he says in the mornings, Moin, he says at noon and, like everyone here, in the evenings, as well. Now and then a brief sentence about the rain and wind, or about the harvest in the fall, is enough to pass for sociability between the stranger and the natives. The newcomers are a nice couple. They don't force their way into the village community, they're not nosy, they only come to marksmen's festivals or firemen's balls when expressly invited. Heiner's twilight walks on the mound's footpaths are discrete – no one can tell how much he observes. He doesn't have to stop and stare to note the window decorations: wooden swans, china dogs, and glass horses, wooden witches on long broomsticks, and turtles whose heads wobble when a draft passes. He knows who sits on the sofa at what time of day, who cooks, who solves crossword puzzles with a blunt pencil. He tells Lena everything he sees later in the evening, over the last glass of wine. Look, Lena…

Heiner has stayed lean, his white curls reach his shoulders, he stands tall, not betraying the pain that plagues his legs, back, arms, and hands – he knows much worse pain. He writes essays on the "Body and Soul in Extreme Circumstances" and accepts invitations to give lectures, but where only a few years ago he was able to speak with just a few notes, on "Ideology Vs. Human Behavior," or "The Truth of Memory," now he has to write the text down and read it word for word to keep from losing his train of thought. He forgets names as soon as he hears them, but has developed a trick. He names the people on the mound after their house numbers, in order to be able to report to Lena what he's seen. He uses English numbers, not wanting to use the German ones. Look, Lena, old Frau Eleven keeps a fake cyclamen with dark green leaves on her windowsill. Over the last few days, a layer of dust has accumulated on the leaves – do you know what that means? Changes.

A week later the ever-blooming cyclamen is gone, the pot is sitting on the top of the garbage can; the next day the ornately ruffled curtains are gone too. This is no spring cleaning – Frau Eleven's house is being readied for a young family to move in. Sad, Lena says, the old woman loved that house. That's the way things go, Heiner said. Today it's her, but one day other people will live in our house too.

Is she going to a home?

What if she is? There are worse transports than the one that takes you to a home for the elderly, right?

If that's the measure, then yes, of course.

The young family's windowsill now holds herbs and spices, and a jar with olive-wood cooking spoons. At the end of his walk, Heiner enters the church, sits in the last pew, and enjoys the special kind of silence found only in churches. San Elmo has stood in this little town for six hundred years, and was thrice battered by storm surges. The church chronicle describes how the torrents pummeled the organ keys, as if to mock the people, releasing eerie tones that sounded, in the roar of the storm, like screams. As Heiner leaves the church, he lights a candle.

There's another man who never misses his daily walk. People call him "the old tailor." He has to be ninety, at the least. No one knows his real name; he seems quite tough – they say he just showed up one day, bought the empty blacksmith's shop on the edge of the mound, renovated it, and turned it into a tailor shop. People brought him their shirts and pants to be mended, and when word got around that he was good with a needle, they brought fabric from the city for him to sew the women's Sunday dresses and the men's suits. When he was spry, people say, he coached soccer – he was a passionate athlete, and the boys flocked to him. Heiner sees the old tailor every night, at a different place each time. On the path through the fields that lead to the water, in front of the workshop he always passes, in front of the church. The man triggers a vague feeling in Heiner. It sits in the pit of his stomach and presses on his heart. They walk towards each other, and where the path grows narrow, sometimes Heiner defers, sometimes the old tailor.

They murmur their short "Moin" and pass each other. Heiner has to stifle the urge to turn around. He knows that after a few yards, the old tailor stops and looks back at him. He feels the man's stare between his shoulder blades.

Before going home, Heiner leans against the tall poplar tree in front of the empty house that used to belong to Herr Twenty, now dead, to smoke a cigarette or two. From here he has a good view into Lena's study. He sees the warm light, and if she's not sitting there, he imagines her. Why can't one erase memories? Kill the pain they cause? Martha left him for his inability to be a normal person. His daughter could have found him, if she had wanted to. Once he stumbled upon the name Kaija Rosseck in Vienna when he was in some waiting room reading a magazine. Dr Kaija Rosseck, marine biologist. His child. The girl with the blond braids. His little partisan. Our Christ child, Martha had said. He tore the interview out of the magazine and read it in a café. His hands trembled. How, the reporter asked, did you become interested in the plight of whales in the Mediterranean? It seems to run in the family, she'd answered. My mother, too, cared for endangered species when she was younger. And your father? I don't have a father. My father never came back from Auschwitz.

He'd known comrades who kept a revolver in their drawer. There were steep slopes in Austria, high mountains, and deep chasms. The Danube was eighteen hundred miles long, every mile an invitation to take a journey to the Black Sea. There were stout ropes and lonely attics, and even foul stuff like Phenol was surely available somewhere. If he were certain about anything, it was this: Without Lena, he would be dead.

Lena isn't sitting at the desk where he's imagining her. At that very moment, she's standing in the darkness in front of their door, watching the gray plumes rising into the poplar branches. He smokes in secret – she finds it touching, but she doesn't lift her ban on smoking. Five cigarettes is better than fifty.

One foggy gray day, the postman brings a letter that he waves fiercely even before he gets close: From Poland, Frau Lena.

Is that unusual?

Oh yes, the stamps are particularly large. Oke collects big stamps.

Lena glances at the envelope. They're boring, she says, just portraits of presidents; they don't even have ridges.

So much the better – Oke can't stand ridges, he cuts them off.

Why does he do that?

There are too many ridges, the postman says. He can't count them.

The letter is from Olga in Gdańsk, and before she reads it, Lena cuts the stamps off the envelope.

Heiner had discovered the postman's son on his first walk. He was sitting on the only windowsill on the mound that had no starfish, conch shells, or straw witches. Oke watches the neighbors working in their gardens, he sees who leaves the house, who comes back from shopping with big bags, who talks with whom. He can tell the difference between tourists who pass his house only once and visitors who stay longer. Oke notices every change – he knew sooner than the others that the strange man who strolled past the houses and farms in the early evenings was no temporary visitor. The stranger had doffed his hat to him and bowed, as before a little prince. Oke pounded the window with joy.

The boy is round in every way. His head is a little too big for his small body, as are his eyes, which evade no one's gaze. He's just like a ball. Oke works like an amplifier, Heiner had said. When I smile, he laughs. When I laugh, he shrieks; when he sees a child crying, he screams as if he's being spanked. No one knows anything about Oke's mother – it's always been just the postman and the boy. How long has he kept watch at the window? Since he could crawl, walk, and sit, the neighbors say. He never learned to talk. The village children let him take part in some of their games. Hide-and-seek is a good one: the seeker puts his face to the wall and calls out "One, two, three, four high-tide, everybody has to hide, in front or behind me doesn't count, one, two three – ready or not, here I come!" Quick as lightning, everyone finds a hiding place and waits silently to be found – only Oke can't stand the suspense and screams and squeaks in his hideout. They let him screech. He doesn't ruin the game, because no one's looking for him. Another game, which Heiner doesn't understand, begins with a counting rhyme: RiaRaRitz, we're sailing on the ship, we're riding on the choo-choo train and you are it! When they feel like being nice to Oke, they let him stand in the circle, and they change the rhyme: RiaRaRitz, Oke's sailing on a ship, Oke's riding on the choo-choo train and Oke is it. They don't mean anything by it.

Of course he can have the stamps, Lena says. Oke is a sweet boy.

He's transparent, the postman says, sticking the Polish stamps in his mailbag.

What do you mean?

He's like a glass ball. You can see what goes on inside him.

Lena reads the letter in the hallway. Olga had organized the letter by subject matter – as systematic in writing as she is with her amber collection. Point one. She's doing great, and there's a new man in her life: named Adam, married, 20 years younger, sweet, interested in inclusions, but most importantly, and thereby leading to point two, Adam is a historian and publisher, and his newest project is a trilogy about three heroes who all had the same name: The Ghost Rider. The first man, Olga wrote, was the main character in a dramatic story set on the Vistula, first published in 1838 in Poland, in a German culture journal called the "Danzig Steamboat." Point two: the story left a strong impression on Theodor Storm; it was the model for his *Rider on the White Horse*, which takes place near the North Sea. The third hero of the trilogy, Olga wrote, was not a character in a novel, but a Polish Resistance fighter. Henryk Dobrzański was a highly decorated major and a famous equestrian. He killed Nazis wherever he found them. He blew up their cars, hunted, ambushed, and shot them down. Himmler called him the head of a hateful band of thugs, and ordered him hunted down and killed. The man and his white horse were unpredictable. They called him the Ghost Rider or the Ghost Major. He was killed by the Nazis on April 30, 1940: shot in the heart. The man is a legend in Poland. Point three: The book will be comprised of three stories – three bold riders, three white horses, three dead heroes, and Adam wants to know if you'd like to do a new translation into Polish of Storm's *The Rider on the White Horse*. Point four: We Poles love catastrophe. We worship our fallen hero and his mystical downfall; we love courage and pain, supernatural phenomena, Polish rebelliousness and the kind of deep despair that moves us to prayer. Point five: The book will be a huge success, Adam says. Point six: Hugs, Olga.

Lena takes her time answering. *The Rider on the White Horse* was required reading in school, and it had been torture. She reads the novella until its characters and language are familiar, and she's forgotten her schoolgirl judgment. She likes the drama of the possessed, pig-headed main character, Hauke Haien; as a translator, she loves the challenge of a story told by three narrators. Storm's landscape is right outside her door, and she has no trouble believing that a dead horse's bleached skeleton could reassemble and rise again on a deserted holm by moonlight. Dearest Olga, she writes, send the contract.

Early in the morning, when Heiner murmurs "Come back, Lena," in his sleep and reaches towards her as if to keep her with him, while he's falling asleep again, Lena leaves the house and walks through the fields to the sea. Lazily, the sheep open their eyes, too tired even to bleat. Lena is accompanied by a cloud of sounds: hoarse crows and chirping sparrows, the hungry calls of the oystercatchers and cries of gulls, who always sound displeased.

To strangers it looks like Lena is singing when she delves into Storm's language, her voice barely audible. The better she understands the melody, the more sensitive her translation will be.

"'Ended,' he murmured softly to himself; then he rode to the edge of the abyss, where below him, the sinister waters were rushing to inundate his village; he saw the light still shining from his window; it was dead to him. He stood up high in the saddle and drove his spurs into the flanks of the white horse; the animal reared up in pain and nearly fell backward; but the rider forced it to its feet again by main strength. Again he spurred the animal; the white horse screamed in a voice that rose higher than the wind and the roaring waters; the moon shone down from on high; but below, on the dike, there was no more life, only the wild water."

Lena speaks to the water. The sea has good ears. It's a mild morning, almost windless. As she quotes the text, she watches a gull trying to pull a fat worm out of the mudflats, but it keeps pulling back as if it's made of rubber. No German author, apart from Thomas Mann, loves the semi-colon as much, or uses it as lavishly, as Theodor Storm. Eight semi-colons in three sentences – she's never seen so many in one text. She's leafed through German, Polish, and English literature – three hundred, four hundred pages, she's even looked through thousand-page novels – without finding a single semi-colon. It's a punctuation mark on the verge of extinction. In a modern grammar book she comes upon the command: Never use a semi-colon! But she's grown to love the little mark. It's a way of dividing equal clauses more strongly than a comma yet more weakly than a period. It's like an engagement: more than a friendship, less than a marriage. It gives sentences a different melody than the final, brutal period. Semi-colons are the free-style event after all the moves have been mastered. Searching for semi-colons in literature, she takes her cue from Goethe: Eat what is cooked; drink what is clear; speak what is true; love what is rare! On the way home, she takes *The Rider on the White Horse* from the pocket of her coat and reads a section she doesn't yet know by heart, a section that would have a completely different rhythm if Storm hadn't used semi-colons. It would have been stiffer, less flexible, not gently rocking, like the waves.

"But now something came toward me on the dike. I heard nothing; but ever more clearly as the light of the half-moon grew darker, I thought I could make out a dark shape, and soon, as it came nearer, I saw it; it sat on a horse, a high-boned, haggard white horse; a dark mantle fluttered across the figure's shoulders, and as he flew past, two burning eyes stared at me out of a pale face."

The clock in the church tower chimes eight, and Lena turns back. She buys rolls at the grocery store: two poppy, two caraway, she makes breakfast. The neighbors, who don't know how the couple spends their time, have given them nicknames. Heiner is "the wandering man," Lena "the singing woman."

That evening, as Heiner leans against the poplar, the old tailor comes to stand next to him.

Moin.

Moin, Heiner says.

May I?

Heiner nods. The old tailor lights a cigarette and holds the pack out to Heiner. Heiner shakes his head: no thank you, three on one walk is enough.

The tailor avoids choosing between forms of address.

Come from where?

Taunus. And…?

Everywhere and nowhere. Long life, long journey.

Heiner casts a sideways glance at the old tailor. He's smaller than Heiner, stocky. He's in good shape for a man who, if you believe the people on the mound, is nearly ninety.

Smoke one with me.

Heiner can't decline. The man is a neighbor. He takes a cigarette out of the pack and the old tailor lights it. By the light of the white flame, the old man looks as if he's lying in wait. He uses the informal.

What's your name?

Je suis Einér.

Heiner doesn't know why he says the sentence he practiced in France. It slips out, unplanned, just like that.

What's your name?

Einer.

The tailor takes a long drag, shakes his head, growls a "Moin," and shuffles off towards the workshop where he lives.

That night Heiner sits mutely in front of the television without commenting on the news of the world. He doesn't seem to be listening.

Aren't you feeling well? Lena asks.

No, no, keep the television on, I just don't want to talk for a bit. He wraps himself tight in the light blue woolen blanket and doesn't wake until the middle of the night.

The next morning Lena asks him who the shadow was, that stood under the poplar next to him.

The old tailor.

And?

Nothing.

Did you talk?

He addressed me in the informal. Smoke one with me, he said.

It can't hurt to have a friend with a sewing machine, Lena says.

Their house is surrounded by a sea of glowing yellow. The fields of rapeseed hide streets and paths. They only see the tall parson on his bicycle because his black hat floats over the stalks, as if blessing them. Since the parson discovered Heiner's church visits, he's been stopping at the Rossecks' on a regular basis, drinking a coffee, and trying to draw Heiner into discussions about faith, because any man who's drawn to the church must be searching for something.

We're all searching for something, Heiner says. I, for example, am searching for the peculiar silence that's only found in churches.

Because it's the house of God.

I love the silence without God. It's in the walls and the pews; it's the stillness of a big room that can be filled with thoughts and memories. The church should have stuck to building big rooms.

Without God?

Without religion. But – Heiner smiles – you can leave me that crucified guy. I look at him to remind myself that every day, in every country, people are martyred, abandoned by your God.

The parson refuses to be intimidated. When his path leads him past Heiner and Lena's house, his gets off his bike. The men begin to take a liking to each other. Explain your God to me, Heiner says.

My God is called humility, the parson says. Humilty in the face of the endlessness that carries us through the universe on our little ball.

The little ball on which I sail through the universe is comprised mostly of people who scream because other people are causing them pain. Does your "God Humility" hear these screams, or is he deaf?

God can't be everywhere, the parson says.

I wish he were anywhere!

Didn't he save you too?

Heiner laughs loud and long. Me? You know, I spent a long time with people who implored God, who screamed, cried, begged him to show himself. No one has prayed more fervently, or with more longing, than my friends. The gods who saved me are called Leszek, Stanislaw, Mietek, and Kosta.

You must believe in something, the parson says.

Who says?

Don't you believe in human goodness?

No, I don't believe in human goodness. Nor in human evil, nor in the power of love. I don't believe in abstract virtues at all. I know that there are good people, and that I know some of them. I know that I love Lena and that Lena loves me – that's more luck than I deserve.

A person can't live without faith, the parson says.

Do I look dead to you?

Goodness gracious, no – I just wonder what gives you the strength to get through life, what gives your life purpose.

Heiner leads the cleric to the door and watches him get on his bicycle. He lays a hand on the handlebars. One thought for the road, parson. Life is an experiment and I'm a curious person. I believe chance makes us many offers, and it's up to us to decide which we accept and which we let pass us by. I observe life: that's what keeps me cheerful.

The parson returns. He listens to Heiner's life story. He wants to know where this man gets the strength to live.

I attribute my strength to good comrades, chance, and luck.

The parson doesn't lock up the church in the evening – he leaves Heiner alone with his silence. Sometimes he leaves a Bible in the last row, open to a section he wants to discuss. Heiner's words about life as an experiment give him no peace he says during his next visit. Anyone who thinks that way puts himself in God's place, and that's…

Blasphemy? Yes, that's my attitude towards life.

But Herr Rosseck – what do you think is the meaning of life, if you don't believe in a creator?

The parson tries fear of death, but Heiner has no fear of death. What comes after that, he says, is nothing, and we don't know much about nothing. Maybe it's made of memories, in which case I'll have plenty to do there. What I fear and hate, parson, is the death of those whom I love.

On his next visit, Heiner says: You're young – how long have you been working in the area?

Ten years.

You know your flock?

Every one.

Even the old tailor from the mound?

The parson nods. He came here thirty years ago, bought the abandoned forge, and renovated it. He has no friends, as far as I know, but many loyal customers. He's an inconspicuous citizen – a loner who doesn't do any harm to anyone. He used to coach soccer, and as long as I've known him, he's been coming to church.

Is he a pious man?

He knows the songs and prayers.

Do you know where he's from?

Are you interested in him?

No.

Why do you ask?

We run into each other sometimes. He smokes with me.

One Sunday afternoon in the fall, the parson invites himself over for coffee. He brings apple pie, but doesn't want to discuss God this time, he wants to tell an old village legend. He found a note, he said, in an old parish register, telling of how many years ago on Christmas Eve, in the middle of the Christmas story, parson Anselm P.'s eyes had glazed over, he'd begun to sway, and had fallen from the pulpit, crying, "I see it, the star of Bellehäm." The local vet, who on that night had had to serve as emergency doctor, determined that the vision had been induced by a bottle of grain alcohol. "I see it, the star of Bellehäm," had become a saying in the congregation. Two men, the parson said, carried the babbling pastor home. It was dead silent in the church. Not a single pew creaked. White clouds of breath floated through the cold nave. And do you know what? Before the congregation could disperse in disappointment, the village schoolmaster stood up, climbed up to the pulpit, and recounted the events of the year. The birth of twins, Ingar and Ingmar, the organist's wedding, the death of old Frau Emma, who had wanted to live to a hundred and only made it to ninety-eight.

Nice story, Heiner said. So?

The custom has continued. After the Christmas story, one of the congregation speaks.

And?

The pulpit's still vacant this year.

You're offering me a sermon?

After the pastor left, Lena said: You'll decline the invitation!

Why?

I know your Christmas stories. They don't put people in a good mood.

Where does it say that Christmas is the holiday of good moods?

Christmas, Lena says, is the holiday of peace and love.

And that's my favorite subject.

If the parson comes back with more pie, Lena says, show him the jar with the bones, and there will be no more doubt about the content of your sermon. Please, Heiner – don't say yes until you're sure.

I am sure.

They drop the subject until the beginning of December. A week before Christmas, Heiner starts making notes on little scraps of paper, and types them up after his evening stroll. He sits in the living room at night and leafs through the big book. He smokes. Lena asks the doctor to forbid Heiner the excitement of a church performance; the doctor refuses to patronize him. She tries blackmail: If you give the sermon, I'll go visit Olga. If you give the sermon you'll be alone on Christmas. Heiner looks unhappy and keeps working.

For my sake, Heiner: Don't do it.

What are you afraid of?

You're not well. And you'll alienate the congregation.

They'll survive.

And our Christmas?

He takes her in his arms. You'll stay with me? Lena, treasure, it will be a beautiful holiday. We'll cook, we'll set a festive table. In good Polish tradition, our house will be open to the unknown guest.

No one will come.

On the contrary. *Einer*.

Heiner's text seems to make him happy. He's in a good mood, and very lively. Lena gives up. He has to do it, even if he goes down in the history of the congregation as the second preacher to fall from the pulpit on Christmas Eve.

Heiner likes Oke and Oke loves Heiner. This, according to Oke's father, is because you can set your watch by Heiner. If he says he'll come at three, at three on the dot he'll be standing on the doorstep. He's the only grown-up for whom Oke will leave his post on the windowsill. On Wednesdays and Fridays, Heiner skips his afternoon nap to take a walk with Oke. To Heiner, Oke isn't a glass ball – Heiner can't see everything that goes on inside the boy, but finds him clever, even if he wouldn't be able to learn anything at school. The school subject in which Oke would excel doesn't exist. After one of their first walks together Heiner tells Lena:

The boy is friends with a lamb.

So am I.

Listen, Lena. We're walking beside a meadow filled with sheep and lambs. Suddenly the boy stands at the fence and starts making strange noises. I watched as one lamb raised its head and ran over to him as if its parents had just given it permission.

Any sheep will come when it's called.

He responds to trees.

Do they respond to him?

On every walk, Heiner feels more and more like he's walking with a human seismograph. For a while, the boy's hand will lie still in his, and then suddenly it will twitch or clutch Heiner's tightly. Has something startled Oke when he squeezes like that, is he scared? What scares him? And when the hand is limp, is he peaceful and happy? What makes Oke happy?

A child isn't an experiment, Lena says.

I want to understand the boy.

Tell the truth: you want to learn from him.

In a way, Lena is right. Heiner credits the boy with an ability to see, hear, and perceive beyond normal ability, as if Oke is some kind of early warning system.

Come, Oke, let's go for a walk.

For weeks Heiner has been observing Oke's reactions. He responds differently to children than to adults. If a child smiles at him, he laughs; if he sees a child crying, he screams, but he doesn't seem to take any notice of grown-ups. Does he just not care about big people? Visits to the baker and the butcher provoke no reaction, but by the sea, where the shrimp fishermen are, Oke's hand moves in Heiner's. It's not the people that excite him, though, it's the fish. He doesn't distinguish between those that flop around in nets, desperate for air, and those that lie peacefully in crates, like sleeping dolls. He squeezes Heiner's hand, and Heiner can't tell whether Oke's agitation means fear or joy or some other sensation he's not familiar with.

Come, Oke, let's visit the old tailor.

They cross the mound, past the house where Oke lives with his father, a few more steps down the slope to the former blacksmith's workshop that the old tailor has turned into a sewing room, living room, and bedroom, plus a shed with five chickens. Heiner enters the workshop like a thief, stealing with his eyes. Maybe something in this room will betray the history of the man that makes Heiner so uneasy. What he sees is banal. Two sewing machines, long racks containing hangers of shirts with no arms, suits with white basting thread; the tables are covered with colorful pins and boxes filled with every color and shade of thread; a tape measure hangs from the ceiling. A tailor shop – what did he expect? On the dresser lies an open pack of cigarettes. Heiner presses Oke's hand and the boy returns the gesture.

A rare visitor, the old tailor says, drawing the curtain to hide a narrow, unmade bed. Coffee?

No.

Hot chocolate for the boy?

No thanks, he doesn't like chocolate.

What do you want?

Heiner isn't prepared for such a direct question. He looks around, feels Oke's hand and says: Can you sew the boy a winter coat? With a hood?

Do you have fabric?

No.

Then come with me.

The tailor goes over to a chest, opens a row of large drawers and points to their contents. There's coarse, brown linen, silvery-gray flannel, bottle-green cotton, and a large leftover swatch of fabric: midnight blue and soft as a rabbit's fur.

Feel this, Oke, Heiner says. Should we make this into a coat?

He guides the boy's hand over the fabric; Oke conveys neither agreement nor rejection.

Italian velvet, says the tailor. Highest quality. Not cheap.

It doesn't matter. I want to give Oke a soft blue velvet coat for Christmas.

The boy submits patiently to measuring: arms, shoulders, short torso. How long do you want the coat? the tailor asks. The boy is puny – barely five-nine.

Oke has turned his head in the direction of the clucking sounds. Go look at the chickens, Heiner says, and to the tailor: The boy is quite round. Can you make him a cape – a cape with a hood?

The tailor nods. Oke is absorbed with the chickens. He imitates their soft clucking, but doesn't try to pet them. He picks up a white feather and sticks it into his sweater.

What are you doing rambling around this place with the dumb kid? the tailor asks.

I like the boy. He'll never do anyone any harm.

The tailor lays a brown egg in each of Oke's hands. The boy carries them slowly and carefully towards the door of the workshop. There he stops short. He doesn't know how to take Heiner's hand.

I'll open the door, Heiner says, you can take the eggs home with you.

Oke considers his hands. Then he lets the egg that the tailor put in his right hand fall to the floor. The other one he brings back to the chickens.

The tailor smirks. Crazy kid. To Heiner, he says: Stay a little while, smoke one with me.

Six points of light make the bedroom look like the evening sun is shining on the floor. The gentle light keeps Heiner's fear of the night at bay and helps calm him after bad dreams. It's been half a century since he's been a prisoner, but the many years can't protect him from terrible images. Nor can Rilke, nor the goodnight prayer for Lena: *I would like to sing someone to sleep, to sit beside someone and be there. I would like to rock you and sing softly, and go with you to and from sleep.* He closes his eyes, sinks into sleep, and can't help wandering into a large chamber at the end of a long hallway. The judge wears a pointed hat like a magician, and a long scarf. His hands lie on top of a large folder. He's wearing gloves. We've been waiting a year for you, he says reproachfully, as Heiner enters the hall. Sit down behind the accused. The accused wears a well-made suit with white basting thread. Heiner has only a wool blanket around his shoulders. Stand up, says the judge. He gets up. No, not you, Herr Witness, the man sitting in front of you.

Are you married? the judge asks.

No, the accused answers.

Were you married?

No.

Why not?

The war.

And after the war?

Especially not then.

Why especially not then?

None of your business.

The accused stands in front of the judge with his legs wide, hands propped impudently on his hips.

What were your duties there?

The accused answers dourly. I'd like to know that myself. A little of this, a little of that. I was bored, mostly.

Were you a witness?

Me? Never! I left before anything happened. Why would I want to see that crap?

Did you throw eighty children into the fire?

The accused shakes with laughter. He rocks forward and back like a bush in the wind. I saw no children there because there were no children there. Listen: I saved one thousand two hundred and fourteen lives.

How do you know so exactly?

Do you think I'm stupid? I can count.

The accused begins to count. One, two, three, four... The judge doesn't interrupt him, he makes tally marks on a piece of paper. The accused says: I gave all those people radishes.

Why radishes?

Potatoes didn't grow there.

Accused, please sit down.

The judge looks at Heiner. Herr Witness, what do you say to this?

The accused is right, Heiner says, standing up. I know him, he was no hater of men. He had a calm, kind way of escorting the children to be injected. He was a respectable SDG.

A what?

A respectable Sanitätsdienstgrad – a medical orderly. I never heard him yell, he never hit anyone. Once he said: How beautiful it looks when the children fall like harvested stalks.

Why would he make such a comparison, Herr Witness?

Because the children were thin. Like stalks of wheat.

Herr Witness, where did you get the pretty blue wool blanket?

They came on the trains from Holland. There were many blankets, I only took one. I was freezing, it saved my life.

Did the blankets travel under their own power?

Yes, Herr Judge, under their own power.

When did the blankets arrive?

September '44, I believe.

Is light blue your favorite color?

No.

What is, then?

I don't have a favorite color.

Please give the blanket to me.

Never!

The accused turns around. He says: Don't get so upset, buddy, smoke one with me.

It's Lena's voice that reaches the room from the courthouse hallway. She calls his name and then, over and over: Heiner, let go! Treasure, let go of the blanket!

Later Heiner could have sworn to having a cigarette in his hand when he woke up, which Lena took from him, before going to the kitchen to fetch some coffee.

It should rain. Heiner wishes for a fine, mean, constant rain that creeps through the cracks in the houses, that the wind drives through jackets and sweaters into every pore. He wishes for bad-mood weather. How is he supposed to give his sermon on a day when the sun shines and thick white flakes fall from a shameless blue sky? They cover branches, blanket streets and fields, the heads of the birds, and the backs of the sheep. It's the 24th of December.

Heiner and Lena sit at the window eating breakfast. The dark shadow beyond the snow flurries is only the distant reminder of a church. Lena fills Heiner's mug with coffee. Pretty, she says. A fairy-tale kind of day.

The flakes floated down from the sky back then, too. They melted on the skin of the naked men waiting patiently for the trucks to depart. Father, father, take me with you. A shameless blue sky vaulted over all.

Heiner stands up. I'll go pick up the coat for Oke.

Quickly he climbs the path across the mound and enters the workshop without knocking. The old tailor sits at the sewing machine with a cigarette in the corner of his mouth; chickens scratch at the ground around him. The tailor holds the pack out to him; he shakes his head – no thanks, not in the morning. The tailor stands up, takes the cape off its hanger and spreads it out on the table in front of Heiner.

Is it satisfactory?

Dark blue velvet. From Italy. Heiner lifts the cape up: it falls like a tulip skirt, and he imagines Oke's face in the hood. Well made, he says, what do I owe you?

Nothing.

The fabric is expensive, Heiner says.

The tailors smirks. I'll take exactly nothing.

Heiner stares at the old man and tries to think of a way to pay for the work anyway. He could lay two hundred marks on the table, which the tailor, if he's stubborn, could shove back in Heiner's mailbox the next day. A silly game. He could send a wire transfer to the old tailor – but that too is no guarantee he wouldn't get the money back. The fleeting idea of buying something for the workshop – expensive shears, colorful thread – is discarded immediately.

I don't want the cape for nothing.

It's not for you, the tailor says. It's for the stupid kid.

Heiner tears the cape from the table and rushes home. He doesn't turn around, but knows that the old man watches him until he becomes a shadow behind the wall of snow. The tailor stands at the window, blows his cigarette smoke against the windowpane and can't understand why the man takes walks with a crazy child, gives him an expensive present, and isn't pleased to get it for nothing.

Heiner slams the door behind him and drinks a vodka to quell his nausea. The tailor has woven himself into the cape, and Heiner doesn't know how to get rid of him. He hates feeling powerless. He curses. You're careful as can be, you plan everything out in advance, and then suddenly someone throws a wrench in it and you're helpless. He wraps the gift in colorful Christmas paper, ties a thick ribbon around it and writes OKE in big letters on the package. Then he walks up the mound again, approaches the postman's house through the garden, sets the gift on the doorstep, knocks on the window, and runs away. He knows that Oke will be out of his mind with joy – that comforts him. The boy won't lower his hood in church, and in the new year, the boy's father will curse Heiner for giving him the cape. The boy wears the magic cape indoors and out, in summer and winter, and since his father insists he take it off before bed, he uses it as a blanket.

At the Rosseck house there's no Christmas tree, there are no cookies, and no Christmas carols. They call the holiday Heiner's birthday: for three days he gets to choose any meal he wants. For weeks, Christmas stars have hung in every window, children's voices sing of the holy night in supermarkets, but as he does every year, Heiner defends his thousand square feet of Christmas-free living.

At midday on Christmas Eve, Heiner sits at the kitchen table scaling a perch. Lena sets the table in the living room the way Olga does, festively, with an extra place for the unknown guest who has no home on this evening. For years, Lena has viewed this place setting with a mixture of curiosity and discomfort: no guest has ever rung their doorbell on this evening, but Olga has had unknown guests twice at her table in Gdańsk. Two Christmases ago it had been a neighbor whose wife had kicked him out that very day, and a year ago it had been two lively girls who'd been bored at their parents' house and wanted to see whether the Polish custom still worked. Both nights were among Olga's nicest Christmases. Lena shines the silver and calls through the kitchen door: Get ready for it to be just the two of us tonight, no one's going to want to eat with us.

Think of the unknown guest.

Who's that supposed to be?

Someone who's drawn to me.

Someone you like?

He shakes his head.

I don't entertain people you don't like.

It won't stop snowing. At sundown they sit by the window and drink cocktails à la Zofia. Snow is a beautiful invention, Heiner says, you can smother the whole world with snow – slowly, quietly, gently, kindly. Snow has no anger, no frenzy, just a beautiful, white, consistent indifference.

The church bells ring in the evening. Around five-thirty they dress for church. Lena takes out her warmest skirt and jacket, Heiner the white suit that he wore for his seventieth birthday.

White, Lena says reproachfully, are you trying to look like a snowman in the pulpit?

The parson wears black, Heiner says. White is the color of innocence.

At around six they leave the house and join the long line of people climbing the steps to the church. The parson had reserved seats for Heiner and Lena in the first row. It's quiet in the old wooden church before the organ begins – only the pews creak, as if reminding them in this hour of the floods that come every hundred years to sweep all the benches out to sea. During the last storm surge, the sea had been forced to return without its prize, since the congregation had hung all the pews from the church's roof. When the echo of the organ's last note dies away, the parson climbs up to the pulpit. He blesses the congregation, sings "From Heaven on High I come to You," with them, then says the names of all the children he baptized in the past year. Liza, Annika and Jule, Max, and Daniel. He remembers the dead they buried together. Inken Peterson left us at the age of one hundred and three. Hauke Asmus, at ninety-nine. Arne Lorenzen at seventy-four. We mourn Sönke Ingwerson, who departed this world at the age of twenty-four. The parson opens the bible. *And it came to pass in those days…*

Heiner looks around. The older people in the congregation fill the first five rows – women and men in black, hands folded in their laps. The youngest ones are around fifty-five, the oldest have to be nearly a hundred. They move their lips: they know the Christmas story, they say it along with the parson like a prayer. In the sixth through twelfth rows sit their children, the generation between thirty and sixty. *And she brought forth her firstborn son, and wrapped him in swaddling clothes, and laid him in a manger; because there was no room for them in the inn.* The children and young people of the congregation sit on the balcony in white shirts and black suits. Are they listening to the parson, or are their thoughts on the presents that they're going to get after the service? Heiner likes the faces of the boys and girls up above – they're beautiful because they're unfinished. Not cheerful, not blithe, but not angry or disappointed, either – they're sketches of faces, masks that can be read. They don't know that the most precious present on this day doesn't lie under the tree. They can see it, if they want to. It's the heads, backs, and hands of their parents and grandparents, which tell the story of how they live and have lived. Those who sit up high can look down on their future, or dream of a different one. Soon the youngest will leave the balcony for the back pews and then, sooner than they expect, they'll find themselves in the first rows, where their grandparents sit now. In front of the first rows is the grave. In between is life, which one either allows to happen, or shapes. The view from above is a view of life itself – what a Christmas present.

The parson closes the bible. Before descending from the pulpit, he reminds them of the old tradition of giving the second sermon to a member of the congregation. Lena doesn't pray, she doesn't beg, she sends orders up to heaven: Dear God, let a fire break out! Send a flood, I know you can do that. Let the roof cave in under the snow, let lightning strike, appear in person or send an angel and let everyone faint, just stop him from speaking! Too late. Heiner stands up and shakes the parson's hand. It's silent inside the church. Heiner stands there in his white suit and searches for Lena's eyes. He looks good, not like a snowman. He smiles briefly at the round child's face in the velvet blue hood on the balcony. Then Lena hears the voice that she fell in love with, over thirty years ago in the courthouse hallway. "Servus," the man who had collapsed before her very eyes had whispered, conveying both charm and scorn. Now the voice is strong and calm. It doesn't shake.

I want to tell you about a Christmas Eve that befell me many years ago. Thereafter I crossed this holiday, the way it's usually celebrated, off my calendar. I declared the three days of Christmas to be my birthdays.

Lena calms down. He stands coolly at the pulpit as if he speaks here every Sunday – he'll acquit himself well. And if every person stands up and leaves the church, Heiner will speak to the empty pews.

Today it is again Christmas Eve, Heiner says, looking into the eyes of the old man who sits behind Lena in the second row.

It was a particularly sad day. Our thoughts were on our homes, we imagined Christmas trees with candles and tinsel, a warm room and sugar cookies – we thought of those we loved, and no one was ashamed to be seen with tears in his eyes.

It's silent in the church

On the Christmas Eve I want to tell you about, the SS men had set up a Christmas tree in front of the kitchen building. A gigantic Christmas tree! Electric candles on the branches; we stared at the tree as if it were a phantom. What was going on with the Nazis? Was the war over? Did they want to cozy up to us now? Make

amends? Had mercy entered their hearts? We could have understood any baseness, but not this tree. Then came evening muster.
Twenty thousand men in striped rags, filled with hope and mistrust. The bells chimed. It was December 24, 1942.

The man in the second row stands up and shuffles slowly down
the aisle towards the exit. Everyone watches. Heiner waits until
the old tailor has closed the church door behind him and the faces
turn back to the pulpit.

The Nazis wanted to give us a nice holiday. We would have
voluntarily stood at attention in front of the tree until the next
morning, that's how rapt we were. I don't know how long they
let us stand there. Ten minutes? An hour? Suddenly, comrades
were picked out: You and you and you and you. They had to
march into one of the barracks, and when they came out, they
were carrying Muselmen. At the command "Drop," they set the
Muselmen on the ground under the tree like Christmas presents. I
don't know how many there were. Muselmen, you have to understand, weren't people to us anymore, yet they weren't dead, either.
They were beings without will – shadows that inhabited the realm
between life and death. No one wanted to get close to them – we
feared them, like a contagious disease. We were a hair's breadth
away from becoming what they were, so we had to keep our distance. The Muselmen were our future. We had no sympathy for
them. If you tried to stand them up, they fell over. Muselmen
were ghosts. Did they have feelings? You couldn't tell. If you ran
into a Muselman, you averted your eyes. We were ashamed of
these people who had so completely lost their dignity. They hung
around the camp like birds without wings; they were the brothers
of death. Our comrades lay these beings under the Christmas tree.
Another miracle? Were the Muselmen going to celebrate Christmas with us? Were the SS men allowing them to see a Christmas

tree one last time? The world was upside-down that day. And as we were staring, hypnotized, at this eerie offering, orders were barked: Buckets! Water! March! It was gruesomely cold that day – thirty below. Christmas Eve. The water was poured on the people under the tree, and after a short while, the Muselmen were encased in a block of ice. I don't know if the procedure took an hour or a night, all sense of time was lost, to me it felt like we stood there a year.

A pew creaks as a married couple leaves the church. Heiner no longer sees the congregation, nor Lena; he's not standing in the pulpit, he's standing on the mustering ground. His voice is barely intelligible.

Killing people…He speaks softly, with bewildered pauses. In such a way…on Christmas Eve…and the killers were Christians…

His gaze returns to the present. He looks at the old people and their children, he looks up at the balcony. None of the young people has left the church. Oke waves with both hands. Heiner wouldn't be Heiner if he didn't tell the story's ending.

There was a voice inside me, a clear voice – neither male nor female, old nor young. It said: If you are still human, lie down with them. Do it for the dead in the ice. My friend stood next to me. I whispered: Leszek, I'm going to lie down with them. He hissed: Dupa. You ass.

Heiner bows. He sticks his notes in the pocket of his suit. My story is a Christmas present, he says, unwrap it – the message is a humble one. Whether we are angels or devils is up to us to decide. And now let us enjoy the meal that awaits us. Merry Christmas.

No surprise visitors have ever arrived at their door on Christmas Eve, yet they hold on to the tradition of the empty chair and the extra place setting. A soup bowl, a plate, spoon, knife, and fork, a wineglass for the unknown guest. Lena doesn't want to set the third place on Christmas Day – the tradition is just for Christmas Eve, she says, but Heiner insists on celebrating one of the nicest customs he knows on each of his three birthdays. Perhaps there will be someone who's not feeling so good, he says, it's possible that someone who was in the church yesterday will want to come talk to me today.

Lena sets the crispy brown duck on the table. The red cabbage is steaming in its bowl, the spoon lies ready in the mashed potatoes. She looks at the clock. She pours white wine in two glasses. The squinting cuckoo shoots out of the clock and opens its shabby beak eight times. Go see who that is, Lena calls a bit later when the doorbell rings, I have the gravy boat in my hands. Heiner goes into the hallway. He stands at the door without opening it. He's known it would happen, he's been waiting for him, yet at this moment he knows that he doesn't want to admit this guest. He doesn't want this man to enter his house. From the kitchen, Lena calls: Heiner, the table is set.

He opens the door. Tracks in the snow, but no visitor. A package lies on the doormat. It's tied with twine and plastered all over with big stamps that have no ridges.

Glossary

Arbeit macht frei: Literally, "work sets you free," a slogan written over the gates of several concentration camps, including Auschwitz.

Arbeitsdienst: "Reich Labor Service," abbreviated RAD. Labor corps founded to alleviate unemployment in Germany, militarize the work force, and indoctrinate Nazi ideology. Six months of service prior to military service was compulsory for men between 18 and 24; during World War II the corps provided auxiliary support for the Wehrmacht.

Augarten: A large public park in Vienna.

Blockführer: "Block Leader." Nazi rank specific to concentration camps. A Blockführer was in charge of one or more "blocks" or prisoners' barracks.

Einer: "One" in German, as well as the French equivalent of Heiner's name.

Hadschi Halef Omar Ben Hadschi Abul Abbas Ibn Hadschi Dawuhd al Gossarah: The full name of a character from the popular German adventure writer, Karl May; being able to recite the full name was considered the sign of a true May fan.

Hitler Jugend: "Hitler Youth" was the youth organization of the Nazi party.

Justizpalast: The "Palace of Justice" in Vienna, which is the seat of the Supreme Court of Austria, as well as housing several lesser courts and judicial offices.

Kapo: Officially called Funktionshäftling, "Functionary Prisoners." Kapos were prisoners chosen to act as guards or supervisors over their fellow prisoners at concentration camps. They were spared harsh treatment and were often just as cruel as the SS officers.

Kasperle: The traditional hero of puppet plays in German-speaking countries. Like *Punch and Judy* in England, Kasperle theatre has a long history, and is comprised of stock characters, including Gretel, Witch, Crocodile, Princess, King, and Robber. Kasperle's roots can be traced back to Italian Commedia dell'Arte, but he developed into such an integral figure in German culture that Kasperle theatre has become synonymous with puppet theatre.

Lagerälteste: Rank held by a Kapo; the highest rank a prisoner could hold in a concentration camp.

Lagerkommandant: "Camp Commander." Highest-ranking officer in a concentration camp.

Muselman: A term used in concentration camps to describe prisoners at the brink of death due to sickness, starvation, and exhaustion. Such prisoners were extremely emaciated, weak, and often barely conscious, thus seemingly apathetic towards their own fates.

Oberscharführer: "Senior Squad Leader." A Nazi paramilitary rank roughly equivalent to American sergeant first class or British company sergeant major.

Ortsgruppenleiter: "Local Group Leader." A Nazi political rank designating the chief Nazi in a municipal area. During Nazi rule, an Ortsgruppenleiter effectively had the power of a mayor; where mayors and similar officials continued to exist, their posts were usually held in name only.

Rapportführer: "Report Leader." Mid-level Nazi paramilitary rank specific to concentration camps. A Rapportführer oversaw subordinate officers (Blockführer) and usually conducted morning and evening roll calls.

Reichsjägermeister: "Reich Master of the Hunt."

Rotfront: "Red Front," the Rotfrontkämpferbund. Originally a proletarian defense organization for the working class associated with the Communist party; later developed into a paramilitary resistance group against the Nazis.

Rottenführer: "Section Leader." A Nazi paramilitary rank roughly equivalent to corporal.

Schutzhaft: "Protective Custody." The official euphemistic designation of prisoners sent to concentration camps. Ostensibly, prisoners needed "protection" from the "righteous anger" of their fellow German citizens. Any such prisoner was a "Schutzhäftling."

Schutzhaftbcfchl: "Protective Custody Order." Mandate sending prisoners to concentration camps.

Servus: Common salutation in many parts of Central and Eastern Europe, including Austria and southern Germany. An abbreviation of a Latin phrase meaning, "I am your servant," or "at your service," but actually quite informal in tone.

Sicherheitsdienst: "Security Service." The intelligence agency of the Nazi regime.

Sonderkommando: "Special Unit." Work group in charge of assisting in the killing of other prisoners, and in the disposal of corpses.

Sturmbannführer: Nazi paramilitary rank equivalent to major, used in various Nazi organizations.

Unterscharführer: "Junior Squad Leader." Nazi paramilitary rank roughly equivalent to second lieutenant in the US or British army. Unterscharführerin is the female equivalent.

Afterword

The newspaper announcement was quite brief: A survivor of Auschwitz had founded a club, for which he sought friends, supporters, and members. The society was called "Camp Community: Auschwitzers and Friends." The founder lived near Frankfurt. At that time (1979) I worked for the Hessian radio, and I thought: Here's a man who seems ready to share his experiences with others – if you don't overcome your fear of the subject now, will you ever? I didn't know much: Hermann Reineck was Viennese, and he'd been deported to Auschwitz in 1942 as a Communist. A stamp on his ID: R.U. Return Unwanted. I proposed doing a profile of him for the radio station.

I'll never forget that afternoon. I parked my car near the house where the founder of the club lived – and didn't get out. How does one greet a person who survived Auschwitz? What is one allowed to ask? What was it like there? In the morning, at noon, through the evening, the night, every day, every month, every year? How does one survive in a place that was conceived and constructed for the purpose of killing? How can one live with such a past? What is one not allowed to ask?

I forced myself to get out of the car and thought: Ring the bell, shake his hand – the rest will follow. And it did. There was coffee and cake, Hermann Reineck talked without waiting for my questions – about his time in the camp, about the Frankfurt Auschwitz trial, about meeting his wife and how they fell in love in the hallway of the courthouse. Anni Reineck poured coffee, set cake on the table, and her husband spoke the sentence that revealed his life philosophy: Help yourself. In this house, plum cake and Auschwitz belong together.

After the interview, Hermann Reineck dismissed me with two questions: Can you drive a truck? Answer: No. Have you ever been to Auschwitz? Answer: No. Before I left, he said: Of course you can drive a truck with your driver's license. And of course you have to get to know Auschwitz. Hermann was charming and authoritarian, and, of course, on that afternoon I became a member of the club. Now I was one of them.

We made the perfect team: A journalist who wanted to see and understand everything, and a man whose health and good spirits depended on talking about Auschwitz – it was a kind of therapy for him. He was a gifted storyteller.

At the beginning of the eighties, when Poland was ruled by martial law, he organized convoys with relief supplies for his comrades – survivors like him. We criss-crossed the country, Hermann thinking only of the well-being of his friends. Their children, reared on their parents' horror stories, showed us, the drivers of the convoy, the real Poland. It was a country that forced its people to go underground.

Heiner, Lena, and their Polish friends are modeled on real people. It was necessary to get to know them so that they'd have a chance of developing into characters in a novel, so that they'd have their own book-life, which functions according to different rules, constraints, and pleasures than "real" life. Which is to say: Heiner isn't Hermann and Lena isn't Anni. Their love, too, is different.

For several years I devoured everything that could be read, heard, or watched about this topic – to the point where my husband asked if I might have some sort of addiction. As strange as it sounds: Yes, horror is addictive. There are so many stories that haven't been told, so many people that one could talk to before it's too late. When you realize that, you have to stop. I put the mountain of books, recordings, and manuscripts in a closet and locked the door.

And then, nearly twenty years later, a friend from Israel said over dinner that he'd weathered his first visit to Auschwitz well: as a precaution he'd avoided standing in any one place for too long. I said: That was wise – lingering is dangerous. How did I know that? The evening ended with the idea of making fiction out of reality. On that very same evening I opened the closet. A note fell out of the first book I grabbed: Monika, don't forget us!

What now? Try to invent a simple story about a complicated love: This place holds no fear.

Monika Held